I0667795

EVERYTHING I
HOPED FOR

A JOURNEY'S END BILLIONAIRE ROMANCE

ANN CHRISTOPHER

BLUE IRIS
PRESS

The Queen's grandson. A beautiful American doctor. An unforgettable royal love story...

Opposites attract. But for how long?

At thirty-five, with both her training and medical challenges finally behind her, Dr. Melody Harrison no longer believes in fairy-tale romances, handsome princes or even online dating. Her single passion? A blossoming career as a pediatric surgeon.

Given his painful past, sexy but awkward Londoner Anthony Scott no longer believes in much of anything at all. Until the night he lays eyes on Melody at a glittering gala in small-town Journey's End.

Sparks fly when opposites attract. As for happily ever after between star-crossed lovers? Anything's possible in Journey's End...

If you love hot and emotional contemporary romance, grab this two-part romantic saga today!

1. No Ordinary Love **(Baptiste & Samira #1)**

2. Beyond Ordinary Love **(Baptiste & Samira #2)**

3. Everything I Hoped For **(Anthony & Melody #1)**

4. Everything I Need **(Anthony & Melody #2)**

5. Untitled **(Nick's Story #1)**

6. Untitled **(Nick's Story #2)**

ALSO BY ANN CHRISTOPHER

The Davies Family Contemporary Romance Series

Book 1: *SINFUL SEDUCTION*

Book 2: *SINFUL TEMPTATION*

Book 3: *SINFUL ATTRACTION*

Book 4: *SINFUL PARADISE*

The Warner Family Contemporary Romance Series

Book 1: *TENDER SECRETS*

Book 2: *ROAD TO SEDUCTION*

Book 3: *CAMPAIGN FOR SEDUCTION*

Book 4: *REDEMPTION'S KISS*

Book 5: *REDEMPTION'S TOUCH*

Boxed Sets

DEADLY Series

IT'S COMPLICATED

SWEET LOVE

BELLA MONSTRUM Young Adult Horror Series

Book 1: *MONSTRUM*

Single Titles

CASE FOR SEDUCTION

THE SURGEON'S SECRET BABY

SEDUCED ON THE RED CARPET

Novellas

TAILS OF LOVE

GIFT OF LOVE

To Richard.
And to EVB. I miss you.

ACKNOWLEDGMENTS

Special thanks to:

Caroline Linden, for the brainstorming sessions and research help;

My copy editor extraordinaire, Martha Trachtenberg, for her eagle eyes;

Earthly Charms, for the gorgeous covers; and

Mom, for answering my medical questions. And for being a great mom.

For information, contact:

Blue Iris Press LLC

7350 Montgomery Road #36476

Cincinnati, OH 45236

www.BlueIrisPress.com

ISBN-13: 978-1-948176-20-0

Excerpt from *Everything I Need* © 2018 by Sally Young Moore

Dear Readers:

You know the old saying about how you only get one chance to make a first impression. Which is all well and good if you're, say, a charming extrovert who loves parties and meeting new people. But what if you're an introvert (like me) who's uncomfortable in new situations? What if you're downright shy? Are you doomed to failure every time you meet someone new?

I *don't* think so.

Say hello to Anthony Scott, our intrepid hero. Anthony first arrived on the scene in *Beyond Ordinary Love*, the second half of Baptiste and Samira's story. You remember Anthony, right? Baptiste's blond and handsome British friend who was a bit rude upon being introduced to Samira's best friend, Dr. Melody Harrison, at the winery gala?

Well, it turns out that there's a lot more to Anthony than meets the eye. He's not a bad person. Just awkward. He's got a bit of Mr. Darcy (*Pride and Prejudice*, anyone? The Keira Knightley version?) in him. Maybe a little Hugh Grant as the prime minister in *Love, Actually* as well.

I don't know about you, but I consider that a sexy combination. ;)

Anthony has been wanting to meet Melody. Why? Because she's smart, accomplished and beautiful. An intriguing woman with a complicated past. And he feels a powerful, instantaneous and undeniable connection to her the second he lays eyes on her.

Melody also feels this connection. Even though Anthony's a bit rough around the edges.

As an eternal optimist, I believe that great love stories can arise from inauspicious beginnings. Turn the page and see if you agree with me...

Happy Reading!

Ann

B loody black-tie events.

    Scowling as he leaned against the nearest pillar, Anthony Scott ran his fingers under his starched collar as discreetly as he could, trying to overcome the feeling of a noose tightening round his neck. The glittering ballroom overflowed with exactly the sorts of yammering society nobs and suck-ups he normally encountered back in London. The sorts that set his teeth on edge. One would think that crossing the Atlantic and traveling all the way to tiny Journey's End in upstate New York would solve this particular problem, but no such luck. One might also think that, given his age (thirty-four) and his background, he might be more comfortable with chatting up complete strangers but, again, no such luck. Honestly, he wouldn't mind giving a nice chunk of his fortune for the pleasure of escaping up to his suite and being done with the whole event.

The only bright spots on his otherwise dreary horizon?

Half the crowd were Yanks, which meant they had no idea who he was.

And *she* might be there.

His skin tightened pleasantly with anticipation, but a quick scan of the crowd revealed no one nearby with that glowing golden skin or tumbling corkscrew hair. No one with that direct gaze, which was as challenging as it was compelling. No one with the smiling eyes and banked laughter that suggested she was the woman you wanted whether you were watching a Wes Anderson movie or sharing secrets in the dark.

A tinge of disappointment made him scowl again before he raised his whisky glass to his lips and drank deeply. He somehow resisted the urge to pull out his phone and stare at her pictures for the millionth time since his longtime mate from boarding school, Jean-Baptiste Mercier, first alerted Anthony to her existence, but it took a great deal of effort.

But Anthony gave his breast pocket a reassuring pat with his free hand, just to make sure the phone, and her smiling face, were still there—

"Anthony."

Startled, Anthony glanced around to discover an exasperated looking Baptiste beckoning to him from several feet away. A surprise because Anthony had thought that Baptiste and their other school chum, Domenico "Nick" Rossi, were still right there beside him.

Anthony snapped to attention, realizing that he had, perhaps, lapsed into a daydream. About *her*.

Baptiste raised a brow and beckoned again. "Do you want to join us, or do you want to continue being rude?"

Anthony hesitated. What he wanted was to leave this gala celebration of Baptiste's new winery merger, go upstairs to his hotel suite, shed the monkey suit and stretch out in bed to watch football with another whisky and a nice slice of New York style pizza. Then he could fall asleep with his Ruth

Bader Ginsberg biography, which was really starting to get good.

Actually, strike that. What he *really* wanted was to be upstairs rolling around in that same bed with the object of his growing obsession, but since what he wanted didn't seem to be on the menu tonight, he braced for another round of small talk and calibrated his expression for polite interest as he walked over.

That was when the crowd shifted and he realized that Baptiste and Nick were standing beside two beautiful women, one with dark skin and short hair, the other with—

Christ. It was *her*.

His mouth dried out. His feet simultaneously turned leaden and clumsy, like flippers on land, and his steps slowed to the point where it was a wonder he didn't trip over himself and plant his face on the floor.

Still, he eventually got there, his mind empty of all intelligent thought.

Well…except for the galling knowledge that he'd probably screw things up. The way he always did.

Put that thought aside for now, Anthony, he told himself, taking a bracing breath.

"Could you be a bit more sociable?" Baptiste snapped when he arrived. "I thought you were with us. Not standing over there holding up some pole."

"I'll try." Anthony cleared his throat and decided that coherence was all anyone could request of him at the moment, let alone good manners or a smile of greeting. He also decided it was best not to look directly at her until he got his features and hoarse voice under control. "I'm not very good at these events, I'm afraid."

"He's a Brit," Nick interjected apologetically, flashing the wide smile (blindingly white and readily available) that always made Anthony seem that much more a buffoon in comparison. Freaking charming Italian. "They show no emotions, ever. What can you do?"

"Don't start, you two," Baptiste warned Anthony and Nick in that silky accent of his, green eyes bright and twinkling for the ladies' benefit. "I'd prefer for Samira to think I have nice friends."

Freaking charming Frenchman, Anthony thought, glaring at Baptiste with rising despair. Moments like these always made Anthony wonder why he'd ever befriended these two suave fellows in the first place. Thirty seconds with them in a social setting and Anthony inevitably sank to bottom of the class in terms of interpersonal skills and making a good impression.

Lobbing a final glare at Anthony and Nick, Baptiste commenced with the introductions. "Anthony Scott, meet Samira Palmer and Dr. Melody Harrison."

Oh, Anthony knew who Dr. Melody Harrison was, all right.

Why?

Because Baptiste had texted him a few weeks ago, saying that if Anthony was still in the market for surgeons willing to volunteer for one of the foundations he chaired, which provided medical services for children in need around the world, then Baptiste had a lead on someone for him to consider. And he had provided a link to Melody's hospital bio.

Since Anthony was always in the market for volunteers, he'd clicked on the link. Seen Melody's hospital bio and picture. Been immediately smitten and researched everything he could find online about her.

And suddenly found himself in the midst of a growing

fascination with this stunning woman standing in front of him.

Melody Harrison, thirty-five. A single, Harvard University-trained pediatric surgeon born and bred here in Journey's End, now practicing at the local medical center.

Anthony had, naturally, watched all her online video snippets for parents, where she discussed topics like the necessity of vaccinations and vision and sight screenings. He'd discovered that she was sharp, funny and compassionate, with a brisk and lovely American accent.

One might think that, with all that information and growing curiosity under his belt, he would be more than ready to meet Melody. One would be sadly wrong. Especially with his heart pounding its way up his throat.

So he focused on Baptiste's new girlfriend, Samira, first.

"How do you do?" he said, noting Samira's doe eyes, gleaming dark skin, high cheekbones and open smile. Baptiste had chosen well. Anthony could absolutely see why Baptiste had lost his head over her. "Pleasure."

Samira murmured something in response. He had no idea what. Why? Because his brain exploded as soon as he turned to Melody and looked into her face at close range.

Christ.

Surely no one present could blame him for needing a moment to adjust to being in the presence of this angel in their midst, much less smile or make conversation. Not with his face frozen like this.

Where to start?

Well, she was of average height, but that was where anything remotely average about her ended. She had luminous brown eyes that dominated her heart-shaped face. A cute nose. A lush fantasy of a mouth. Black corkscrew curls, piled on top of her head tonight, with a tumble trailing down one side of her face and along her neck. Honeyed skin, a gift from her white mother and black father (he'd seen them in her social media pictures), that glowed gold in the ballroom's romantic lighting. A filmy and fiery strapless red dress that left a healthy portion of her cleavage visible to admiring eyes, like his.

For a couple of the most deliciously excruciating moments of his life, he had zero idea what to do or say.

But then a small portion of his brain returned from break and reported for duty.

Right, then. Greet her, Anthony, you bloody moron. Don't screw this up.

Everything happened in slow motion.

He nodded at her.

A smile turned up the corners of her mouth, revealing the promise of dimples.

Excitement swooped low in his gut.

They shook hands, her soft palm sliding against his.

Her eyes widened as a shiver of something passed between them.

A secondary explosion racked his brain, leaving nothing useable in its wake.

Her lips moved.

He heard nothing.

She waited, a flicker of something indefinable crossing over her expression.

And…that was when everything zoomed to regular speed again and full awareness slammed back into his body.

Just in time for his social awkwardness to be revealed in all its glory.

She said something, you dolt.
Answer her!

"Pleasure," he said, dropping her hand and stepping away from this female flame before he truly hurt himself.

She stared at him, her expression inscrutable, before hastily looking away and smoothing her hair where it ran down her cheek.

With that, all the air seemed to go out of the room. He knew he'd taken it with him, but he couldn't quite figure out how to get it back. He never could.

A long and uncomfortable pause followed.

"So…" In a valiant attempt to get the mood back on track, Melody took a deep breath and encompassed all the men in her sweeping glance. "I have one dance partner for later, thanks to Nick. Who else is with me?"

"I am, as long as Samira can spare me," Baptiste said. "She's so easily eaten alive by jealousy. You understand."

"You *wish,*" Samira told Baptiste, and the two lovebirds made eyes at each other.

Melody looked to Anthony, her expression hopeful. "What about you?"

His heart sank. Every time he stepped onto a dance floor, he somehow managed to expand his two left feet to his entire body, generally spasming about like a man being electrocuted.

The only thing worse than his social graces? His dancing.

"You'll have to do without me," he said. "I don't dance."

As soon as the words were out of his mouth, Anthony wanted to find a shepherd's hook and yank them back. He'd meant to sound regretful. Instead, he'd sounded like a curt arse, even to his own ears. His poor sinking heart bottomed out at his feet.

"*You* don't dance? Well, there's a surprise," Melody said tartly.

"Mel…" Samira said, shooting her a look.

Ignoring this interruption, Melody stared up at Anthony with an open combination of amusement and mild irritation. Not at all the kind of thing he usually encountered with society women, who fell about simpering at him and laughing at every half-baked joke he told.

He stared at Melody, feeling a powerful surge of adrenaline as everything in him waited at strict attention to see what she would say.

"Pardon me?" he asked, his voice acquiring a husky edge.

"The life of the party, such as yourself?" Melody asked sweetly. "Hard to believe *you* don't enjoy dancing."

Anthony gaped at her.

"You might want to try dancing, Anthony," Baptiste said. "Samira and I danced together the night we met, didn't we, Samira? You never know when chemistry will strike."

"Well, it's not striking *here*." Tipping up her nose, as though she found the merest whiff of Anthony intolerable, Melody pivoted on her sky-high heels, firmly turning her back on him. "So don't waste your time."

She. Turned. Her. Back. On. Him.

On. *Him.*

Oh, she was spicy, this one.

Anthony liked that. He liked that a lot. And God help him, but she smelled like some heady and expensive combination of lemons and flowers. His belly tightened with spiraling desire.

He watched her, bemused and speechless.

"I think I need more champagne," she added. "Great to meet *you,* Nick."

The subtle emphasis was lost on no one, Anthony was sure, least of all him. He choked back a startled laugh.

With a final scowl in his direction, Melody swept off, giving Anthony the time and the opportunity he needed to admire her backside and shapely legs through the slit in her dress as she walked off through the crowd.

"I *believe* I mentioned that Melody is the surgeon who wants to donate her time and talents to your foundation? The one that treats sick children?" Baptiste asked Anthony blandly. As if Anthony hadn't told him, earlier this very evening, that Anthony was keen to meet the lovely Melody for reasons that had nothing to do with the foundation. "Or perhaps you've forgotten already?" Baptiste continued, eyes glimmering with mischief.

Anthony frowned at him, but couldn't get worked up about the teasing. Not when he felt this vibrantly and unreasonably alive in the wake of Melody's set down.

And also—let's face it—ridiculously deflated and disappointed with himself.

His entire body sagged with the weight of his failure. What a royal cockup.

He discreetly tried to keep Melody in sight, blinking and looking away only when Nick thumped him in the stomach with the back of his hand.

"Well done," Nick said brightly. "Now you've alienated people on six of the seven continents. We must book a trip to Antarctica so you can finish the job. Come on. We need drinks."

"We'll see you in a bit," Baptiste said, clearly eager for a minute alone with Samira.

"Great to meet you," Samira called after them.

"You, too," Anthony and Nick told her, setting off.

Anthony scanned the crowd again for signs of Melody, some of his surging hormones easing back until he felt stunned by the speed at which he'd crashed and burned. See? He'd screwed it up, just as he'd feared.

In his mind, meeting Melody could have unfolded so differently tonight.

He'd envisioned it all perfectly:

He would arrive and have a drink or two to shore up his courage and help overcome his embarrassing awkwardness with new people. He and Melody would lock eyes from across the room and somehow drift closer to each other, equally trapped in a haze of sensual awareness and magnetically drawn to each other. They would have a drink. Laugh. She would be every bit as beautiful and intriguing as her photos and videos promised. He would, for once in his misbegotten life, be as witty and smooth as Baptiste, Nick or, hell, George Clooney. She would like him for *him,* not knowing or caring about his family fortune or his grandmother. And then —he was a little hazy on this part—he and Melody would somehow find themselves upstairs in his suite, where they would fuck and fuck and then fuck some more, ravaging each other until the sun came up.

He could almost laugh.

In that entire well-spun fantasy, the only part that had come true was that Melody was far sexier and more intriguing than his poor mind could ever imagine.

And now?

And now she thought he was the toilet paper that got stuck to the bottom of her spiky heels when she visited the loo.

And he felt frustrated. Defeated. But also determined to try again.

What was it that Nelson Mandela had said about just such a situation? Ah, yes.

A winner is a dreamer who never gives up.

"I want you to know," Nick said, clapping a hand on

Anthony's shoulder to steer him to the nearest bar, "that that was a pathetic performance—"

"I know," Anthony muttered.

"—and you have embarrassed yourself—"

"I know."

"—*and* your family." Nick tipped his head and studied him with thoughtful concern. "Possibly for generations to come."

"Yet you stood silently by and watched it all happen," Anthony said bitterly. "Why haven't you and Baptiste taught me anything after all these years, I wonder?"

"We try!" Nick cried. "But you are absolutely unteachable."

"Fair enough," Anthony said, turning to the bartender. "Two whiskies. Neat."

They took their drinks and waded back into the crowd. Still no sign of—

"Stop craning your neck," Nick said around a sip of his drink. "You'll give yourself an injury. And it's pathetic."

"Yes, all right. We've both agreed that that was not my finest performance." Anthony shot daggers in his direction. "Perhaps we could move on."

Nick shrugged, sipping again. "Agreed. But I of course reserve the right to talk about it again with Baptiste."

"Wouldn't blame you." Anthony tossed back his entire drink, relishing the head-clearing burn as it worked its way down his throat. "I've got to go back in and try again."

"Yes. Because you've been wanting to meet that woman, staring at her videos and mooning over her—"

"I didn't *moon*."

"—and you can't let someone else swoop in and steal her out from under you tonight. You're as good as anyone else."

"Well, the jury's still out on that one," Anthony said, wishing he had another drink.

Nick snorted. "Just tell her who you are. I would. I would tell every woman within seconds of meeting her, and then just collect the panties the way people collect neckties or shoes." He paused, making a show of smoothing his hair and preening. "Of course, I *do* already collect the panties. But I would collect *more*."

This was the kind of thing that always made Anthony flare up.

"Yes, well, I'm not *you,* am I? I don't have the whole Sophia Loren smile—"

"My smile *is* excellent, I admit," Nick said, grinning in a blinding display of teeth.

"—nor do I want women who only want me for my family connections or money—*oh, for God's sake*." Spying the pair of women headed toward them, Anthony winced and wished he was back at his pillar so he could hide behind it. "Speak of the devil."

"What?" Nick asked quickly, dropping his voice and leaning closer.

"It's a bloody matchmaking mama from London who thinks I should marry her daughter. She stalks me at all these —oh, hello, Mrs. Carmichael." Anthony pieced together about 30 percent of a pleasant smile and plastered it on his face. "Lovely to see you both tonight."

"How are you, sir?" Mrs. Carmichael, whose plump face was difficult to make out what with all the sparkling diamonds ringing her neck and dangling from her ears, beamed at him as they shook. "I was *hoping* you might be here tonight."

"Indeed?" More like the old bat had hired someone to hack into Anthony's personal assistant's computer and steal

Anthony's engagement calendar. "But you mustn't call me *sir*, Mrs. Carmichael. We've talked about that. I'd prefer *Anthony*."

"Oh, I couldn't." Mrs. Carmichael flapped a hand, tittering like a finch on a power line. Then she all but planted her hand between her daughter's shoulder blades and shoved her forward in her eagerness to put her in front of Anthony. "And you remember my Annabella, don't you?"

As if he could forget.

Annabella was actually rather lovely in a toothy, freckled and outdoorsy sort of way, which was fine if one overlooked the fact that she was only twenty-one or so (one of these days, Anthony would have to verify that the girl was, in fact, of age) and had the personality of Sleeping Beauty before the kiss.

Anthony's interest in her, accordingly, ran far more toward adoption than marriage.

He shook the girl's hand. "Of course. How are you, Annabella?"

"I'm really good." She giggled. "We're going to Eleuthera for the holidays." Giggle. "So I can't wait for that."

Anthony nodded, wishing both the Carmichael females would notice, just the once, that he had absolutely zero interest in either of them, take the hint and leave. But then it occurred to him that he might be demonstrating the kind of rude behavior that frequently got him in trouble and decided to make more of an effort.

"And have you both met my school chum, Domenico Rossi?" he asked tiredly, motioning Nick forward.

And there went the wide and startling flash of Nick's smile, right on cue, leaving both the women looking a bit dazed.

"Delightful to meet you, Mrs. Carmichael. Annabella."

Nick's discreet once-over, honed to a razor's edge by years of practice, skimmed Annabella from head to toe, assessing her for relative fuckability. "*Such* a pleasure. Call me Nick."

"And *you*, Nick." Mrs. Carmichael's cheeks, normally rosy, went bright red as she beheld the Roman god. "And what a lovely accent you have. I take it you're from Italy?"

"Forgive me, Mrs. Carmichael." Anthony didn't have the patience to keep the crisp finality out of his voice, but painful experience had taught him that the matchmaking mama wouldn't hear it anyway. "But I've just spotted, ah, someone I need to introduce to Nick. You'll excuse us, won't you?"

Without waiting for any response, he clapped a hand on Nick's shoulder and steered him away.

"Dio Santo," Nick muttered when they were out of earshot, shuddering. "Fucking that one would be as exciting as a blow-up doll. Is she even a legal adult?"

"God knows."

"I was afraid the mama was going to offer you a fifty-thousand-pound dowry and some cows for her."

"I'm sure Mrs. Carmichael has considered it," Anthony said darkly. "She's not exactly subtle—hang on. There she is again. *Melody*."

Anthony froze as he watched Melody join the end of the queue at one of the carving tables, his heart skittering like a fox mid-hunt. Nick followed his line of sight, then eagerly turned to face Anthony, placing both hands on his shoulders and leaning in close.

"Now, listen," Nick said, skewering Anthony with that gray-eyed look of his. "This is your second chance, eh? Don't blow it. You're a good guy. A handsome guy. Stop being your own worst enemy. You're too old to be this shy. Go over there, talk to her and be yourself. And if that doesn't work? Pretend you're me. Okay? *Andare*."

With that, he took Anthony's face between his hands, gave him smacking kisses on both cheeks and turned him loose with a slight shove to get him moving.

Anthony glowered over his shoulder at him. "Stop kissing me. I'm British. We hate that."

A shrug from Nick. "I'm Italian. That's why I do it."

Chuckling, Anthony hurried the rest of the way. He slipped into line behind Melody and helped himself to a plate, praying she wouldn't notice him for a second or two. Just long enough for him to think of something to say.

But Melody, naturally, saw him immediately.

She stiffened, stabbing his flagging morale directly in the heart with her dinner fork.

That was when he shored up his courage and gave himself a swift kick in the arse. He'd been a captain in Her Majesty's service, for God's sake. He'd served overseas. He wasn't going to let a case of nerves keep him from getting to know Melody better while the opportunity presented itself. He could be brave when he needed to. This was clearly one of those moments.

He took a deep breath.

"It seems we've got off on the wrong foot," he told Melody.

"We did *not* get off on the right foot." Melody shot him a sidelong glance as she also took a plate from the stack. "I think we can agree on that. In fact, why don't we just pretend we don't see each other here in line and call it a day?"

Ouch. Another direct hit to his ego.

"That would be the best thing *you* could do," he said, his pulse thumping in his ears. "Obviously. But then *I* might miss out on getting to know an interesting new person. Not very fair to me, is it?"

"*You're* the one who dug this hole for yourself." She reached for a roll. "*I* was very pleasant to you."

"Yes, and pleasant persons, such as yourself, often give, ah…"

"I believe you Brits call them *arses*?" she supplied delicately.

She had him there.

"Fair enough. I believe you like to give arses like me a second chance now and then."

"Well, I would. Just because you and I will probably be seeing each other a fair amount—"

His pulse rate sped up like the horses out of the gate at Ascot.

"—if things keep up at this rate with Baptiste and Samira. But the problem is, I don't know what kind of arse you are."

"Pardon me?"

"Maya Angelou—you know her?"

"Of course I know her. What kind of a cretin do you take me for?"

"Not sure you want me to answer that right now. Anyway, she said that when a person shows you who they are, you should believe them the first time."

"Ah." His pulse rate crashed and burned. "I see where you're going with this."

"I figured you would. So are you an arse down in your soul, or are you a situational arse?"

She stared up at him as she waited for his answer, all wide-eyed and amused interest with those glorious brown eyes. He eased closer, happy to have this woman reel him in. Honestly, if he were a fish, he'd hook her line through his own cheek just so he could be on the boat with her.

"I'm strictly a situational arse," he said, doing his best to remain undistracted by the plump swells of her baps where her dress dipped in front. But he *did* have quite the spectacular view. He'd hardly be a man if he didn't notice. "You have my word."

"Hmm." She studied him closely. "That remains to be seen. And unfortunately for you, you can't just *announce* what kind of person you are. You have to demonstrate it."

"Understood. But can I offer a tiny explanation? About my gruffness earlier?"

"Feel free." She craned her neck and looked around,

noting all the people still waiting to be served. "Since this line doesn't seem to be going anywhere anytime soon and we may be forced to order a pizza if we want to get fed tonight."

"You see, the problem is that I'm a very poor dancer. The kind who leaves carnage across the dance floor and ruins parties." He shuddered. "No one here wants *that*."

"Ah." Dimpling, she passed him a set of silverware from the basket as the line finally shuffled toward the chef carving his giant roast. "Well, thank you for saving several lives tonight."

Anthony stared at her, feeling a bit lost. The sight of one almost-smile from this woman should not make his blood surge and hum through his veins, heating him from the inside out like some sort of emotional microwave.

But it did.

He studied her downturned face as he watched her spoon potatoes and horseradish sauce onto her plate, wondering if he should call the night a triumph. He'd spoken to her again; she'd given him half a chance; he'd seen a glimpse of her smile. Why not retire with full honors before he mucked it up again and said something to convince her he was as beastly as she'd initially feared?

But he didn't want to retire.

He wanted to bask in her glow for a few minutes longer. See if he could earn a full smile from that amazing mouth.

After all—no guts, no glory.

So he helped himself to potatoes and salad, thinking hard as the line inched forward.

Keep it nice and easy, Scott, he reminded himself. *Don't blather.*

He cleared his throat. "You should probably know. I'm not at my charming best at big parties like this. Or with new people in general. That's what makes me an arse."

More dimples, then she looked up, her bright eyes smiling even if her mouth wasn't.

"Do you *have* a charming best?"

"No. Not that anyone's ever detected."

That did it.

To his immense gratification, she burst into laughter. The kind that made her eyes dance and lit up not just her face but, honest to God, this entire corner of the ballroom and the darkest corners of his being. And he would have smiled back, but he was frozen inside the twin possibilities that he might get to know her, just a little bit more, or that he still might cock this whole thing up before she ever smiled at him like that again.

"See?" She nudged him with her elbow. "*That* was charming and funny."

"And accidental."

More of her laughter.

His heart skittered like beads of water across a hot griddle.

Then she sobered, giving him a crisp nod. "I really like Baptiste. He's got great taste in girlfriends—"

"Yes, because you and Samira are best friends, I believe?"

"—right. And if he's got good taste in girlfriends, maybe he's got good taste in best friends, too."

"That is the case with me. Not at all the case with Nick."

"Ah, *Nick*." She grinned again. "I knew he was trouble."

"You've no idea," he said, wincing dramatically.

"Well, anyway. You'll be happy to know that I've decided to give you another chance."

Oh, the irony. If she knew exactly *how* happy he was to know she hadn't completely written him off, she'd probably drop her plate and run screaming from the room.

"I'm delighted to hear that, Melody," he said, relief and excitement making his voice husky.

Nodding with unmistakable satisfaction, she balanced her plate and cutlery in her left hand and extended her right to him. "Melody Harrison. Great to meet you."

He frowned. "*Doctor* Melody Harrison, isn't it?"

She shrugged that away, flushing. "No need to be pretentious. My title isn't who I am."

Whoa. Had truer words ever been spoken?

He blinked, fighting the sensation that he'd received a mild shock from an outlet. He also battled the urge to look up and ask God if he could possibly be serious by sending Melody across his path, or whether He was just messing with Anthony the way He had during the holidays when Anthony was thirteen. That was the year his beloved mother had seemed to suffer no ill effects following a rough fall on the slopes in Klosters, then died the next morning from a brain bleed.

Melody couldn't possibly be the spectacular woman she appeared to be.

Could she?

Somehow Anthony shook off the dazed sensation. Then he shook this remarkable woman's soft hand for the second time that night, praying that some of the tightness in his throat would ease up a bit, at least enough for him to continue talking to her.

As for the prickling nerve endings in his nape and the goose bumps still flaring up and down his arms?

Nothing to be done about that.

"Melody Harrison." He said her name with relish. "It's a great pleasure to meet you."

She stared up at him, her smile fading as that indefinable *thing* arced between them again, twice as strong as before.

He held her hand, lingering in the moment—

"Excuse me," the woman behind him said in her harsh New York accent, "but the line's moving."

Sure enough, behind Melody's back, the line had moved ahead a meter or so, and the chef was serving the man in front of Melody.

Melody blinked and flushed, dropping Anthony's hand and hastily closing the gap.

He flexed his fingers, feeling deliciously scalded.

Good God. Electrified and scalded. What on earth had got into him tonight?

"Do you have a rare piece?" Melody asked the chef as he sliced for her. "That's perfect. Thanks."

And she stepped away from the carving table with her dinner, lingering several feet away as she searched the ballroom for an empty place to sit without ever looking back over her shoulder at Anthony.

"Rare for me, too," he quickly told the chef, wishing the man would hurry up a bit and not daring to hope that Melody might be waiting for *him,* let alone that she might feel the chemistry between them as acutely as Anthony did. "Great. No, that's plenty. Thanks."

Good fortune was with him. A couple walked away from one of the high-top tables surrounding the dance floor just then, giving him the opportunity he needed.

He hurried over to Melody. "I've found a table. Now that we're practically best friends, I feel certain you'll want to share it with me."

Melody looked round, her expression brightening. Perhaps the whisky he'd drunk had begun to distort his reality, but he could swear she looked excited to spend more time with him.

Almost...*pleased.*

"You're finished being an arse for the night? Because we've still got a fair amount of gala to go," she said very seriously.

"I'll do my best." He steered her to the table, deciding there was no time like the present to make sure she was single. The Internet and Baptiste had already told him that she wasn't married, but that didn't mean she had no significant other. "And are you here with someone? Do you want to go find him and let him know where you are?"

Repressed laughter made her eyes gleam as she set her plate down. "I'm good."

There was only one response to this nonanswer: a doleful look.

"You're sure you're not a barrister or a politician?" he wondered. "I've rarely heard such an evasive reply."

"And I've rarely heard such a poorly veiled question." Her lips twitched at the corners. "If you want to know something, why not ask a direct question?"

Anthony tried to look innocent. "I thought I did."

"No, you didn't—*Baptiste*. What's wrong?"

Baptiste hurried over to their table, looking pale and worried.

"There you are. I've been looking for you," he told Melody.

"What's wrong?" She put a hand on Baptiste's forearm. "Where's Samira?"

"She is, ah..." Baptiste ran a hand through his hair, making the waves stand on end. "She's not feeling very well all the sudden. It's her, ah, stomach."

"Oh, no," Melody said. "There's a nasty virus going around. Do you want me to take a look at her, or...?"

Shaky laugh from Baptiste. "I would love for you to take

a look at her, but she'd have my head for suggesting it. She insists she'll be fine."

"I'm sure she *will* be fine in a couple days. As long as she gets some rest and keeps pushing clear liquids so she doesn't get dehydrated. Are you taking her home?"

"Yes, but she's insisting on staying until after the remarks on the winery merger."

"Well, she works for the winery," Melody said. "It's her job."

"Yes," Baptiste said shortly, looking distracted.

Melody and Anthony exchanged concerned glances. Anthony was about to say something when Melody took the words out of his mouth.

"Baptiste, is there something else going on? Do you think it's something other than a stomach bug? You look so worried."

Baptiste blinked and came out of it, dividing his attention between them and trying to give them a reassuring smile. "I'm sure she'll be fine."

"Will *you* be fine?" Melody asked, squeezing Baptiste's arm. "That's the question."

Baptiste frowned. Shot a wary glance over his shoulder at Anthony.

"I'm not going to tease you, Bappy," Anthony said quickly. "We're not in school anymore, and even *I'm* not that big a prat."

Baptiste's tense face eased into the beginnings of a smile to accompany his nod of thanks. Then he turned back to Melody, sobering.

"The thing is, Samira's everything to me." He swallowed hard, making his Adam's apple bob, and if Anthony didn't know better, he'd almost think he saw tears in his mate's eyes. Which would be the first time ever. "*Everything*. If anything happened to Samira—"

"Nothing's going to happen to her," Melody said firmly. "And she can't take care of herself if she's worried about *you* falling apart. You need to get it together, okay?"

Baptiste took a deep breath and stood a bit straighter. "Yes, of course. You're right. I'm okay now. I'll take good care of her."

"I know that." Melody beamed at him and patted his face. "Why do you think I've been your biggest supporter, *Bappy*?"

"Merde." Baptiste scowled over his shoulder at Anthony, who tried to look apologetic, before leaning down to give Melody a double-cheeked kiss and big hug. "If I'd known we were using school nicknames tonight, I would have told Melody yours earlier, *Stocky*."

Anthony froze, wishing he'd kept his fat mouth shut. He shot Baptiste a warning glance as threatening as he could make it. Baptiste had the decency to look somewhat chagrined, but the damage was already done.

Melody looked at the both of them with keen interest and open amusement. "*Stocky?* I can figure out where *Bappy* comes from, but what's *Stocky* about?"

"Old family name," Anthony said quickly, before Baptiste revealed any further information that Anthony preferred to keep quiet for now. "Please give Samira my best. She's very lovely. I can see why you're so taken with her."

"Indeed." Baptiste's eyes narrowed with speculation, which was never a good sign. "Melody is *also* very lovely. But you seem to have already noticed that."

Anthony's face and ears burned white hot. He tried to look politely puzzled and regretted that they were out of school, where it would have been more acceptable for him to lunge for Baptiste's throat and wrestle him to the ground.

"Don't let us keep you," Anthony told Baptiste through gritted teeth.

Chuckling now, Baptiste clapped him on the back and hurried off through the crowd, leaving Anthony to wish he had a fire extinguisher to put out the flames of his embarrassment as he faced Melody again.

"I've never seen him like that over a woman," he said, jerking his head in Baptiste's direction. "I'd had the impression that things between him and Samira are quite serious. This proves it."

"I think you're right. I've heard people talk about feeling like they got zapped by electricity or lightning or something—"

Anthony tensed, his hand hovering over his silverware.

"But this is the first time I've ever seen it in action. I probably shouldn't speak out of turn, but I'd be surprised if they don't wind up getting married."

Ah, *marriage*.

As the child of divorced parents who'd scorched most of the earth beneath his feet leading up to and following their split back when Anthony was ten, he'd spent a lot of time alternately insisting that he wasn't ready to get married and/or feigning deafness when people like Mrs. Carmichael or, God forbid, his grandmother raised the topic.

So it was with a great deal of surprise, on what had already been a surprising night, that he found himself loosening up enough to spread some horseradish sauce on his meat and say the following:

"Well, we're all in our mid-thirties, Baptiste, Nick and I. I'll be thirty-five next year. Probably long past time for us to settle down and start families."

She glanced up from her careful arrangement of prime rib on her bun. "You like children?"

"'Course. What about you? Do you want to get married one day?"

"Nope. I've sworn off men," she said blithely. "I've decided to embrace my old maid status."

"Excuse me?" He choked on his bite and had to cough. "What the bloody hell are you talking about?"

"I'm serious. I work roughly a million hours per week. When I'm not working, I'm too tired to play online dating games with men who may or may not want a real relationship and may or may not even bother to show up on time for coffee or drinks after I've gone to the trouble of putting makeup and a nice outfit on. I'm over it. I'd rather stay at home and catch up on my medical journals. I've been married to my career for years. Now I've accepted that that's the way it's going to be. In fact, my dream house might be hitting the market soon—it's a gorgeous Colonial about a mile from here —and I'm hoping to buy it. I'm damn sure not going to hold off on that while I wait for a man to show up in my life. I might even get a cat or two. I've always wanted one."

Anthony had a great deal of difficulty getting his lower jaw off the floor. The idea of this intriguing woman rattling around in some lonely house with only a couple of cats and a stack of medical journals to occupy her because of a lack of worthwhile male companionship struck him as every bit as wasteful as tearing down Sandringham House because it had so many windows to clean.

Just in case his head hadn't completely exploded off his shoulders, she went back in to finish the job.

"It would take a great guy to make me jump back into *those* waters," she said, slathering more horseradish sauce on her sandwich and completely unaware of the consternation she'd just caused him. "A really. Great. Guy. *Cheers.*"

With that, she took a bite of her sandwich with relish.

He put down his fork, appetite ruined.

"And what about children?" he demanded. "Don't you like children?"

"Me? I hate children." She wiped her mouth. "That's why I became a pediatric surgeon. Now I can cut on them all day and hear their little screams."

He burst into startled laughter that helped dissipate some of the clouds that had just settled over him.

Melody watched him as her own smile slowly faded.

"What?" He rubbed his mouth with his napkin. "Don't tell me I have food in my teeth. I've barely eaten anything."

She blushed, all that golden skin taking on a rosy glow that seemed to steal all the ballroom's light from other sources and concentrate it on her face.

"You have great smile. I'm just wondering why you keep it on such strict lockdown."

Most of the air whooshed out of his lungs. She'd sworn off men, yet she complimented him like *that*? Was this a mixed message, or had he let his ego run away with him? And why did it feel so important to get the bottom of the matter?

He cleared his throat, determined to stay on topic. "And how do you expect to have children if you're single at the ripe old age of...?"

He already knew her age, of course, but he waited for her to supply it. They were almost the same age. That seemed like an important fact.

"Thirty-five," she said.

"Thirty-five. What's your plan, then?" he asked, recovering some of his appetite and taking a bite of potato.

She shot him a disbelieving look. "You may not realize this, but in the twenty-first century, women can adopt or use sperm donors."

The potato turned to rancid roadkill in his mouth. This just got worse and worse.

He dropped his fork with a clatter.

She looked up from her food, frowning at him.

"Children need a *father,*" he said flatly.

She shrugged. "Plenty of children of divorce turn out just fine."

He was Exhibit A on that point, he supposed. Still, he felt the inexplicable but powerful urge to take up arms and vigorously defend this point.

"Nevertheless, a male presence in the household—"

"I'm too busy to think about that now," she said, waving a hand. "And there's a bit more to my story. I wouldn't care if I never dated again, but Samira got a bee in her bonnet about wanting me to find someone and not be a single mom. So she signed me up for Doctor Love dot com. We'll see what happens."

"Doctor Love dot com?" he blurted on a surge of outrage. "What, some crackpot page for online hookups?"

A cold front swept into the ballroom. The eye of the storm centered over Melody's face. She put her sandwich down.

"It's not a *crackpot page for online hookups,*" she said slowly, icicles trailing spiky points from every word. "It's a well-respected dating website where doctors are matched with other doctors. Their statistics on successful matches are well above industry standards. Samira thinks I should check it out."

Successful matches?

What a disaster. This woman planned to either never date or only date men from the Internet. He couldn't think when he'd heard a more ridiculous idea. And what about *him*? A decent looking real-world man with a credential or two sitting right in front of her! What, was he no better than spoiled haggis?

She had him so flustered that he couldn't think straight. Or at all.

Which perhaps explained why he didn't pick up on social cues and keep his fat mouth shut.

"Yes, but why would a glorious woman like you need to stoop to such nonsense?" he cried. "Now every unworthy man with a medical degree and a computer with Internet access gets a go at you? And what if your best match isn't a doctor? You'd miss him entirely, wouldn't you?"

Melody's expression closed off.

"Does it even occur to you that you're complimenting me and insulting me in the same breath?"

He leaned in, his words clipped and his face hot.

"Does it even occur to you that your plan is illogical nonsense?"

She stiffened. "And the insults just keep on coming."

He belatedly realized that he'd veered into awkward territory again and winced. Impatiently flapped a hand.

"I obviously don't mean to insult you. If I did—"

"*If?*"

"It's purely by accident—*hang on*. Why are you taking your plate? Where're you going?"

"I'm leaving." She stood, her face the vivid red of the guards' jackets during their changing ceremonies outside Buckingham Palace. "And thank you for only wasting ten minutes of my time while you show me that you are, in fact, an unmitigated arse. And for us Americans in the crowd, you're also a *jackass*."

Hurt and anger at himself—because he was always his own worst enemy, wasn't he? —made him sharper than he needed to be.

He also stood. "And you, Dr. Harrison, are a judgmental hothead."

Another humorless laugh. "Yeah, okay. Screw you."

She moved so abruptly as she turned to go that the one side of her hair shifted away from her face.

That was when he saw them:

The raised and mottled marks that ran over her cheek and down the side of her neck like the fingers of a hand.

The sight of the pink and brown striations next to her radiant golden skin was so jarring and unexpected that he couldn't hold back the words as he put a hand on her arm to stop her.

"My God, what's happened to your face?" he said, even though he'd spent more than enough time in overseas war zones to recognize scars like this when he saw them. He'd seen his men alight. Heard their screams in the field, their moans in the hospital and smelled the sizzle of their flesh. And *Melody* had…? He couldn't even let himself finish the thought. It was far too painful. "Were you *burned*?"

Once again, he wanted to yank the words back. Especially when he glimpsed the bright red patches staining her cheeks. Her flashing eyes and flaring nostrils.

But then he saw the hint of steel and realized that he'd angered rather than humiliated her.

She looked as though she wanted to take his head off.

He could hardly blame her for that.

Hell, if there'd been a block nearby, he'd have laid his head down on it for the big chop.

As the wave of her quiet fury rolled over him, he took a moment to put down the shovel he'd used to dig himself this massive hole and admire her all the more. It would take more than the bumbling likes of him to humiliate the beautiful, intriguing and proud Dr. Melody Harrison. Oh, yes, it would.

"I'm sorry," he said quickly, with no way to explain that the sight of that obscene scar on her face was as upsetting as watching someone take a blowtorch to one side of the *Mona Lisa*. No way to tell her that the thought of her ever having to endure that sort of excruciating pain made him want to vomit into the nearest potted plant. "I didn't mean—"

"Save yourself," she said coolly. "I couldn't care less about what you mean."

Stunned stupid, he watched her storm off for the second time that night, thinking about what an idiot he was and how overmatched he was with this one.

And how determined he was to change her opinion of him.

3

"Freaking *jackass*." A few minutes later, Melody helped herself to the healthiest slice of white chocolate raspberry cake she could find from the dessert table, not bothering to keep her voice below a loud mutter. The gala was in full raucous swing by this point anyway, and anyone close enough to hear her ongoing rant about Anthony Scott was probably too drunk to care about the crazy woman's opinions. "Arrogant *jerk*—"

"Oh, Lord." Samira materialized at her side, looking pale and grim. "She's talking to herself."

"Hey!" Melody gave her best friend a medical once-over. Samira's dark complexion had a green tinge to it, so that wasn't good. Her forehead gleamed but wasn't diaphoretic, and her eyes were bright but not necessarily febrile. Just to be sure, she pressed the back of her hand to Samira's neck, only to have Samira scowl and smack it away. "Well, you don't feel warm. Are you lethargic? Nausea? Vomiting?"

Samira's scowl deepened. "I don't need a diagnosis, Meredith Grey. I just don't feel so hot at the moment. No need to order any CBCs or MRIs."

"Well, tell that to your boyfriend. Baptiste looks like he's on the brink of a nervous breakdown." Melody crossed her arms and tapped her chin with her index finger in an exaggerated thinking pose. "And isn't *this* the guy who hasn't raised the issue of what's going to happen with your relationship when he goes back to Paris for meetings this week? The guy you're *so* sure is going to dump you at the first opportunity? Weren't you crying on my shoulder about *that* earlier in the evening? Yeah, I can see why you're so concerned. Baptiste is just not that into you. Clearly."

"Now is not the time for your sarcasm." Samira sipped from a giant glass of ice water. Then she tilted her head ever so slightly in the direction of the tables ringing the dance floor. "Is he still over there? Watching me?"

Melody looked around. "Who? Baptiste?"

Sure enough, Baptiste, who was now reunited with Anthony Scott (freaking jackass), had his moody attention pinned to Samira and her glass of water. The Jackass had, meanwhile, reverted to regarding Melody with the glowering and unblinking expression with which you might expect a panther in a tree to regard an antelope right before jumping down to snap the poor animal's neck in half.

"Oh, Baptiste is watching you, all right," Melody said darkly, looking away from Anthony and returning her attention to Samira.

Samira rolled her eyes. "I'd better talk quick. He only let me come over here if I promised to drink all this water and come right back."

"Well, you don't want to get dehydrated," Melody said.

"Whatever. I want to know what's going on with you and the very sexy Anthony Scott? Seemed like there might be some chemistry there when you met."

Melody gaped at her. "You got up off your deathbed to come over here and be nosy?"

"Of course. And I'm feeling a little better. Now what's up?"

"Absolutely nothing." Melody refused to remember the way her naughty bits had swelled with feminine appreciation a little while ago, when she first met The Jackass, or to consider the way shivers of awareness prickled over her skin even now, knowing that he was still in the room. Still watching her. "He's every bit the arrogant jerk with the British flagpole stuck up his ass that I initially thought he was."

Samira lowered her glass, looking startled. "Whoa. That's a lot of vitriol for someone you just met. Looks like I was right about the chemistry."

"You were *not* right," Melody barked. "He acted like I was an idiot loser for trying Doctor Love dot com. And *you're* the genius who signed me up for it. Like I haven't suffered enough at the hands of online jerks in years gone by."

"Yeah, but this is a better site for you than some of those others you tried." Samira snapped her fingers. "That reminds me. I got your profile up and running."

"You did? That quick?"

"Yep. I used the pic with the red sweater. Red suggests passion and sexual availability. *And* it makes you approachable."

"Yeah, yeah." Melody put down her plate and watched Samira pull out her phone. "Let's see it."

The profile pic, a fun and breezy shot of a smiling Melody, had actually required a photo shoot with Samira operating the camera. Melody looked like a fun woman who was a good choice whether your goals were a leisurely afternoon hike, dinner and a movie, or an unforgettable afternoon in bed.

She had, of course, made sure her hair fully hid her scar. No need to scare all the men off before they gave her a chance.

Although, to be honest, did it matter whether she scared them off in the picture rather than scaring them off when they saw her in person? No, it did not. Either way, in her painful experience, the men treated her to staring, pitying looks and, inevitably, ghosting. No, she didn't want to go down this road again, but she'd promised Samira she'd try to be a more rounded person and give it a shot.

So she'd give it a shot.

Melody studied the profile for several long seconds, looking for cracks in the facade, before making her pronouncement:

"Not bad."

"Thank you." Samira favored her with a dignified nod. "Hopefully, you'll be engaged by Monday."

"You know I'm only doing this to get you off my back, right? I don't want to do this again."

"Don't start," Samira said firmly. "We've been over this a million times. Doctor Love dot com caters to a better clientele than those other sites you've been on. None of the men here are going to freak out when they meet a woman with a little scar."

Melody smoothed her hair with a fidgety hand, making sure it fully covered her cheek. "It's not a little scar, and you know it. And if one more man gets an *emergency phone call*"—she made quotation marks with her fingers— "and dashes out of his blind coffee date with me when he sees the scar, I will not be responsible for my actions."

"Maybe they're dashing out because they've put you in the friend zone. Ever think of that?" Samira deadpanned.

Melody had to smile. Better that than let Samira see how much these incidents hurt her feelings and damaged her morale. Seriously, Melody had thought she'd be over it after all these years. She'd had the damn scar for most of her life, for crying out loud. When was she going to get over caring about people's reactions to it?

"Be grateful you're sick," she told Samira. "It's saving you from a beatdown right now."

"You're *beautiful,* Mel." Samira gave her an arm squeeze and quick kiss on the cheek. "Inside and out. I wouldn't lie to you."

Melody rolled her eyes and repressed a grateful smile. Moments like this made her glad she'd been smart enough to make Samira her best friend all those years ago. "Whatever. You're just trying to make me feel better because you're going home with a sexy guy and I'm not."

"You will be soon, though. That scar's not going to matter to the right man, honey. We just have to find him."

"Well, we can rule out Anthony Scott," Melody said without thinking. "He just freaked out like everyone else does."

"Oh, no." Samira made a face. "Sorry about that."

"Eh. Who cares?" Melody said airily.

Samira cast a wary glance at Baptiste—holding her eye, he pointedly tapped his watch—and sighed. "He's going to come over here in a second. Can you do me a favor, please? I left my black velvet cape in the winery's suite upstairs on the eighth floor. You know the one I'm talking about, right? Can you go get it for me? Baptiste offered to go, but he'll never find it."

"Of course."

"You're awesome. Thanks."

Melody set off for the elevators. And it wasn't that she wanted to know what The Jackass was up to now, because she *didn't,* but her keen peripheral vision happened to notice that he was no longer standing with Baptiste.

Something inside her deflated, which made her doubly glad she had her profile ready to go. That was the thing about being a single career woman in the twenty-first century, wasn't it? You could have a great career or a great man, but you damn sure couldn't have both. You worked hard to get to where you needed to be, but by the time you did, your dating options had narrowed down to divorced men, baby daddies, ex-felons and blue-collar guys who might be perfectly nice but couldn't keep you in the style to which you'd already gotten yourself accustomed. And they all acted like they were doing you some grand favor if they called or showed up when they said they would.

Plus, she had her stupid freaking scar to deal with.

Oh, she'd sworn off men and recommitted to her career, sure, but she was only human. She had weak moments and relapses when she dreamed that her prince might still come. So when she met a seemingly handsome, sexy and well-educated guy like The Jackass, she was primed and ready to hang all sorts of girlish hopes on his unworthy ass.

Well, thank God he'd shown his true stripes so early in the process.

And now that she was on DoctorLove.com? Things *could* change for her, couldn't they? Eligible men might become like planes at LaGuardia now. Another one might be along any second.

And the right one wouldn't be repulsed by her scar.

Normally she didn't like to get too hopeful about her prospects for romance, but the thought cheered her up enough to grin as she made her way through the hotel lobby. She was still grinning when she dashed into a waiting elevator and settled in a back corner of the car just as the doors slid closed. Her grin lasted all the way until she detected movement out of the corner of her eye and heard that bored upper-class British voice.

"Fancy meeting you here."

Melody froze.

Her worst fears were, of course, confirmed when she looked at the mirrored doors and saw Anthony's figure, slouched in the other corner, reflected at her. Her heart sank even as another of those maddening shivers raced up her spine and prickled with the nerve endings in her nape and scalp.

"Oh, come *on,*" she muttered to the ceiling.

"Don't worry." He'd been checking his phone, ankles crossed, but now he stood up straight and shoved his hands in his pockets, moves that inexplicably seemed to result in him taking up far more than his fair share of the space. "I'm sure we can tolerate each other for thirty seconds or so. Which floor?"

"Eight," she said sourly.

He punched the button and stared at her, his jaw tight and his expression impenetrable.

She watched him from beneath her lashes, trying to regulate her suddenly sketchy breathing.

If only he weren't so tall and handsome. Those were the real issues here. Tall and handsome on the outside, with unmitigated jackassery through and through.

Ah, well. The Lord giveth, and the Lord taketh away.

It was *such* a shame, though.

Six two or three if he was an inch, Anthony stood well above her five seven, even in her spiky heels. And he had, as far as she could see with his clothes on (now why was she thinking about taking off his clothes?) the broad-shouldered and toned physique of a swimmer.

As for his coloring, he possessed the blond-haired and ruddy good looks of a lifelong outdoorsman. He was blessed with laugh lines (not that he ever laughed!) bracketing his mouth and fanning out from the corners of his eyes that made him seem all the more interesting and experienced.

The lighting wasn't good enough for her to tell what color his eyes were, but they were light. Fringed with dark lashes and darker brows that seemed particularly striking in combination with his golden sun-streaked hair, which was cut short. He had a long and straight nose, granite-carved cheekbones and a cleft in his chin. His lips were surprisingly full, and he had a movie star smile when he unleashed it long enough for it to come out and play.

The overall effect? Stunning.

She wasn't immune. No woman would be, least of all one who hadn't had sex in the last six months, following the abrupt end of her longtime friends-with-benefits arrangement with one of her former med school classmates after he started dating someone seriously.

Bottom line? Anthony Scott was a Nordic god. Thor came to mind.

He was also a jerk, and *that* was the part she needed to bear in mind if she wanted to keep her wits about her.

They rode for a good second and a half in silence. Well, except for the sound of him systematically cracking his knuckles.

Crack-crack-crack.

Then he lowered his hands and cleared his throat.

"I'm sorry about my reaction to your scar. I just hadn't—"

"Let's not and say we did." Big of him to apologize, but she wasn't in a forgiving mood. "Just forget it."

"I mean it, Melody," he said, his voice husky. "I'm very sorry."

They stared at each other in the mirror.

She blinked, a little taken aback by his evident sincerity. Something inside her relented.

"I appreciate that," she said, beginning to wonder if she'd have to reevaluate her reevaluation of his character.

For God's sake—was this guy a jerk, or wasn't he? Why couldn't she get a decent bead on him?

He nodded and took a deep breath.

"As for that, ah, dating website, I simply meant that I'm surprised that a woman like you needs to resort to—"

Melody snorted. *Unbelievable*. Back he went into the jerk category.

"You know what? Don't bother. You only make it worse."

They glared at each other with a force strong enough to ricochet off the mirrors and make spiderweb cracks shatter the glass. Her neck and face burned with such seething anger it was a wonder smoke didn't come out of her ears and activate the overhead sprinklers. A distant corner of her mind wondered why she was experiencing such a violent reaction to a complete stranger, but a more immediate part of her focused on how nice it would be to bop him on his perfect lips and silence that snooty voice.

"I'm *trying* to apologize," he said.

"Maybe spend less time apologizing and more time thinking about what you're saying in the first place," she snapped.

"Happy to. Only you might want to give a chap some latitude for being a bit nervous around you."

This was so patently ridiculous that she couldn't repress a startled bark of laughter.

"Oh, please," she said, abandoning her corner so she could get in his face and confront him directly. "The guy who's been glaring at me like I'm something he found on the bottom of his custom shoes claims that *I* make *him* nervous?"

He quickly joined her in the center of the car. They met like opponents in a boxing ring just as the bell rang for round one.

She hitched up her chin and put her hands on her hips.

He loomed over her, eyes flashing.

"If you don't know the difference between glaring and staring," he said, his resonant voice acquiring a rough edge that made butterflies flitter in her belly, "then I'm afraid you don't know a damn thing about how beautiful you are or your effect on men."

Wait, *what?*

He couldn't just lob a compliment like that into the middle of their perfectly good argument! What was she supposed to say to *that?*

She stiffened. Opened her mouth with her thoughts on a ten-second delay—

Just as the elevator shuddered to a sudden stop, making her wobble in her heels.

He quickly caught her upper arm in a grip that was warm and sure.

"All right?" he asked.

She nodded shakily, pulling her arm free and trying not to blush when he looked at her like that, all chivalrous concern. "Look what you did. All your negative energy broke the elevator."

There was no smile, but his eyes gleamed with amusement as he pressed the red button.

"Yeah, hello?" said a craggy male voice over the intercom. "Security here."

"Yes, hello," Anthony said. "We seem to have got stuck on the elevator. Any chance you could spring us out of here sometime soon?"

"I sure hope so, buddy," Security Guy said. "That car's been acting up. I'm surprised they let people on it tonight, to tell you the truth. Lemme see if I can get the repair folks on the horn. Give me a few."

Anthony shot her a quick *oh, shit* glance and ran a couple of fingers beneath his starched collar. "You've been having problems with the elevator, you say?"

"Oh, yeah." Security Guy sounded several degrees too cheerful, as though he got paid a commission every time the repair people showed up. "That particular car's been out of order all week."

The car chose that exact moment to drop several feet in silent confirmation.

Melody cried out and grabbed the brass rail for support.

Anthony flattened his palms against either side of his original corner, bracing himself.

"I'll be right back," Security Guy said. "You folks hold tight."

"You *will* hurry?" Anthony called, but no answer.

Several seconds passed with only their harsh breathing to break the silence.

"Well, this isn't how I saw things going down tonight," Melody said, trying to laugh.

"Nor I. I thought I'd be showered and in bed by now, flipping through dreadful programs on the telly and trying to find a football game to watch."

"You like the Pats?" she asked hopefully. "A guy who likes the Pats can be redeemed."

"I was referring to Manchester United." He paced a couple of steps, rubbed the back of his neck and paced back. "Although I probably should pretend to like the Pats just so I don't give you yet another reason to write me off forever."

She rolled her eyes. "I wish you Brits would speak American. It's *soccer*. Not football."

"Thank you for that crucial correction. I'll try to remember it in these last precious minutes before we plunge to our deaths."

She had to laugh as she leaned back and crossed her ankles.

Anthony yanked his bow tie loose and undid the top couple of buttons of his shirt. A closer look revealed a sheen of sweat across his forehead and a vague flare of panic in his eyes.

"You okay?" she asked warily.

"Never better," he said, now taking off his jacket and slinging it over the rail.

The cufflinks went next. He put them in his pocket and rolled up his shirtsleeves, revealing muscular arms fuzzed with that honeyed hair. He paced back and forth again, muttering something she couldn't quite make out, then ran the back of his hand over his forehead.

"You sure?" she asked, noting the way the color continued to leach out of his skin. Another few minutes at this rate and he'd look like her med school cadaver. "Because you're starting to look a little pale to me."

"I'm sure it's just the…" He flapped a hand at the ceiling. "Poor lighting."

She was about to argue the point when her cell phone buzzed. She pulled it out of her little beaded bag and checked the display. Samira.

"Hey, Sami," she said. "Sorry, but I'm stuck on the elevator. With, ah, Anthony."

Who was now leaning into the corner, bent at the waist with his hands braced on his thighs.

"Stuck? Oh, no! Is someone coming to rescue you?" Samira asked.

"That's what they claim. But I haven't seen or heard any sign of it. But don't worry about us. You folks go on home so you can get some rest."

"We'll check with the manager and make sure the cavalry's on the way," Samira assured her.

"Sounds good."

"And you should take a minute or two to get to know Anthony better."

"Is *now* the time for that kind of nonsense?" Melody snapped.

"Not really, but you *did* throw me to the wolves with Baptiste several times, so turnabout's fair play."

Melody scoffed. "Yeah, okay, well, when I plummet to my death, you'll be sorry that your last words to me were about karma."

"Not true. Call me when you get sprung."

"Bye," Melody said gloomily, hanging up.

By now, beads of sweat had broken out across Anthony's forehead and he'd begun breathing through his mouth.

"I'm so glad you're not having a panic attack," she told him, thinking of Baptiste, who'd freaked out on her a few weeks ago, overwhelmed by the speed with which his feelings for Samira had turned serious. "I was with a friend of mine when he had his first panic attack recently. I wouldn't want to think it was *me*."

He raised his head and gave her a baleful look and wry smile as two bright patches of color resolved over his sharp cheekbones. "It probably… *is* you. What else could make a… manly man such as myself…lose my breath like this?"

A part of her heart—a really tiny part, practically negligible—softened toward him.

And her long years of medical training of course required that she comfort the afflicted.

So she walked over to him and put a hand on his shoulder for a supportive squeeze.

"Manly men such as yourself have testosterone to spare. So you're allowed a touch of claustrophobia."

There.

She'd been a nice medical professional and done her duty. No one could require anything more of her under the circumstances.

But with him doubled up like this, there was nowhere else to look but directly in his face. Nothing else to see but his spectacular eyes, which were finally close enough for her to detect the color.

They were blue. The unforgettable color of the earth when viewed from space.

And the unwavering attention from *those* eyes caused her breath to stutter.

"To tell you the truth," he said, gasping, "I'm not…not that fond of closed spaces."

She blinked. Tried hard to view him as a patient rather than a man who made her heart thump with excitement.

"But you ride in elevators all the time, right? And you know that nothing bad's happening. It's your mind playing tricks on you."

"Yes, well, my mind's a… It's a devious bastard. Because it keeps telling me that…if something bad did…if something bad did happen, I couldn't… couldn't escape."

"Shhh," she said, now smoothing the hair at his temples,

which felt like the finest spun silk, warm and somehow vibrant beneath her fingers. They hadn't *technically* taught this method of patient care in med school, but she couldn't seem to help herself. "I'm sure the elevator has an emergency brake system to prevent it from falling—"

"I'm not...it's not *falling*."

"Then what?"

"Fire." He said the word quietly, as though he knew the sound of it was enough to lock her down with fear. "I can't stand the thought of *fire*."

She stared at him, her mind blanking out as she felt a phantom flare of pain across her cheek—

"So, hey, uh, I've got some bad news for you folks." Security Guy's voice burst back over the intercom, startling them and thankfully snapping Melody back to the present. "You're going to be in there for a while. At least an hour. The on-call elevator guy's working on some issue over at the hospital, and they get priority 'cause they're moving patients. They've called in the backup guy, but you might want to make yourselves comfortable."

4

"At least an hour?" Anthony slid to a seated position in the corner, rested his arms across his knees and put his head on his forearms. *"Christ."*

Melody, who still had her hand on his shoulder, felt him begin to tremble.

"Thanks for the update," she quickly told Security Guy. "What's your name?"

"Roy," said the disembodied voice.

"Thanks, Roy. I'm Melody." She kept an anxious eye on Anthony. "Is there any chance someone could, I don't know, pry open the doors or something? Is that the issue?"

"Nope. Sorry, Mel. The car's between floors from what I can tell. Even if we could get the doors open, you'd have to muscle your way up to ceiling level and you'd only have about a foot of space to work with. Unless the guy with you's Tom Cruise in between *Mission: Impossible* movies, no one's getting out that way."

Melody grimaced. "Wonderful. Well, what's the ETA on backup elevator repair guy?"

"He's on his way."

"Thank God," Melody said.

"From the city," Roy added.

"That's *two* bloody hours," Anthony said, his voice muffled.

"Yeah. Sorry 'bout that," Roy said. "You folks holler if you need anything."

"*Could* you get us anything?" Melody asked hopefully. "Some water, maybe?"

"Not really, no," Roy said. "I was mainly trying to be polite. Keep your morale up."

"Yeah? Well, my morale's plummeted through the bloody floor." Anthony raised his head, now gasping through his open mouth like a caught marlin. "Have you got anything else for us?"

"Yeah, okay, thanks, Roy," Melody said quickly, frowning at Anthony. "We'll let you know if we need anything."

"Why would we...why would we bother?" Anthony asked her, looking incredulous.

"Good luck to you there, Mel," Roy said, his subtext (God bless you for being stuck in there with *that* asshole) coming through the line loud and clear. "Over and out."

Melody rounded on Anthony, which was hard to do with him slumped against the back wall down around knee level. "There you go being a jerk again. It's not Roy's fault we're— Anthony? Anthony!"

But Anthony was staring straight ahead with a fixed expression of horror, his face damp with sweat and his body shaking like a dog on his way to the vet for shots.

"I can't get out." His voice sounded scraped. Broken. Ruined. "I'm going to die like this."

Melody had seen this before. Many times. Especially when she did a rotation at the VA hospital back during her residency. She sank to the floor beside him and arranged her skirt as best she could with the deep slits in each side.

"You were in the military, weren't you?"

A muscle in his jaw twitched. He nodded.

"Overseas?"

Another nod.

"Afghanistan?"

He stiffened and didn't answer.

"What happened to you?" she asked quietly, leaning against him and wrapping her arm around his back so he'd know he wasn't alone. He blindly reached for her free hand and held it. His hand was big and warm, she discovered, with nice fingers and well-kept nails. "Anthony? What happened?"

He shook his head.

"You can tell me. *Anthony*. I'm a doctor. You can tell me anything."

He blinked and came out of it enough to look at her, his expression bleak.

"I don't want to go there. Not with you."

"I think you're already there. Why not get it out of your system a little?"

His expression turned stony, slamming the door and turning the bolt on this idea.

She held his gaze. Waited patiently.

He opened his mouth, surprising her. Activated his voice after a long delay and an unsteady breath.

"Something went wrong." He cleared his throat. "With the rotor."

"Your helicopter?"

A sharp nod.

"You crashed?"

"I had to abort the takeoff. And there was…" He broke off, the word working in his mouth. "There was…"

"There was a fire?"

He hesitated. Nodded.

"And you were trapped?"

Another nod.

She squeezed his shoulder and waited again.

"I couldn't breathe. The smoke was the blackest thing I've ever seen. Great clouds of it. Like it was alive. Like it was coming for me. It wanted to cover my face and get all that petrol inside my lungs." He paused. "It was hot, you know? The smoke itself was *hot*. And I got my belt off, but I couldn't work the door latch. It was…it was jammed or something."

She nodded.

"People were shouting. I could hear some of my boys pounding. Screaming."

She nodded again.

"And the flames were…" His laugh was humorless. Shaky. Bewildered. "You think fire is just orange, but it's not. It's orange and red and gold and yellow…and it's fast. It's over there, and you think you have a few seconds, but…" Incredulous laugh. "It's right there, chasing you."

"What did you do?"

"My…the windshield had cracked. I was able to kick through it and…once I hit the ground and I got some air, I…I had to go around to the side and help…"

"You got your men out."

He swallowed hard, looking dazed. Stunned. "Yeah. The crew on the ground was there, and we did what we were trained to do. We got everyone out. Fifteen besides me."

"Any fatalities?"

A sob crept up on him, making his face contract and a strangled sound escape before he mastered it with a serrated breath.

"Burns. Broken bones. Lacerations. Concussions. Smoke inhalation." He wiped his mouth with the back of his hand. "No fatalities." He covered his face with his hands and let his head fall back against the wall. *"No fatalities."*

This man was a war hero, she realized. The first she'd ever met.

He was prickly, arrogant, intermittently funny and charming, handsome, sexy and fascinating.

And he was a war hero.

Maybe her thoughts were louder than she'd hoped, because he dropped his hands and glowered at her, his eyes sparks of blue with black striations.

"Don't go looking at me like that. I did my job."

She tried to wipe some of the admiration off her face.

"Great. Well, thanks for doing your job. You're just like a plumber who unclogs a toilet before it overflows, thereby preventing a tragedy for the people on the floor below."

He made a sound that may have been part of a startled laugh.

"I did what I had to do. I'm not a hero."

"Whatever you say," she told him.

"I was scared out of my fucking mind."

"'The brave man is not he who does not feel afraid, but he who conquers that fear.'"

His jaw dropped.

She felt a twinge of unease. "What? It's Nelson Mandela."

"I know," he said, staring at her. "Mandela's one of my personal heroes. You know him?"

"Of course I know him. Anyway…We'll have to disagree about how brave you are or aren't."

Anthony hastily looked away, flushing until his ears turned red.

"America's a free country. You're free to have your opinion and free to be wrong about it. Only I wish you'd stop looking at me."

She flapped a hand at the elevator in general.

"My options for things to look at are fairly limited at the moment. Sorry."

He snorted and swung his head back around to stare at her again.

"And speaking of looking at people, maybe you could stop looking at me like *that*," she said. "It's like being glared at by a pissed-off bald eagle. And then you've got that whole voice thing going on. I'm afraid you're going to launch into *Richard III* or something. 'Now is the winter of our discontent made glorious summer by this son of York.' It's unnerving."

He blinked. The corners of his mouth twitched. "I would never do anything so cruel."

"Well, how do I know that? I just met you. I'm not used to surly Brits."

He seemed taken aback.

"You *do* realize that you just told me your entire story and you're breathing fine? You're not sweating. You're not shaking. You're still alive."

"And humiliated beyond words," he muttered.

"Why? Because you have bad memories of a bad thing that happened to you when you were doing your job and saving your men?"

Something in his expression eased all the way to the outskirts of a smile.

There was a long and delicious pause.

"No. Because there's this woman I'd love to impress. But I haven't managed a decent thirty seconds with her all night."

"Oh," she said faintly, all the breath whooshing out of her lungs.

That was when she felt it again—that touch of electricity to her nape and down her spine until it radiated from her fingertips and all the way out her toes. He didn't smile a lot, but he did such extraordinary things with those eyes of his. Freezing her out one moment, then luring her closer the next.

And all of it with a dizzying earnestness she'd never encountered before.

"Can I explain something to you?" he asked quietly.

"There's *more*?" she asked, trying to keep her tone light. The intensity level between them had already reached critical levels in the last minute or so, despite the fact that they were complete strangers. She wasn't sure how much more she could take.

"The thing is…" He swallowed hard, making his Adam's apple bob. "The thing is…I've seen fire. I know what it can do. And what I said before? About your scar? It was my inelegant way of expressing that I can't stand the thought of a fire marring this amazing face. I can't stand the thought of you in pain. Even if it was a long time ago."

Melody blinked. Tried hard to keep her walls up and not lose herself in those remarkable eyes or his powerful words. Something warned it would be way too hard to find her way out again.

"Tell me what happened to you," he said.

She automatically shook her head and started to slam that particular door shut the way she always did. She never talked about her scar if she could help it. It was a rule.

"I can't—"

"*Melody*. I just told you my story. Fair is fair."

He watched her, waiting patiently and without apparent judgment.

And the story rose up, whether she wanted it to or not.

"It wasn't a fire. I was, ah, playing tag with my yellow lab one day before school. His name was Charlie."

She paused, taking a moment to compose herself before she crept up on the rest of the story. The way she imagined a snake charmer took his time before lifting the lid on a dancing cobra's basket.

"And what happened with Charlie?" Anthony asked gently.

"We ran into the kitchen. I tagged him. Then it was his turn to chase me. My mother yelled at us to stop running. Just as he clipped my heels and tripped me. I, ah, fell into the stove. Caught a pan handle with my hand. Flipped a pot of oatmeal over. It hit the side of my face. My mother screamed. Charlie barked."

"Jesus," he muttered.

She caught herself reaching for her cheek. Put her hand down again.

"But I didn't burn my hands. And I didn't burn Charlie. So I was glad about that. Mad that I couldn't go to school, but glad about that."

"How old were you?" he asked, his expression bleak.

"Six." This was a good stopping point for her little tale of woe, but it suddenly seemed important to get it all out there. "It was a couple months before I went back to school. And the kids treated me differently after that. As you can imagine."

"I'm, ah..." He rubbed his forehead hard enough to make the skin peel. "I'm sorry you went through that."

"Don't be," she said crisply. "It made me who I am. That's why I went to medical school. I wanted to help little kids and be like the doctors who helped me."

An unmistakable gleam of admiration lit his eyes. "I see."

"Don't look at me like that," she said. "It's no big deal. What else was I going to do? Shrivel up and die?"

The gleam intensified. "Ah. So you only did what you had to do."

"Yeah," she said, keeping her responsive smile on maximum security lockdown. "I did what I had to do."

He nodded, his amusement fading away.

They stared at each other, the intimacy of their positions penetrating her consciousness in slow waves.

They were sitting side-by-side on the floor. She had her right arm around his back and her entire torso pressed against him. Her left hand lay on top of his where it rested on his knee. Their fingers were laced. His face was *right* there, half a whisper away.

If she wanted to, she could lean in a tiny bit more, angle her head and kiss those full lips.

And she wanted to.

She *wanted* to.

This man was a complete stranger, she reminded herself. She'd sworn off men.

Yet everything about what they were saying and doing in this elevator felt as right as brushing her teeth when she got up in the morning.

"I'm very glad I met you tonight, Dr. Harrison," he said quietly.

She tried to work her lungs. Tried to smile. Reached for words that darted just outside her reach.

"Don't try to sweet-talk me now."

Wry smile from Anthony. "Have we met? I doubt I could manage sweet talk if I tried."

She had to laugh. "Well, that's sadly true."

He suddenly sobered, his grip tightening on her hand.

"You're extraordinary." The husky urgency in his voice

perfectly matched the relentless focus of those eyes on her face. "I've never seen anything like you in my *life*—"

"Great news, folks!" Roy's cheery voice boomed through the quiet car like a marching band in a funeral home, startling them. But it was just the interruption she needed, right on time. Time to come to her senses. She and Anthony were experiencing a moment out of time following drinks at a party. Not the birth of some great love affair. A smart girl would remember that. So she quickly pulled her hand free and scooted sideways enough to put a little daylight between them, trying not to notice the way a light dimmed in Anthony's expression, or the way his hand clung to hers, just a little, as she broke the contact between them. "The repairman's just arrived. He got finished at the hospital sooner than he expected. He's getting set up."

Sure enough, there was the clang of metal somewhere nearby.

Something sank in the pit of her belly, greeting this good news the way she would if she'd just discovered, post family dinner, that her Thanksgiving turkey had been laced with botulism. The realization hit her that if they could slip a pizza and some Malbec into the elevator with her and Anthony, and maybe a bench to sit on, she'd be happy to stay there for several more hours.

"Thanks for the update," Anthony said sourly.

The loss of Anthony's touch and body heat suddenly made her aware of her bare shoulders. She shivered and rubbed her upper arms, feeling a little bereft.

"Here." He grabbed his jacket, shook it out and slung it around her shoulders before she could protest. "No need for you to catch your death."

"Thanks," she said, although she was a lot more grateful to be able to touch something of his than she was to ward off the chill. His scent infused the jacket's fine wool—something earthy and sophisticated, with maybe a little pepper thrown in —and she gratefully wrapped it closer. Appreciatively sniffed a sleeve. And the words zoomed up and out of her mouth before she could clip a leash on them and yank them back. "It smells like you."

Hang on.

What the hell had she just said?

She winced, briefly harboring the hope that maybe she'd been thinking loud thoughts again.

The subtle hitch in his breath told her otherwise.

She blushed hard enough to melt his poor jacket off her body. He stared at her all throughout a pregnant pause. The weight of his attention made her sizzling face burn even hotter, forcing her to duck her head as she issued her apology.

"Sorry. I don't know what made me—"

"Take down your hair," he said quietly.

The command (there was no request in it), issued in that deep voice and proper accent, made illicit images seethe to life in her mind.

Her head came up.

She met his smoldering blue gaze, seeing all her sudden desires reflected back at her:

Anthony's naked body stretched out on the bed beneath her as she straddled him. His hands gripping fistfuls of her hair as she leaned down to lick one of his nipples. Her hair trailing over his belly, making his muscles leap as she eased lower…

She cocked her head, stalling for time because she was fairly certain she'd do anything this man asked her to do in that voice and she wasn't ready to cede control just yet.

But did control really matter when you were only doing the thing you already wanted to do?

"Excuse me?" She infused her tone with a challenge, half expecting shy and awkward Anthony to back away from his words and claim that he didn't know what had come over him.

But Anthony, whom she'd already discovered was full of surprises, was much more alpha male than she'd suspected. He didn't blink and he damn sure didn't waver.

"You heard me."

The modern career woman in her was outraged.

The only problem was that the primitive cave woman side of her wanted to be dominated. Wanted to find a man as strong and sure as she was. And Cave Woman was, let's face it, much more powerful than manicured Modern Woman, who wouldn't dream of getting into a street brawl and possibly breaking a heel.

Still, she wasn't quite ready to go quietly. "I thought you were shy and awkward."

He shrugged. "The ice seems to have been broken between us. And you *did* mention that you prefer direct communication."

Fair enough.

With that, Cave Woman punched Career Woman in the nose, knocking her out cold, and dragged her limp body into the nearest closet, where she slammed the door.

And Melody reached for the pins in her hair.

Funny how a style that had required four viewings of a YouTube video, an hour of her time and a forty-dollar salon gel could be undone in three seconds, but she threw all her hard primping out the window without regret. Her hair slid back to its default position, which was exploding in spirals around her shoulders and lower. For good measure, she fluffed it up and tossed it a little, releasing its scent of fancy flowers and God knew what all.

Her reward for her compliance?

The way Anthony's pupils dilated and his face flushed with unmistakable desire. The slight flare of his nostrils as he leaned toward her, tipping his chin up to catch her fragrance from the air. His rapt attention as he took a strand, studied it closely as he rubbed it between thumb and forefinger, then let it bounce free while he trailed his fingers down the side of her neck.

And Mr. Shy and Awkward damn near made her come on the spot.

She waited, breath held, to see what he would do next.

5

"Happy now?" Melody asked, surprised to hear how much sex kitten had snuck into her normally brisk voice in just those few seconds.

Crooked smile from Anthony.

"I am content." Pointed pause. "For now."

"Is *that* so?" she asked, her heart pounding into overdrive as another illicit image—Anthony's sweaty body levered over her and his hard dick inside her, thrusting deep—filled her mind.

Funny how her voice got raspier the longer he looked at her like that.

"Yes. Now you're much more girl next door. Much less unapproachable goddess."

What? *Her?*

"Anthony…"

"Either way, I'd be all over you right now, but I'm guessing this elevator has video cameras. How do you feel about that?"

Her first instinct was to suggest that he see what he could do to disable the cameras. But that probably wouldn't be a smart girl move, and she prided herself on being smart if nothing else.

"Video cameras? They keep public places safe, don't they?"

That got him. He laughed.

She damn near swooned. What else was a woman to do after receiving a dizzying compliment and glorious laughter from a man like *this*?

"Consider this discussion bookmarked for later," he said firmly.

"If you insist."

"I definitely insist." He adjusted his position until he sat cross-legged facing her. "Can I get your picture?"

Her mind blanked out. "My picture?"

He pulled out his phone and looked a little sheepish. "If you don't mind."

"You want my picture but not my number?" She fluffed her hair and prayed her forehead wasn't too glaringly shiny. "Not sure what to make of that."

"Oh, I want everything I can possibly get from you." His voice turned to pure velvet as he tapped his phone. When he flicked his smoldering gaze back up to hers, she felt the same kind of thrilling shiver she'd expect if he trailed his lips down her torso and dipped his tongue into her belly button. "But this seems like a good place to start."

He aimed.

She hiked up a shoulder and turned her head to look over it, favoring her good side. Since she was prone to taking shots that either featured her lids half closed mid-blink or her lips curled as she asked the photographer whether s/he planned to count to three or not, she had no idea where the Tyra Banks attitude came from. Other than the fact that she felt like the sexiest woman alive when Anthony looked at her with all that banked heat.

"Shoulder or no shoulder?" she asked, her voice husky.

"Oh, we definitely want that shoulder," he murmured.

She posed. He clicked. Checked the display.

"You have to delete it if I don't like it," she warned.

"I've never hurt a woman before, but you would be the first if you tried to delete this shot from my phone."

"What?" she said, laughing.

He clicked again, then nodded with grim satisfaction. "That should do it."

"Let me see."

She scooted forward on her hands and knees, her hair shifting over her shoulders, well aware both that her dress gaped significantly in the front and that he was all sudden stillness, wide eyes and focused attention.

"You're not being rude, are you?" she asked softly as she looked down at the photo.

His gentle fingers sifted through her hair, making shivery goose bumps erupt up and down her arms.

"I'm being unspeakably rude."

She glanced up from his phone, where a miraculously radiant snap of her glowed up at them, and looked him in the eye.

He leaned a little closer. Watching. Waiting. Clearly hoping.

If she had any doubts about what he was hoping for, they dissipated when his attention dipped to her lips.

As for *his* lips? They were ripe. Tender.

And they *were* right there.

Something came over her.

"What would you do if I kissed you right now?" she asked quietly.

His gaze met hers again, blazing and direct.

"Die of happiness."

She would have smiled, but she was too busy taking a deep breath and licking her lips…easing forward that last little bit…tilting her head just enough…

Ah, *God.*

His lips were soft. Firm. Unspeakably tender and delicious.

She lingered as long as she dared, wanting more, and her hot blood surged even harder in response to the gathering tension in his body. She broke it off just as a rough hum began to vibrate in his chest and her breath turned to a rasp.

Slowly sitting back again, she raised her lids to discover him watching her with glazed eyes. He sat absolutely still, not moving or breathing for so long that she began to wonder if she'd made some terrible mistake.

Until vivid color concentrated in his cheeks and he blinked.

"Fair warning," he said, unsmiling. "Never do that again unless you want me to fall in love with you."

Melody gasped.

He seemed so sincere.

And something about him tugged at her as though he'd found a giant S-hook and used it to bind them together at the waist.

"I already told you. I'm married to my career. Why would I want to change my mind for a handsome Brit who may or may not be a complete arse?"

That amazing mouth of his didn't smile at her, but his eyes sure did.

"Because he would adore you." His voice grew hoarse. "Absolutely adore you."

Whoa.

With that, they both seemed to realize that they'd inadvertently waded into deeper waters than either of them had intended.

He quickly looked away, rubbing the back of his neck.

She quickly looked away, feeling scalded.

This wasn't normal, was it? Feeling this kind of connection to a guy you'd just met? She'd dated, yeah, but her skills were rusty, which was what happened when you lapsed into the lazy routine of hanging out with and having sex with someone who was primarily a buddy. In situations like that, your heart never came off the bench, much less bothered taking off its jacket to warm up and step onto the field.

But *here…*

Why did she have the terrifying feeling that the sky was the limit?

"So, ah…" Anthony rubbed a hand over his head and blew out a breath. "You grew up in Journey's End, I believe?"

The segue caught her off guard. She tried to think.

"Yep. Local girl, born and bred."

"College? Med school?"

His open curiosity made it easy to mirror his posture and sit cross-legged, arranging her fluttery skirt around her and resting her wrists on her knees.

And from there?

It seemed the easiest thing in the world to loosely twine her fingers with his when he reached for her.

"Stony Brook." She kept her chin up rather than surrender to her unfortunate tendency to duck her head and hunch her shoulders when this particular topic came up. "And, ah, Harvard."

His brows shot up. "Why d'you say it as if you're ashamed? As if you got a mail-order degree from someone printing diplomas in their cellar?"

"Because I get a variety of reactions when people hear where I went to school. Everything from affirmative action comments—"

Anthony's expression flashed murder.

"—to people assuming that I'm a trust fund baby, which I'm *not*—"

Anthony's expression turned speculative.

"—to people assuming I'm a snob and being preemptively snotty to me about it."

He claimed her other hand, holding both. Their fingers slid together in different combinations, teaching them the feel of each other, and her skin tingled with the contact.

"Yet you think *I'm* an arse."

"Well, what's *your* reaction to hearing that I went to Harvard med?"

He seemed offended. "I think it's brilliant, obviously. You're far too smart for me, which I find incredibly sexy. I could only ever marry a very smart woman."

She grinned. "Well played."

"I thought so. And you do seem to be developing a soft spot for me."

"Not at all. I'm just pleased that you have a valid reason for not liking stalled elevators. I was worried you were going to blame it on accidentally locking yourself in a dark closet for ten minutes when you were a little kid or something."

He burst into laughter, the most exuberant of the night, and something inside her contracted, hard.

God. He was spectacular. Worse? The chemistry between them flared too big. Too bright. She wanted to run away from it almost as much as she wanted to lose herself in it.

Meanwhile a crucial question had already popped into her mind:

What if he wanted her to spend the night with him?

Actually, that was a foregone conclusion, wasn't it? Men always wanted women to have sex with them. Which meant that the real question was:

Did she plan to sleep with this man tonight?

And the answer was:

No...?

Yeah. She was pretty sure—well, a solid 51 percent sure, anyway—that the answer was...

No.

His laughter slowly faded. Reaching out, he filtered his fingers through her hair and made her flesh sing with pleasure. When he looked her in the eye again, he seemed a little troubled.

"What's going on here, Dr. Harrison?"

"I wish I knew," she said on a shaky laugh.

There was a clatter just then. A scraping sound. The elevator shuddered, possibly deciding whether it wanted to go up or down.

If she'd had a vote, Melody would have chosen for the elevator to stay put indefinitely.

Anthony hesitated. "Maybe we could—"

His phone buzzed.

"That's me. Sorry," he said, pulling it out of his breast pocket and frowning at the display. "I've no idea who this could—yes, hello?"

He listened, his expression clearing.

"Granny! Wonder why my phone didn't tell me it was you?"

More listening.

Sorry, he mouthed to Melody.

She quickly shook her head, smiling and bemused by her luck in discovering a handsome and intriguing man who was also a war hero and close with his grandmother. Maybe she'd also discover a phoenix riding a unicorn before the night was over.

"You cannot be serious," he said, now practically levitating with delight. "They gave you a mobile? What on earth is the world coming to?" He listened, then laughed. "Yes, well, you'd better call me first for a heads-up before you send me a text. Otherwise, I'm likely to keel over in a dead faint. And the one thing I don't ever want to see from you is a selfie."

He laughed. Melody also heard the braying of hearty female laughter from the other side of the line.

He checked his watch. "And what are you doing up? This is an ungodly hour, even for you. Uh-huh. Well, that'll teach you to have all those chocolate bourbons before bed, won't it?"

Granny said something Melody couldn't quite hear.

"So, listen, I'll be in town by, ah…" Anthony held Melody's gaze, his laughter dimming a little. "Let's say Tuesday at the latest." He listened. "Yes, well, something's come up. It's only a day. What do you mean? Nothing I'd like to get into with you right now, that's what." His face and ears turned red; he tugged on one lobe, his gaze slipping away from Melody's. "No, I'm not getting into it, Granny. Forget it. You're far too nosy."

He made a *what can you do?* face at Melody. Listened again.

"Tea?" He frowned. "That all sounds very formal, doesn't it? Everything okay? But…Okay. Okay. Okay. Wednesday tea, then. Right. Bye."

He hung up.

"Sorry," he said to Melody. "Grandmothers. What can you do?"

"Don't apologize. I love grandmothers. You're close to yours?"

"Very. But don't get me sidetracked. We were talking about what's happening between—"

Without warning, the bottom seemed to drop out of the elevator, leaving Melody to wobble and grab Anthony's forearms because they were the only things she could reach. And then what began as a potential nightmare scenario turned into a smooth ride as the car began a graceful descent. Anthony recovered almost as quickly as the elevator did, holding the brass rail as he surged to his feet, bringing Melody with him.

The doors slid open to the bustling lobby from whence they'd come just as Melody stood, got her heels under her and arranged her skirt back into some semblance of normalcy. Rarely had a dramatic rescue received such a glum reception. Feeling shell-shocked by this unwanted intrusion from the rest of the world, Melody noted the chattering passersby, some of whom were happily sipping champagne or using their teeth to pull shrimp off skewers...the sudden and unwelcome infusion of brighter lighting...and the relentless thump of pop music over the speakers now that the dancing portion of the evening had begun.

She hated it all. Had to fight the overwhelming desire to punch the Close Doors button and keep punching it until the doors shut out all this nonsense and left her alone with Anthony again.

He didn't seem to be faring much better. He stood there, his body utterly still while his expression eased into blank inscrutability. On the bright side? At least he wasn't glaring again.

Melody watched him, trying to hide at least some of the dismay creeping across her face.

"Well, folks, looks like the doors are open." Roy's disembodied enthusiasm over the speaker only intensified Melody's desire to find the nearest baseball bat and smash the panel's lighted buttons. "We didn't keep you too long, after all, did we? You're free to go. Enjoy the rest of your night."

Melody plastered a smile on her face and tried to pretend this was good news. "Thanks, Roy."

"Yeah." Anthony, whose lips had thinned into near invisibility, shoved his hands deep into his pockets. *"Thanks."*

Neither of them moved.

Until at last some of Melody's wits crept back into her brain and started cranking dials and flipping levers again. Sudden burning awkwardness made her tinker with an earring and smooth her hair as she strode past Anthony to rejoin the real world.

All she could think was:

What the hell happened between them now?

6

A nthony trailed Melody off the elevator, his entire existence divided into the primitive caveman part that wanted to carry her up to his room—*now!*—so they could get started fulfilling the promise of that red-dressed siren's kiss, and the gentlemanly part who wanted to ask her to have a drink with him so he could make sure he got her number and further make sure that he handled their budding relationship with the kid gloves it deserved. Because Melody felt important. *This* felt damn important. But his hormones buzzed in his veins and his pulse. And the rest of the world kept insisting on getting in the way.

For example? The friendly neighborhood elevator technician in his blue jumpsuit, tools littering the floor as he worked on some master panel to one side of the elevator.

"Worked as quickly as I could, folks," the man said. "Hope you're none the worse for the wear."

Melody stopped and smiled. Only the telltale bursts of color over her cheekbones told the tale of how flustered she was at the moment. Maybe almost as flustered as Anthony was.

"Thanks for riding to the rescue. We appreciate it."

The *we* was a lie. Anthony *didn't* appreciate being unwillingly liberated from his intimate little cocoon with Melody. But that wasn't this poor guy's fault.

"Thanks, mate," he said, shaking the man's hand and keeping one eye on Melody as she walked a few steps away, to a seating area near the reception desk. "Sorry for the trouble."

"No worries. That's what they pay me the big bucks for."

Anthony nodded and hurried after Melody who had, by this time, taken off his jacket and folded it neatly over her arm. Her downturned face was pensive as she smoothed a sleeve but, to her credit, she managed a fairly convincing smile as he walked up. If he hadn't spent so much time studying this exquisite face tonight, he might almost be fooled into thinking their interlude hadn't unsettled her the way it had him.

"Thank you for letting me borrow your jacket," she said, handing it back to him.

"My pleasure."

He had so much more he wanted to say to her—questions to ask about her life and career, whether she'd give him her number, whether she'd let him see her tomorrow—but it wasn't so easy now that she didn't belong to him alone anymore. Now that they were out of the elevator. In there, where it was just the two of them, it was fine to ask her to take down her hair and to request a picture. In there, he was just a guy, the same as any other. Out here? There was every possibility that she'd discover who he was before she got to know him any better and judge him on his own merits, such as they were. Out here, she probably had friends waiting. Other people to catch up to. Appetizers to nibble and cocktails to drink. For all he knew, she was eager to get home and put her feet up so she could scroll through the pictures on DoctorLove.com.

But maybe she wanted to linger a while. With him.

There was something steady in her shining eyes as she looked up at him. Something vulnerable and hopeful.

"Have a drink with me, Melody," he said before his courage evaporated.

"Well, *finally*." She grinned, looking relieved. "I was afraid you were going to let me slip away into the crowd now that you have your jacket back."

She was afraid—?

"I'd have to be a much bigger fool than this to let you slip away into the crowd."

"Well, you're back to glaring at me again. It's hard to tell what you're thinking."

He had to smile, even if doing so in that moment left him feeling incredibly exposed.

"I was thinking that life was so much simpler on the elevator."

"Agreed," she said, laughing. "You were very bold on the elevator."

"*You* kissed *me* on the elevator. Did you forget that part?"

"Did I forget kissing you?" A blush blazed its way across her breasts, up her neck and all the way to her forehead and ears. "Let's call that a *no*."

He felt a wild rush of satisfaction. It gave him additional courage.

"I want to take your hand again. Or is that strictly elevator behavior?"

There was a pause.

Then she held out a hand.

He took it, marveling at the soft skin and delicate fingers, so different from his own.

"You have good hands." He ran his thumb over her knuckles as they turned toward the ballroom. "You really should think about surgery as a career. I'm sure you'd be quite good at it."

She laughed. "Noted. Speaking of careers, you haven't told me what *you* do for—"

"I hate to interrupt," said a new male voice coming up behind them, "but—"

The Texas twang made Anthony cringe and drop Melody's hand even before he turned to verify the owner of that deep voice. *Dear God. Not him. Not* now. But it *was* him, of course. Like a spot appearing on the tip of a teen's nose the day of class pictures, the man invariably showed up at the worst possible time.

Melody also glanced around at the man, looking bemused.

Anthony let his eyes roll closed and rubbed his temple in anticipation of the pending headache.

"—I feel a moral obligation to let you know, ma'am." As per usual, the man focused on the woman in the group. His charm level was always directly proportionate to a woman's beauty, which meant that he laid it on particularly thick tonight to impress Melody. The sparkling eyes, flashing teeth and grooving dimples were therefore all on full display in the man's weathered face, and the silver hair was coiffed to slick perfection. He looked trim in his custom tux, Anthony noted with clinical detachment, which meant that he still spent a good portion of his days lifting weights at the nearest gym. An added benefit of the gym? There were always gym bunnies on the lookout for a sugar daddy, so the arrangement was win-win for all parties concerned, at least until the inevitable nasty breakup and/or divorce. Tonight's pointy boots were a glossy alligator rather than the pebbly ostrich of the last time Anthony had seen him. Oh, and the man's spray tan was especially healthy tonight, although it was too pumpkin-esque for Anthony's tastes. "A stunning woman such as yourself can do a lot better than *this* bozo." The man jerked a thumb at Anthony. "If you have any interest in a *real* man, let me know."

Anthony opened his eyes and dropped his hand in time to see the man toast Melody with his glass of bourbon and much glimmering of his diamond-studded pinky ring, then drink deeply.

"I will bear that in mind." Melody divided her attention between the two of them. "And do you have a name? In case I need to come calling?"

The man finished his drink with a smack of appreciation, whipped his enormous white handkerchief out of his breast pocket and patted his lips. Then he replaced it and beamed his dazzling toothpaste commercial smile directly at Melody.

"I *do* have a name. But maybe Junior, here, would like to make the introductions."

Melody and the man looked to Anthony, who considered the relative merits of making a run for it. It would be hard to explain later, of course, but surely no harder than explaining his genetics. On the other hand, Melody already knew a good portion of the worst about Anthony, having witnessed one of his panic attacks. Why not bite the bullet and get more of the worst out of the way now?

He sighed. Girded his loins.

"Dr. Melody Harrison, this is Tony Scott." Anthony tried to get the rest of the information out, but it felt trapped behind his clenched jaw. "My, ah, father."

"Your *father*?" Melody took a closer look at both men, then nodded with dawning comprehension. "I see the resemblance now. You have the same noses and chins. And your face shape. It's great to meet you, Mr. Scott. But, Anthony, I thought you were British through and through. You didn't tell me you're as American as I am."

"I'm, ah…" Anthony cleared his throat. "My mother was British, so I'm half and half."

Tony winked at Melody. "Half the time, he doesn't claim me. The other half of the time, I'm disowning him because none of his halves have any Texas in 'em. Things get complicated around here, darlin'. You might as well learn that early in the game."

"I see," Melody said, raising a delicate brow.

Anthony crossed his arms and tugged on an earlobe, which was a better option for his hands than, say, lunging for his father's throat. "I didn't hear why you're here."

He couldn't bring himself to add *Dad.*

"I got word that Baptiste was throwing himself a little party and decided to put myself on the guest list. Baptiste is always happy to see me. Almost like the son I should have had."

Melody frowned as she listened to this speech.

"And I figured I might catch you here, too," Tony concluded.

"You do realize that catching me is a great deal easier when you pick up the phone and call once every six months or so," Anthony said.

"You're no better on the communicating," Tony said easily, flapping a hand. "But we don't need to get into all that now. We *do* need to discuss your grandmother, though. Word is, she's up to her shenanigans again."

"You know what?" Melody said brightly. "I should let you men—"

"No," Anthony said quickly, as alarmed at the prospect of being left alone with his father as he was at the idea of

Melody either slipping away while he wasted time with this nonsense or Melody learning more about his grandmother tonight. "You shouldn't." He shot his father a pointed look. "Why don't we try to catch up in a day or two?"

The one good thing about Tony (if, indeed, there was anything good about him at all), was that he was extraordinarily sensitive to matters pertaining to impressing women. The light of understanding brightened his eyes immediately.

As did the light of mischief.

"Sure, son, but I was fixin' to buy a couple drinks for you and your beautiful date, here."

"Oh, we're not on a date," Melody said quickly, cheeks flushing.

The clarification made Anthony feel a twinge of annoyance.

"Yes, but that's a distinction without a difference at this stage of the proceedings, isn't it?" he murmured silkily, now aiming his pointed look at Melody as he retook her hand and drew her back to his side. He pressed his thumb to the pulse in her wrist, noting with satisfaction the way her heart rate sped up when he touched her. Then he turned back to his father. "So we should plan on speaking soon, then?"

Tony eyeballed their clasped hands with open amusement, causing a further spike in Anthony's annoyance level. "I was hoping to get to know Miss Melody a little better—"

So am I, for Christ's sake, Anthony thought.

"—but I can't blame you for wanting to keep her to yourself. Glad you appreciate your good fortune. A woman like *this*? Plenty of men would be happy to snatch her away from you."

"Funny how I've been living my whole life thinking I was a real human being," Melody said tartly, "only to discover at this late date that I can be snatched just like a car. Who knew?"

"Oho! Miss Melody's a spitfire! But we could look at her hair and her red dress and tell that, couldn't we, son?" Another wink at Melody, who received it the way flood victims receive weather forecasts calling for more rain. "You'll have to forgive me, ma'am. I'm just an old country boy. Hard to teach me new manners at this late date."

"If you call me *ma'am* again, I'm never forgiving you anything," Melody told him, eyes glinting with a warning look.

Anthony snorted.

Tony exploded with laughter as he clapped his son on the back. "You'll have to keep this one, son."

There it was at last. Something he and his father could agree on.

Anthony tightened his grip on Melody's hand and steered her away from all the raucous laughter before it drew any more attention than it already had. "I'll wait to hear from you soon, then, shall I?"

Tony tipped his invisible cowboy hat and waved.

Scowling, Anthony steered Melody back to the ballroom, the silence between them mushrooming into awkwardness. And there was another good thing about his father, Anthony supposed. Ten seconds in his presence, and Anthony was no longer the most ill-mannered person in the room.

The thought was strangely cheering.

"Sorry about that," he muttered when he could no longer stand the suspense of wondering what Melody thought of him now. "Sometimes I console myself with thoughts that my mother had an affair with the rubbish man and I'm therefore not related to Tony at all."

"Oh, you're related," she said cheerily. "You look like him."

"But you're not holding that against me…?"

"Wouldn't dream of it. You think he's the only character I've ever encountered?"

Somehow Anthony resisted the urge to drop to his knees and kiss her feet in gratitude. "You're too good to be true, surely."

She beamed with unmistakable pleasure. "Surely."

He looked around, discovering that they were near the sushi bar. "Shall we get something to drink? Are you hungry?"

"Sounds good to…"

She trailed off as the music changed, a frisson of excitement running from her hand to his.

He knew why. It was Joe Cocker's raspy and haunting "You Are So Beautiful," the perfect soundtrack to mirror what ran through his mind every time he looked at Melody tonight.

She looked back over her shoulder at him, a woman's sultry smile beginning to curl her lips as she tugged him with her to the dance floor. "You're not going to tell me *no* again, are you?"

His heart contracted, hard.

Probably because that was the one moment, in a night full of moments, when he realized how vulnerable he was to this one woman's looks and smiles, her humor and laughter. Her smarts. Her light. And if it turned out that she wasn't the person he suspected she was, if she decided she wanted nothing further to do with him or if she let her glorious light shine on some other bloke's face…

In that one moment, he really had to wonder if he would recover.

"Anthony?"

"We both know I have no intentions of telling you *no,*" he said, reeling her in.

Her laughter was soft. Triumphant. The way he imagined she'd sound if she made him come until he shouted her name.

A helpless shudder rippled through his body as she settled inside his arms, her breasts firm against his chest and her thighs brushing against his as they shifted back and forth. She was ridiculously feminine, in every possible way. Her fragrant warmth. The scent of expensive flowers in her hair and on her bare skin. The silkiness of her dress as he rested his hand on her waist. The entirely different silkiness of her flesh as he ran his hand under the heavy fall of her hair, to her nape. The way she cooed her approval from her throat, like a dove. The way she turned her face into him, snuggling closer, allowing him to press his eager lips to her forehead and leave them there while they swayed back and forth.

Much to his surprise, he managed to dredge up a little rhythm and stay on the beat.

The night was, clearly, a glorious success.

He let his eyes roll closed, praying there was no photographer nearby memorializing this intimate moment for the tabloids and not really caring if there was.

She eased back enough to look at him, leaving his lips bereft. His consolation? The fact that her glittering eyes and high color reflected every bit of the lust he currently felt for her.

"I thought you said you couldn't dance."

"Don't get complacent," he said, stroking the side of her neck for the pleasure of feeling her shiver. "Still plenty of time for me to break most of your toes."

She laughed. "I'm glad you said *yes* this time. I'd have to wonder about a man who claimed to be attracted to me, then missed the opportunity to hug me while pretty music played for five minutes."

"Don't waste your time wondering anything about how much I want you. It's going to make me break out in a sweat in a minute."

More of her throaty laughter made his muscles tense with the effort of keeping his hands to himself. He wanted to clamp them on her delicious arse. To run them up and down her bare arms. To hold her face still so he could kiss those unbelievable lips.

"And yet you're still glowering at me like a great horned owl from the top of a barn."

"Or perhaps my features are strained with the effort of trying to control a monstrous erection. Ever think of that?"

Regret or something like it shadowed her eyes.

"That's good, because I'm not coming up to your room tonight."

He made lazy circles on her neck, enjoying the way her breath hissed.

"You sure about that? I was just about to make a direct request. I know how you like those."

She stared up at him, unsmiling, while several beats passed.

Yeah. It was definitely regret.

"I'm sure," she finally said.

"And if I developed a medical emergency?" He shifted his hand so he could massage her shoulder. Her lids lowered to half-mast. "Perhaps required some assistance upstairs?"

She laughed. "I would call 911 for you."

"Ghastly woman."

"It makes sense for us to get to know each other a little bit first, don't you think? Unless…" Her face fell. "If you just want a quick hookup—"

"Shhh." He pulled her closer so he could kiss her forehead again. "I think we're getting things mixed up here. Do I want you? Yes. Would I be deliriously happy if you joined me upstairs tonight? Or any other night? Yes. And do I also want to get to know you much better? Yes. If you joined me tonight, would that stop me from wanting to get to know you much better? No. Just so we have things straight."

He felt the apple of her cheek swell against his chin as she smiled. But then she eased back enough to look him dead in the face, and her shadowed expression told him exactly what was coming.

"Where do you live, Anthony?" she asked quietly.

He opened his mouth. His brain floundered, stalling for time, but there was no sugarcoating this.

"London."

Dr. Harrison had a serviceable poker face, but he felt her shoulders droop.

"London," she said, looking away and putting a bit more daylight between them.

He couldn't quite smother his harsh sigh at this appearance of a brick wall in his face. But he'd come this far with her. He wasn't going to go down in flames now. Not without a bloody good fight.

"Let me guess," he said. "You don't want to get too attached to a man who lives on another continent."

She glanced his way again and attempted a wry smile. "What would be the point? Between my scar, my work schedule and the usual game-playing between men and women, I've done very poorly with the men who live on *this* continent."

Much to his surprise, the answers rolled right off his tongue for once. Absolutely no awkwardness. Only heartfelt sentiment.

"Then maybe you should try someone who doesn't live on this continent and also doesn't play games," he said, staring her in the face. "And in terms of us getting too attached to each other? I believe a great deal of damage has been done already. Back on that elevator."

Melody went very still, her gaze sliding out of focus.

Meanwhile, Joe Cocker's unmistakable growl faded away as the song ended. Anthony tightened his hold on her, ready to stay right where they were until they reached some kind of accord. Besides that, there really *was* something to be said for dancing, wasn't there?

"Melody."

She looked at him, her expression inscrutable.

"Give me a chance. Let's see what happens," he said.

It was tough to regulate his breathing and pretend as though this was a standard conversation about, say, their dinner or movie options for a date night. Tougher still to let her decide and not plead his case like a salesman on some lot for used cars.

They stared at each other. He aged a thousand years with each passing second.

But then her eyes crinkled at the corners, generating a wild swoop of relief in his belly.

"I live here. You live in London. You're going home in a couple days. What could possibly happen?"

He snorted out a laugh. Honest to God, when she looked at him like that, he felt the distinct possibility that it, whatever *it* was, had already happened.

"I'll take that. Thank you."

She worked hard to repress her answering smile. "Don't get too grateful just yet. I have to go."

"What? *Why?*"

"Well, for one thing, the song's ended and we're standing

in the middle of the dance floor. Plus, I have an early shift tomorrow."

"But tomorrow's *Sunday*," he said, well aware that he sounded like one of the brats from the *Willy Wonka* books. "And you promised me a drink."

The thing was, he didn't want to let her go. He didn't want to stop touching her or let her out of his sight. He wanted to prolong this magical night forever if possible, but at least until one or two if it wasn't. And the thought of turning her loose in the world, where she might find out much more about him than he was ready to tell her just yet, made all the long muscles in his body tighten with tension.

"I know it's Sunday," she said. "I keep explaining the days of the week to sick kids, but they just never listen. We should get off the dance floor. We're in the way."

"Let's go over here," he said, holding her hand as he took a step—

And nearly collided with Mrs. Carmichael, whose hideous Medusa stare threatened to turn him and any other unfortunate men inside her blast radius into stone.

Acting reflexively, he stood in front of Melody and tried to protect her from those horrible prying eyes.

"Mrs. Carmichael." It was a real effort to keep his voice pleasant. "You'll excuse me, won't you?"

As it turned out, she wouldn't. He could almost see her implanting her feet in the floor like a time-lapse video of an oak tree growing roots.

"Evidently you *do* dance, after all," she said, tipping up her chin and craning her neck—albeit in as well-bred a manner as possible—in her effort to get a good look at Melody. Melody, he saw out of the corner of his eye, ran a hand through her hair, making sure it covered her scar. He instantly disliked Mrs. Carmichael all the more. "Maybe now you'd like a dance with Annabella. If your lovely friend can spare you, of course."

Annabella, who stood off to one side, looked a bit hurt. But, to her credit, she kept her chin up and flashed Anthony an apologetic smile as she put a restraining hand on her mother's arm. "Come on, Mummy. Let's leave the man in peace."

Anthony's heart sank. He felt bad. He'd never wanted to hurt the girl's feelings, and it wasn't *her* fault her mother saw dollar signs and a ticket to the higher ranks of society every time she looked at her.

"Another time, Annabella," he said quietly.

"Yes, of course," Annabella said brightly.

"You won't forget?" Mrs. Carmichael asked Anthony.

"*Mummy*. For God's sake."

"Wouldn't dream of it." By now, Anthony had depleted his supply of patience and begun dipping into the reserves for tomorrow—he didn't have time for this marriage-minded mama's nonsense! Melody had to leave! He had to figure out when he could see her again!—but he somehow kept it all polite. "Until next time."

Tightening his grip on Melody's hand, he led her toward—

"Oh, but you haven't introduced us to your friend, Anthony," Mrs. Carmichael called after them.

Anthony mouthed *sorry* to Melody (she raised a brow at him, looking amused) and turned back.

"Another time, Mrs. Carmichael." He infused his expression and voice with a finality that even this old fool couldn't mistake. "Good *night*."

7

Anthony plowed through the crowd, determined to physically harm and perhaps maim the next person who tried to prevent him from saying a proper good-night to Melody.

She held tight to his hand and leaned closer, laughter heavy in her voice. "Who were *they*?"

"Just a silly woman from back home," he said as they finally emerged into the lobby. "She's been trying to pawn her daughter off on me since the poor girl was in pigtails."

"Are you sure you're not already betrothed? Mama Bear seemed very proprietary to me."

He led her to a quiet spot between the reception desk and the elevator, where there was, thankfully, no further sign of the repairman, and turned to face her and all her banked amusement at his expense.

"I can assure you there's not—and never will be—a match between myself and Annabella."

"If you say so. But I'd never want to get you in trouble with your future mother-in-law." She paused. "Or keep you from your one true love."

His one true love.

The words snagged in his brain, sending a frisson of something dancing across his skin.

He frowned, trying to snap himself out of it. "Annabella could never be my one true love, and we've wasted enough time with those two—*oh, for God's sake.*"

"What?"

He tipped his head at the scene unfolding behind her. She turned to look just as Nick, who was several feet away and had evidently had his lips surgically attached to a busty redhead's and his hands to her ass, came up for air. Catching their eyes, he gave them a sheepish, *what did you expect?* shrug and wolfish grin.

"I see you've convinced Melody to give you another chance," he called. "You're not as hopeless as I'd feared."

Anthony shot him a repressive glare. "Thanks for that overwhelming vote of confidence."

Nick laughed, one hand tracing lazy circles low on the redhead's bare back while she nuzzled his neck. "You're very beautiful and accomplished, Melody. I understand Anthony's interest. A shame for *you,* of course. A woman like you prefers a sexier man. I, myself, could—"

Melody snorted. "Don't you have your hands full right now, Nick?"

"Yeah," the redhead said, pouting as she smacked Nick's arm.

Nick laughed, then gave the redhead a soothing kiss to her cheek.

"There's always room for one more," he told Melody, alight with more mischief than a family of leprechauns. "If you'd like to ditch Anthony and join us…?" Nick trailed off, shrugging.

The redhead glanced around and regarded Melody with increased interest.

"No, thanks," Melody quickly said. "I'm good."

"Bugger off," Anthony told Nick at the same time, pulling Melody closer for good measure. This wouldn't be the first time that a woman he'd had his eye on defected in favor of Nick's Mediterranean charms. He wasn't taking any chances with Melody. "This one's spoken for."

Tart frown from Melody.

"This one?" she told Anthony. "Well, *this one* can speak for herself."

Anthony gestured to Nick. "Be my guest, then. Tell him."

"Bugger off, Nick," she said.

They all laughed.

"Next time," the redhead told Melody with a wink.

More laughter from Nick. "Melody, if you have a sister, you must introduce me to her right away. Although I doubt she could be as fascinating as you."

"I *do* have a sister, and I'm going to make it my life's work for you to never lay eyes on her," Melody said with a dramatic shudder.

"Buona notte, amici." There was a lazy wave and final laugh from Nick, who pressed the Up button and dove back in where he'd left off with the redhead.

"Typical," Anthony muttered, facing Melody again and trying not to hate Nick for teasing him like that and, more to the point, for succeeding tonight where Anthony would fail. Yet Anthony felt a soaring lightness in his chest every time he looked at Melody, and that went a long way toward soothing his aching blue bollocks. "That could have been us, you know."

"With the redhead?" Melody asked brightly.

"No. With each other. I hope you're happy."

"Eh." Melody's expression turned a bit melancholy as she tore her gaze away from Nick and his conquest and focused on Anthony again. "Happy is overrated. I'm smart. Isn't that so much better?"

"No," he cried. "It's not *remotely* better."

They laughed together for a delicious moment. Until he remembered that he was being selfish for not letting her go when she had an early day tomorrow.

"Shall I drive you home? I have a rental."

She shook her head. "My car's out in the parking lot."

He nodded, trying not to feel too disappointed at this loss of the chance to spend a bit more time with her tonight. To see where she lived so he would know where to find her.

Then he eyeballed the big dark world on the other side of the lobby's sliding doors and thought about Melody driving herself home at this late hour. He'd never been particularly protective about anything, unless you counted his attachment to his first dog, a border collie he'd named Fitzroy, or his first car, a royal blue Aston Martin, but the idea of Melody out there by herself did not thrill him.

"You don't live far, do you?" he asked.

"Just five minutes."

"You'll drive safely, won't you? Really, it would be better if I drove you."

She studied him with dawning incredulity. "You're not worried about me getting myself home safely, are you? How do you think I've managed my late-night shifts and being called into the hospital in the middle of the night for all these years before you showed up?"

Christ.

The idea tied his gut up in knots.

"If you're trying to reassure me, you ought to rethink your strategy," he said darkly.

"I'm a *grown woman*. In a perfectly safe small town."

"Only think of all the drunks that will be hitting the streets once this party lets out."

"I'd rather take my chances with them than with a guy who may or may not know how to drive on the correct side of the street," she said, laughing.

The urge to kiss her in that moment damn near tackled him to the ground and pummeled him into submission. Some of his sudden tension eased back, leaving him to feel sheepish.

"My driving is perfectly fine. I'm as American as you are. I believe I've mentioned that already. It's just that…"

He paused, not wanting to get into it.

"Just that *what*?"

"It's just that…" He ran a hand over his nape. "When you've been overseas, you quickly learn that things can happen to people. And I don't want anything to happen to you before I can get to know you better."

She stared up at him, looking a bit shaken.

Probably because she'd realized what a nutter he was.

"Sorry," he said, cheeks burning. "I didn't mean to—"

"It's okay. Thanks for telling me."

She seemed sincere. And her quiet understanding felt as though someone had gifted him with a few of the lesser Crown Jewels.

Now *he* felt a bit shaken. Because this woman and her reactions and understandings shouldn't loom so large in his life. Not this fast. This couldn't be healthy.

He cleared his throat. "Right, then. Coat?"

She quickly blinked and pulled a claim ticket out of her little bag. "In the cloakroom. I'll be right back."

"I'll get it for you."

"Oh, you don't have to—"

Yeah, he did.

He gave her a look. She hesitated, then handed him the ticket. He retrieved her coat and helped her into it, breathing in her hair's fragrance when she pulled it out from beneath the coat's collar.

When she faced him again, sudden unsteady nerves made his throat burn and the words stick.

He cleared his throat, pulled out his phone and strove for some modicum of nonchalance.

"I don't have your number."

Melody hesitated. Ducked her head. Looked down at the floor, then back at him, eyes shining. He felt relieved and grateful that her nonchalant routine wasn't any better than his. They were in this thing, whatever it was, together. There was a great deal of comfort in that.

"This really isn't a good idea, Anthony. I live here. You live in London. I'm focusing on my career. I'm perfectly happy with that. Why muddy the waters?"

"I thought we'd settled this," he said quietly. "Our waters are already muddy."

She shrugged. "Maybe, but they're only a little muddy. Why not quit while we're ahead?"

How quaint. She'd somehow deluded herself into thinking they could each go on their merry way as if tonight had never happened.

"You're in denial," he said. "And I don't have your number."

They stared at each other. He found himself fascinated by the slight flare of panic in her eyes and the way it so perfectly matched the growing tightness in his chest.

This thing between them could be big. She had to know it. Why fight him so hard, otherwise?

"Plus, this is where men blow it," she said with a shaky

laugh. "They ask for your number, then they never call again. Or they ask for your number, but they wait a month before texting *Hey* so they can show what hard-asses they are. Meanwhile, women are stuck trying to decode these signals and figure out what it all means. It's exhausting. A man should never ask for a number unless he intends to use it."

Unless he intends to—?

Anthony wanted to ask her if she was insane. Wanted to confess how close he was to prostrating himself and clinging to her ankles so she'd have to drag him along with her when she tried to leave the building. But it was all too soon, and this thing between them felt terrifyingly real. It seemed incredibly important to keep himself on lockdown until he had a better handle on it, lest he scare himself any worse or scared her away.

So he blinked back the hot yearning currently scorching his face, met her eye and held out his phone.

"I don't have your number," he repeated quietly.

Her lips curled. A vivid blush brightened her cheeks. She took the phone. Input her information. Handed it back with a wry smile.

"It'll be fine." He returned the phone to his pocket with a tremendous surge of satisfaction. "You'll see."

"Will I?"

"Yes," he said firmly.

They stared at each other for an endless beat or two, heat simmering between them. Honest to God, he could have stayed there all night, memorizing the way her eyes turned up at the ends and the light made her skin gleam like rose gold.

"Well." She took a serrated breath and nodded crisply. "I should get going—"

He raised a brow at her. She didn't honestly *think*—?

She stopped talking.

He reached for her hand. She hesitated before twining her fingers with his.

They headed for the sliding glass doors, falling into stride together. The early December night's frigid air felt good against his face, but did nothing to cool him down as she led him down the sidewalk and past several rows of cars.

He stroked the tender skin of her wrist, drunk with anticipation.

She gasped. The clicking of her heels sped up.

The deserted parking lot grew maddeningly larger the longer they walked.

She finally slowed as they approached a nice Acura SUV.

"This is—" she started to say, turning toward him.

He couldn't wait another second and pulled her in with a low growl, his hands already going to the sides of her head.

"Oh, God," she whispered, tipping her chin up to meet him.

8

The first lingering brush of their lips caused an electrical charge to flash through him, the kind of power surge that knocked out grids and left entire city blocks in the dark. He made some kind of incoherent sound—of surprise? Recognition? Unadulterated joy? —and pulled back to get a better look at this siren and try to figure out what he'd got himself into.

He didn't lose his mind about women or anything else. Ever.

Kisses didn't burn like this.

This—*she*—wasn't normal.

But when he looked down at her, all he saw was the same bewilderment mirrored back at him. The same heavy-lidded gaze, hot with lust. Her mouth looked tender and dewy, ripe for more kisses. Her coat was open in the front, revealing the lush rise and fall of her breasts against that sexy red dress as she tried to catch her breath.

And her glittering *eyes*…

"Anthony."

There was no mistaking her plea or the answering clench

of his gut. He reached for her again, incapable of any pretense of gentlemanly behavior or a man in charge of his reactions.

Yes.

This.

Her.

He claimed handfuls of that glorious hair, sifting through the warm spirals because he needed to claim it all and touch every single strand. He stroked the sides of her neck, which was satiny on one side and rough from her scar on the other, both sides equally thrilling. He cursed himself for a fool because he was the genius who'd retrieved her coat and put it on her, blocking her body from his touch. Slid his hands beneath the sides of the coat, stroking over the filmy material of her dress in his search for her breasts. Her hips. Her round arse. Her round arse. Her round *arse*. He claimed it for his own, clamped a hand on each half and thrust against her, the ridges of his zipper cutting into his rigid erection and causing him a significant amount of discomfort.

He didn't care in the slightest.

Why?

Because she *fit* in his arms and against his body. Her mouth needed his as much as his needed hers, and she needed it with the same rhythm and urgency. Her cries and her croons had to be music for his ears alone.

They each belonged exactly where they were, doing nothing else but *this*.

But if they kept up like this, he'd be taking her against the side of her car, and she deserved so much better.

So he broke the kiss—the loss of her eager mouth felt like an amputation—and rested his forehead against hers, trying to catch his breath as it continued to sprint away from him.

"Come to my room with me." His voice had degenerated to less than half a rasp. "I'm *begging* you."

She snuggled closer, her arms tight and strong around his waist, and shook her head. "I want to. In case you hadn't noticed. But I can't."

He meant to respect her wishes. Honestly, he did. But she didn't actually think that they could resist *this* for very long, did she? It would be like rigging a system of buckets at the bottom of Niagara Falls and trying to get the water back up.

What was the *point*?

"Why?" He eased back so he could see her face, keeping his voice gentle. "Tell me why."

She smoothed her hair and blew out a breath, her lips swollen from his kisses.

"For one thing, I'm not looking for a quick hookup."

"Nor am I. I want to *see* you."

"Yeah, well, you live in *London*. Even if I didn't work all the time, it's not exactly an easy day trip. If nothing else, we need to be slow and careful about whatever we're doing with each other."

"Melody…"

"And we barely know each other. I don't even know what you do."

Stymied, he dropped his gaze and said nothing. She bloody well had him there, didn't she?

"You're angry with me?" she asked.

"What? *No*. Of course not. But…I feel like there might be some other reason as well. Something else going on."

She ducked her head. Looked off across the parking lot. Back at him.

"I had a friends with benefits situation with one of my med school classmates for a while."

"Friends with benefits situation," he echoed dully. Well, of course a woman like *this* had had sex in her life. But as a man whose hormones were still singed and smoking, he didn't particularly want to hear about another man who'd fully enjoyed her delights when Anthony had only had a taste. "You still have feelings for him?"

"No. I never had feelings for him. I mean, he was a buddy. I never thought it was going to be anything else. Never wanted anything else."

"But…?" he asked, his ears perking up.

"The thing was, he wasn't special to me and I wasn't special to him. At all. He basically took one look at the woman he's engaged to now and dropped me like a bad habit." She snapped her fingers. "I don't think he's thought twice about me. And that stung."

Anthony frowned, beginning to see where she was going with this.

"Seeing the way Baptiste is with Samira really solidified this for me," she continued. "He's crazy about her. *Crazy*. I meant what I said earlier about being married to my career. But if I *were* to open myself up again, I'd want someone who could lose his head over me and I could lose my head over him. I'm not settling again."

Anthony wanted to put up his hand and mention that he was more than pulling *his* half of that equation, but now didn't seem to be the time. She probably wouldn't believe him yet, anyway.

He took a deep breath.

"Understood." Actually, that was only partially true. His head understood completely, but his private parts had seized up with frustration. "It's too soon to make love. But can I see you tomorrow?"

"Not tomorrow," she said with unmistakable regret. "I'm at the hospital, remember?"

"What? All bloody day?"

"Yes, all bloody day," she said, laughing, in her best British accent.

"Can't they let you out to eat dinner?"

"You'll have to forgive me. If I'd known you were going to show up in my life, I would have dropped everything and rearranged my whole schedule."

"As well you should," he said sternly, scrubbing his hands over his head in frustration. "There must be something we can do before I fly back to London on Monday night. Please tell me there's something we can do."

She thought it over. "Well, it's not thrilling, but maybe you could meet me at the hospital for breakfast Monday morning. I'll have a little bit of a window—"

"Done."

She brightened. "Really?"

He snorted. "Did you think I wouldn't grab any chance I could get?"

"I wasn't sure."

"And you also weren't sure whether I would kiss you good night or not, I believe?" Running his hands beneath her coat and around her waist again, he eased her closer. "On second thought, I'm not sure that Harvard degree's done you much good at all."

A sultry woman's laugh from Melody.

"I'm not sure *kiss* is the right word for what we just did."

"Agreed. I believe the word you're looking for is *foreplay*." He ran his nose down the side of her face and neck, breathing her in before he worked his way over to her ear and nipped it. "And I did warn you not to kiss me again unless you wanted me to fall in love with you. So now I can proceed with impunity."

"Ah," she said, tipping her head to the side to give him

better access. "But *you* kissed *me* that time. Not the same thing at all."

He laughed. Held her tighter as they swayed together.

"I don't want to let you go, Dr. Harrison."

"I don't want to go," she said, sighing.

"Will you think of me tonight?"

She tipped up her chin and stared him in the face. "I think you know the answer to that question."

He stared at her for a minute, lost in her big brown eyes and the way they shone at him. The thrilling feel of her against his body. The promises that felt like they were forming between them. The only cloud on his otherwise perfect horizon had to do with his family and the desperate hope that, just this once, a person could want him for *him*.

"I wonder if you could do me a favor?" he asked.

"What?"

"Maybe we could, ah, get to know each other a bit without doing online searches and background checks and the like. Just see how much we like each other on our own merits."

"Now you're making me nervous." She narrowed her eyes at him. "That's the kind of thing pedophiles and Charles Manson would say."

"It's nothing like that," he said quickly. "Ask Baptiste if I'm okay if you like. You trust him, don't you?" She nodded. "It's just that I have sort of an unusual family. As you could probably tell from my dad. And sometimes it's hard to know whether people like me for me, or whether I'm just a sideshow attraction. Am I making any sense?"

"But you're not married…?"

"God, no. Never married. No children. Clean record. Upstanding citizen. Kind to puppies and other small animals."

A couple of beats passed while she studied him closely.

"As long as this doesn't come back to bite me in the ass."

He thought that over. Wondered if he should confess everything now.

But he couldn't. Not with Melody. Never in his life had it been this important to verify that a woman wanted him for *him*.

"I feel reasonably certain it won't come back to bite you in the ass. And I'll tell you everything you need to know about me. In my own time."

She rolled her eyes. "Fine. I hope you appreciate this gesture of goodwill. I'm way too soft."

He stroked over her arse again. "You *are* soft, aren't you?"

"Stop that," she said, grinning as she pulled free.

"What about my good-night kiss?" he cried, outraged.

"What was *that*?"

"Warm-up."

"You've had enough kissing for tonight," she said, laughing as she turned her back on him, pulled out her key and opened the door. "And I need to get home."

He scowled and shoved his hands in his pockets lest they try to reach for her again. "Cruel woman."

She hesitated, a seductive smile playing at her lips as she faced him again. Then she leaned in and gave him a sweetly lingering kiss that he planned to add to his treasured memories of tonight.

"Good *night*," she said firmly, getting into the car.

"Good night, darling."

She looked surprised. "Did you just call me *darling*?"

Yeah, he'd surprised himself with that one. His ears burned, but he didn't want to retract it.

"I believe I did."

She raised her brows, grinning, as she shut the door.

He backed away, watching her pull off with a wave. When the red pinpoints of her taillights disappeared around the corner, he fought off a wave of loneliness as he matched up one of her pictures with her phone number in his contacts, then sent her a text.

Just to assure you I don't think I'm a hard-ass.

Grinning to himself as he set off walking, he'd just made it back to the lobby when his phone buzzed.

Good to know, she said.

Laughing, he sent her another one:

You're not texting while driving, are you?

He waited, but no answer.

So…what now?

Anthony surveyed the lobby—the gala was still in full swing, from the sound of it—and considered his options.

Off to bed? No. Didn't think he could sleep just yet. Or at all tonight. Too excited.

Drink, then.

But rather than go back to the gala, which had far too many people and the distinct and horrifying possibility of running into Mrs. Carmichael and Annabella again, he headed for the sedate and elegant bar down the hall, where a pianist plinked away on some melancholy tune. Ordered his whisky. Slid into a booth in the corner, where he could wallow in his thoughts of Melody and sip in peace.

He'd just raised his glass to his lips when a movement across the way caught his eye. It was his father, he realized with a sinking heart. By himself in another booth, looking morose as he stared down at his drink.

Christ.

Anthony was just weighing his chances of sneaking back out without having to deal with the old man again, when

Tony glanced up and saw him. With a wry twist of his mouth, Tony toasted him and drank deeply.

Anthony sighed harshly and decided there was no time like the present for getting it over with. So he walked over and had a seat opposite his father, taking care to put his phone on the table so he'd be sure to notice if Melody texted him back.

"Where's Miss Melody?" Tony asked, swirling his bourbon in its tumbler.

"She's gone home."

Derisive snort from Tony. Which was his lifelong default response to pretty much everything Anthony said or did. "So you couldn't close the deal, eh? Why am I not surprised?"

It was no good telling himself not to rise to this bait. Not to give this man any more control over his emotions. Not to allow these old wounds to open up again.

So much for getting it over with, Anthony fumed, his spiking temper making any sort of a productive conversation impossible now. Not when he wanted to hit the old man about the face. No surprise there, really. Tony and he had always got on like Churchill and Hitler, the only question being how much earth they'd scorch between them on any given day.

"Why are you not surprised? Probably because you've never taken more than thirty seconds to get to know a woman and can't conceive of why that should matter." Anthony downed his drink and reached for his wallet, tossing some money on the table. "Lovely as always to see you. I look forward to you popping up again in another year and a half or so. Actually, let's try to make both of us happy and stretch that out indefinitely. And if I pass any half-clothed nineteen-year-olds on the way out, I'll send them your way, shall I?"

Anthony planted his hands on the table and levered himself halfway up—

"You just might get your way this time." Tony's jaw tightened. "I'm sick."

Anthony froze. Then he slowly lowered himself back to sitting.

A server breezed by just then. "Can I get you two—"

"We need doubles," Anthony said, beginning to recover from his shock.

He took a deep breath and tried to think.

This must be bad. Really bad. As a man's man who could sever his arm with a chainsaw and call it "a little scrape," Tony would have to be at death's door before he admitted having so much as a cold.

"A whisky and a bourbon," Anthony told the server. "Thanks."

The server left. Tony fiddled with his cocktail napkin.

"What's going on?" Anthony asked.

"Eh." Tony looked up at last, his expression carefully neutral as he flapped a hand. "Got heart disease. Had a little heart attack. And a bypass."

"What? *When?*"

"Few months back."

"And you didn't think to mention it?"

"That's what I'm doing," Tony said evenly.

Anthony tried to lock his feelings into some semblance of control, no easy task when he'd already lost his mother and felt the flare of an orphan's panic at the thought of losing his remaining parent, even if he was a poor specimen.

"Well," he said gruffly. "Looks like you're taking care of yourself. Your spray tan is firmly in place, I see. You must be feeling fine."

Self-deprecating smile from Tony. "Let's hope I can keep myself healthy. Since that's the only way I'm going to live to torment you another day."

Anthony's lips started to smile, but only made it halfway. They didn't quite remember how. Not in his father's presence. "Anything I can do?"

"Yeah." Tony leaned in, all neutrality slipping away from his expression. "You can come back home to Houston with me."

Well, there it was: Tony's hidden agenda. It never took too long to raise its ugly head, yet it was always a nasty surprise when it showed up.

"I was thinking more along the lines of chicken soup or a new pair of pajamas and slippers. Maybe a visit at the holidays," Anthony said.

"You could see about dipping your toe in the business. Or get started on another career."

"I have a career," Anthony said flatly.

"No, you don't." The old man's upper lip peeled back in the beginning of a sneer. "You have your grandmother's charity work. Not the same thing at all."

Anthony had no intentions of opening up *that* Pandora's box tonight or any other night. Not with his father. And if there was a nasty twinge of truth to his father's words, Anthony would put it aside for now. There was no point getting into it. He'd made his choices long ago.

"I'm not discussing my work or my grandmother with you."

Frustrated sigh from Tony followed by a beseeching wheedle.

"I'm getting old, now, son. You're the only kid I got. Family means something."

Anthony glared the man down, appalled both by his father's never-ending hypocrisy and his own ongoing animosity toward this man. It would take a hell of a lot more than an alleged diagnosis of a serious illness to mend *these* bridges.

"Family means something to *you*? Since when? Not when you cheated your way through your marriage with my mother or made her life miserable during the divorce or didn't show up to her funeral, surely. And probably not when you haven't been bothered with *me* since, except for random appearances, phone calls and the occasional threat to cut off the income from the trust fund that *my mother left for me*."

The words hung in the air, ringing with enough truth that Tony actually had the decency to look ashamed.

"Fair enough." Tony bowed his head. "How about this: family *should* mean something. Will that work?"

Anthony worked hard to loosen his clenched jaw. "Agreed."

Tony moodily stared into his glass. "And your mother made me your trustee. To do with your money as I see fit for the term of the trust. Thanks to me and my investments, you'll be knocking on the door of a billion dollars when you get control next year when you turn thirty-five."

"Yes, well, I appreciate your diligence, but you'll have to forgive me if I'm a bit anxious to be out from under your financial thumb."

"You wouldn't have been under my thumb if you had a career. Which I've been telling you for years. Don't you want something of your own that you can be proud of?"

"You're a broken fucking record."

They glared at each other. In those toxic few seconds, it probably wouldn't have taken much for either of them to lunge across the table and throttle the other.

The server reappeared with their drinks, and not a moment too soon. Anthony downed half of his in one sinus-burning gulp, but Tony picked his up and swirled it.

By then, Anthony was feeling no pain and no mercy.

"Come on, now," he said, reaching across the table to thump his father on the shoulder. "You're not going to let your lame-ass son drink you under the table, are you?"

Tony sadly shook his head. "I can't drink like I used to. Doesn't set right with my belly."

"There's a *tragedy*," Anthony muttered.

Tony put his glass down and nailed Anthony with the piercing gaze that had shone disapproval down on him all his life. "Will you think about it? Will you come home?"

"Try to pay attention. Houston's not my home."

"It was after your mother died." A muscle pulsed in Tony's forehead. "For about ten minutes."

"Yes, and that was more than long enough for us to nearly kill each other, which was why I took myself off to boarding school. And I'm not an oilman like you."

"Nope," Tony said bitterly. "You're nothing like me."

"There it is at last." Anthony downed the rest of his drink. "Something we can agree on."

"Doesn't it matter to you, son? That I might be dying?"

Anthony spoke without thinking. "You're far too hateful to die."

Tony stared him down until Anthony's gaze wavered and fell.

He considered his father and thought of all the hard feelings and years wasted. All the slights, perceived and real. The occasional laughter—the time they spent a mud-splattered day together racing around the ranch in their all-terrain vehicles came to mind—quickly followed by endless silences and phones that never rang.

And now his father had heart issues.

"Of course it matters to me," Anthony said, his voice husky.

Tony leaned forward. "You're gonna let me do that alone?"

Anthony couldn't meet his father's gaze, so he eyed his empty glass and came up with a deflection.

"Where are all your teenaged ex-wives and playthings?"

Tony barked out a laugh. "You think one of them is gonna stick around for some sick old man?"

Anthony shrugged, every atom inside his body determined to never show this man his vulnerable underbelly lest Tony rip it out like a lioness with a zebra kill.

"That seems like the kind of thing you might have thought about twenty years ago, when you were a middle-aged man trying to fuck every co-ed in the University of Texas school system," Anthony said. "So I guess this is a case of reaping what you've sown?"

Tony's face twisted into a snarl of bared teeth, lowered brows and flashing eyes.

"This is about your grandmother, isn't it? You open your mouth and her words come out! She's brainwashed you! She clicks her bony old fingers, and you can't go running fast enough! Why don't you try being your own man for once?"

The hypocrisy remained thick as shit in a cow pasture through here. Too bad Anthony hadn't brought his Wellies with him.

"I've *always* been my own man," he said, his voice shaking with a lifetime's worth of repressed anger as he pointed a finger in his father's face. "*That's* why you could never stand the sight of my face."

Tired smile from the old guy, who raised his drink again.

"I can't stand the sight of your face because you look just like your mother."

Anthony froze. What? *What* did he just say?

Tony toasted him and downed his entire drink in a rough gulp, generating a hacking fit.

"Jesus." Anthony watched helplessly for a moment, then signaled for the server. "Can we get some water over here, please?"

"I don't need any *water*!" Tony coughed again, then cleared his hoarse throat. "I need my *son*!"

Anthony grimaced and stared the old man in the face, noting the deep under-eye circles. The craggy lines that now stayed one step ahead of the Botox treatments. The veiled fear and despair in those familiar eyes.

And he felt…numb.

He couldn't decide whether that was better or worse than the usual blind rage.

"I don't think I can help you," he said. "I'm being honest."

Tony's face fell.

Anthony's phone buzzed just then. Grateful for the distraction, he snatched it up to discover another text from Melody:

I was at a stoplight! Home now. Sleep tight.

She ended with a kiss-blowing emoji that made him unreasonably happy, especially after the turmoil of the last several minutes. He started to grin but caught himself, mindful of his father's unhappiness and rapt attention.

Sure enough.

When Anthony raised his head again, those watchful eyes were everywhere, seeing everything all the way down to the dark and hidden corners of Anthony's heart. He looked hopeful for Anthony. Excited. Possibly even proud.

That, in a nutshell, was the most insidious thing about spending time—any time at all—with Tony. Sometimes he acted like the kind of father a bloke might want to have around. And he was a good enough actor to really fuck with Anthony's head.

"She special to you? Miss Melody?"

Just like that, the bubble of warm feelings that Anthony had accidentally and temporarily felt for his father popped like a balloon meeting a razor blade. Anthony thought back to the girlfriends he'd had over the years, most of whom Tony had charmed, some of whom he'd actively tried to seduce and one of whom he'd actually fucked back when Anthony was in college. An event that had come to light when Anthony foolishly ran out to pick up pizza, then returned to his dorm room a bit sooner than the lovebirds had probably expected.

He barked out a laugh. "You don't actually expect me to discuss Melody with *you*?"

"Fair enough," Tony said sadly. "How about a word of advice?"

Annoyed at being cast in the bad guy role tonight, Anthony impatiently twitched his shoulders.

"You care about that girl? You hang on to her." Tony pointed at Anthony's face. "Don't you let your grandmother, me, Miss Melody's kin or anyone else keep you from her. You got me?"

Against all odds, the numbness inside Anthony gave way to a twinge of affection for the old guy.

"Looks like there are two things we agree on tonight," he told his father.

9

Anthony: Saved any youthful lives today?

Melody: Let's hope so. 5 y.o. with significant liver lacerations following car accident. Emergency appendectomy. Rounds. Paperwork. Another day in paradise. ;) You?

Anthony: Can't answer. Too exhausted reading about YOUR day. When do you sleep?

Melody: Sleep? What is this concept?

Anthony: I was going to complain about Nick standing me up for breakfast in favor of the redhead, but am now rethinking…

Melody: LOL! So what did you do all day? How do you like Journey's End?

Anthony: Wonderful town. I kayaked. By myself. Nick skived off because he was "low on fluids." I'll leave that to your imagination. Baptiste is with Samira. Says she's better today.

Melody: Yeah. Talked to her. You should try Pub 221B for dinner. Fish and chips. Let me know if they're authentic.

Anthony: Will do. We still on for quick breakfast at hospital in morning?

Melody: Yep. Meet me in the atrium at 9:30.

Anthony: Looking forward to it.

Melody: You might want to reconsider. I plan to grill you about your career and city of residence.

Anthony: Still looking forward to it. And to hello kiss.

Melody: G-rated only in the workplace, pls.

Anthony: Alas!

10:16 p.m. Sunday

Anthony: Fish and chips NOT authentic. At home, skin remains on the fish.

Melody: What? That's disgusting!

Anthony: Not at all. You'll see when you come to London to visit me.

Melody: ?

Anthony: Sorry? I was under impression English is your first language?

Melody: We just met! Now you're planning trips?

Anthony: Too soon? Save trip planning for tomorrow or day after?

Melody: W-O-W

Anthony: Your noncommittal answer is duly noted. Demerits given. You will receive stern talking to tomorrow morning.

Melody: So you're still coming?

Anthony: Did you think I wouldn't?

Melody: You might ghost me.

Anthony: Ghosting you is the last thing on my mind. Did

you think about me today? Sorry. Wine from dinner is making me needy. So did you?

Melody: I'm a busy surgeon and a consummate professional! I was working all day!

Anthony: Did you think about me today?

Melody: I thought about you ALL day. Curse you and your clever questioning! Did you train with 007?

Anthony: I cannot reveal that information. Will they let you sleep tonight?

Melody: Hopefully. Speaking of—time for me to grab some ZZZZs.

Anthony: I'll let you go. Try to think of me when you get into bed. Because I'll be thinking of you.

Melody: No "darling"?

Anthony: Try to think of me tonight, Darling.

Melody: XO

WHEN MELODY HURRIED AROUND THE CORNER AND INTO THE soaring and sunny hospital atrium the following morning, she had no problem locating Anthony. He was the one holding a shopping bag and a drink carrier and sandwiched between two smiling and pretty med techs—she thought they were from radiology—who stared up at him with red hearts where their eyes had been.

Not that she could blame them.

She checked him out as she came closer, her heartbeat lapsing into a wonky pattern that made her glad she was in a hospital and therefore easily resuscitated when she keeled over in a dead faint.

He'd traded in his tux for a pair of faded jeans that showcased his long legs and stellar ass to perfection. Weathered brown leather bomber jacket. Sweater. Scarf. A ridiculously sexy five o'clock shadow.

All she could do was glance sorrowfully down at her blue scrubs and lab coat, smooth her ponytail and thank God that she had clear skin—the unscarred part, anyway—and time to swipe on a little lip gloss before she came down.

They didn't have scarred faces, she noted, eyeballing her would-be competition with a sinking heart. *They* looked fresh and clean and weren't wrapping up a ridiculous no-sleep shift that created a whole set of Louis Vuitton luggage under your eyes. A man like Anthony rightfully belonged with a woman like one of *them*.

Her steps slowed.

She reached for her ponytail again, longing to pull the elastic out and fluff her hair around her face and neck so she could at least approximate someone who didn't make small children stare. As a person who worked with many small children, she periodically had to question her masochistic tendencies.

On the other hand, she'd never been a coward and she wasn't going to start now. And the best way to get Anthony to reveal his true colors—and true intentions—might well be to force him to confront her scar head-on, with no filters and no rosy glow from good lighting and a few drinks.

She squared her shoulders the way a confident woman would do and completed her approach.

"Thanks so much, but I'm…" Anthony saw Melody and brightened, his breath hitching audibly as his avid gaze swept her up and down. To his credit, he seemed much more interested in her eyes than her scar. "Here she is now," he told the med techs. He spared them a quick glance, then returned his attention to Melody. "Appreciate the help, though."

The women looked crestfallen. Honestly, if they tried to

make a living playing poker, they'd be homeless and destitute by the end of the first round. They didn't do much better when it came to checking Melody out. In a standard reaction, they saw the scar, recoiled slightly, caught themselves doing it, then recovered and overcompensated with smiles that were a bit too broad and overenthusiastic. This time, there was added puzzlement in their expressions, a distinct *what's he doing with* her? vibe that plunged an ice pick straight through the center of Melody's fragile ego.

They can't hurt you, Mel, she reminded herself, employing the mantra that had gotten her through a thousand of these awkward encounters in her life. *Nothing can hurt you unless you let it.*

Unfortunately, her mouth wasn't listening.

"Just a kitchen accident when I was a kid," she told the women in a prickly knee-jerk reaction before she could stop herself. "No need to stare."

By this time, they'd caught sight of her name badge and all but died of embarrassment.

"Sorry, Dr. Harrison."

"We didn't mean to—"

"No worries," Melody said, now fighting her own embarrassment. Why did she always have to spout off at the mouth? Why couldn't she trot out her best behavior for ten seconds in front of Anthony? She managed a quick smile. "Have a great day."

"You too," they said, leaping on the opportunity to put their heads together as they hurried off, probably whispering about the scarred doctor whose sanity was questionable at best.

And leaving Melody alone to face a now unsmiling Anthony.

"You get that a lot?" he asked quietly.

"It's okay." She attempted her most offhand shrug. The last thing she wanted was for this man to feel sorry for her. "I'm used to it."

"Not sure you could be," he muttered, frowning as he stared after them.

"Eh. I'd be a fool if I let staring people ruin my day. Don't you agree?"

His head came back around. His expression was so full of surprise and admiration that there was no room for pity.

Her breath caught. She hid it as best she could, but she couldn't help but stare. Just a little.

The glorious morning light hit him just right. His eyes were bluer than she'd thought, his gold-streaked hair blonder. And she absolutely could not think when he looked at her like *that,* with such unwavering and relentless focus you'd think she'd shown up with a potion for orgasms on demand in her pocket.

"So…good morning," she said, trying to smile. Which wasn't easy when a blush roared up her neck and set her face on fire.

"Good morning." After a beat or two, he blinked some of that intensity into submission. His voice softened when he spoke to her, she noticed. "It's really great to see you."

"You too," she admitted, feeling her expression morph into the same sort of unfortunate simper the med techs had just exhibited.

He hesitated, then leaned in to press a lingering kiss on her scarred cheek, right by her ear.

Just dove right in and kissed her thickened skin in the cold light of day.

She froze, stunned.

Clearing his throat, he slowly pulled back.

She, meanwhile, resisted the urge to touch the spot, which

now tingled, and awarded him a million points for finesse. Was the kiss only a clever maneuver designed to get him laid sooner rather than later? Possibly. That didn't stop her heart from thumping or a delicious shiver from racing over her flesh.

"See? Perfectly G-rated," he said.

She laughed. "Well done."

His eyes shone at her. It seemed like a real possibility that they'd lapse into another bout of mutual staring, but he snapped his fingers.

"Before I forget to ask, how is your little car accident patient with the lacerated liver?"

She grinned, both at his interest in her life and career and at the memory of the drowsy and angelic little girl she'd just left upstairs.

"You remembered."

He looked vaguely offended. "'Course I remembered."

"She had a bleeding complication in the night, but her color was good on morning rounds, so I'm hoping she's turned the corner. She's adorable. Excited because her family just got a puppy."

He nodded with unmistakable satisfaction. "I'm sure you're taking good care of her."

"I'm trying."

"This is a lovely hospital." He glanced around with approval. "Everyone here is so kind and eager to make sure I'm not lost. Three different women pointed me in the right direction."

She shot him an incredulous look. "If you think those women wanted to help you out rather than come in for a closer look, then I've got a nice river nearby that I'd like to sell you."

He grimaced, flushing and looking sheepish.

"Right. Well, thanks for that."

Laughing, she decided to let him off the hook before he expired from embarrassment. She pointed to the white shopping bag he carried, which was from Java Nectar, the local coffeehouse.

"What's all that?"

"Breakfast. I thought you might like a change from the cafeteria food. Java Nectar is a nice little gem, isn't it? They have twin boys, about eight, working there. They're a bit cutthroat, to be honest. They each insisted on a tip for handing me my cutlery and napkins."

"Ah, yes. You met Jonah and Noah. The owner's sons. Let's sit over here."

She led him to a quiet spot with some modicum of privacy next to a giant pillar and a potted palm. He handed her the drinks and set the shopping bag on the little table between them as they sat.

There were four coffee cups.

"Are we expecting someone else?" she asked.

"Ah, no. I may have, ah, gone a bit overboard. This one's coffee for you. This one's decaf for you, just in case. And this one's English breakfast for you. Also just in case."

"No Earl Grey?"

Poor Anthony looked so crestfallen that she didn't have the heart to tease him.

"Just kidding," she said quickly. "I hate Earl Grey. I'll take the English breakfast."

He snorted out the laugh of a good sport. "*English* breakfast. Well played."

"I strive. You're very thorough."

"Or perhaps a bit manic. I didn't want to get anything wrong, so I brought, well, you can see—"

She peered in the bag. "Bagels. Scones. Danish. Yogurt—"

"All busy surgeons need their protein."

"—fruit—"

"And their vitamins."

"—and, *yes,* a couple of egg sandwiches."

"Just in case you eat like a lumberjack. Do you see anything you like?"

"I like everything," she said, touched by his effort as she smiled across the little table at him. "Thank you."

He'd been distributing napkins, but now he stopped and stared at her, arrested.

"Can I tell you something?"

"Yes." Her heart thudded. "Of course."

"You're *beautiful.*" He hesitated, the tips of his ears turning bright red. "And I've really missed you. So that's two things, isn't it?"

Funny. She felt spectacularly beautiful with those vivid blue eyes sparkling at her that way. Just like any other woman in the throes of a new crush. She didn't even feel the urge to smooth her hair and make sure the side of her face was covered. But she was no goddess and the moment felt far too meaningful for this early in their relationship.

Naturally, she reached for her default defense mechanism.

"Is it the bags under my eyes? The unkempt hair? The complete absence of makeup?"

"It's *you,*" he said flatly.

She gaped at him, her entire vocabulary abandoning her.

God, this *man.*

He caused such a sweet ache in her heart.

The stern warning she'd given herself earlier—*it's just a quick breakfast, girl; don't lose your head*—flew right out the atrium windows. With a quick glance around to make sure no one noticed, she half stood, leaned over the table and kissed his eager lips. She'd meant for it to be a quick peck, but his hands swiftly came up to cup her cheeks, holding her there long enough to elicit a helpless coo of pleasure from somewhere deep inside her.

When he let her go, his lips were dewy and smiling, his eyes heavy-lidded.

"You *definitely* don't think I'm as big an arse as you used to," he said with unmistakable satisfaction.

"Eh," she said, grinning. "Let's see how you did on the bagel and cream cheese selections, shall we?"

"Fair enough."

They got settled, picking out their food and prepping their drinks. Then she pulled out her list, unfolded it with a flourish and laid it on the table.

"Uh-oh." He eyeballed it warily. "What's all this?"

"My questions for you. Since I've been forbidden from looking you up."

He made a face around his bite of egg sandwich. "Can I eat first?"

"No! Question number one: where did you go to school, and what do you do career-wise?"

"Perhaps you'd like a copy of my résumé?"

"Clock's ticking," she said, tapping her watch.

"Eton. Cambridge. The Royal Military Academy and my training. Overseas for a bit. NYU Law."

"Hang on. You're a lawyer?"

"I've never practiced. I wasn't quite sure where I wanted to settle, and then I sort of fell into what I do now. I help my, ah, grandmother with her charity work when she needs it, which is quite often these days. Especially the foundation."

"What does the foundation do?"

"Provides medical care for underprivileged children

worldwide. Primarily in Africa. I thought Baptiste had told you at least that much about me."

"Oh, that's right!" She snapped her fingers. "You're the friend of his who's always looking for doctors willing to volunteer."

"Right. That's how I knew about you."

"Knew about me?" she asked blankly, sipping her tea.

Anthony stiffened. His expression slid into distinctly *I've said too much!* territory.

"Yes, well…" He tugged on an earlobe. "I had, ah, glanced at your bio and watched your videos before I met you the other night."

Wait, *what*? He looked her up online?

"You did?"

"You might as well know the whole story. Before Nick blurts it out in his ongoing campaign to embarrass me at every opportunity." There was a long pause while he drummed his fingers on his knee, took a deep breath and stared her in the face with those vivid baby blues of his. "I was very keen to meet you, to be honest. I thought there was something about your eyes. I mean…There *is* something about your eyes."

Melody's brain blanked out. Something about *her* eyes?

When *he* had the most striking blue eyes that God ever conferred on a human being?

The possibility that a man like *this* would be excited about meeting her was far too thrilling and overwhelming to meet head-on.

"It's the scrubs, isn't it?" Not bothering to hide her incredulity, she swept a hand down her body with a flourish. "You knew how sexy I'd look coming off a long shift with no sleep, didn't you?"

He stiffened. There was an awkward pause while something in his face closed off, causing a corresponding and painful twinge in the area of her heart.

He shook his head and looked across the atrium. Tried to smile. Failed miserably and looked back at her.

His eyes weren't so bright and sparkly now. They were subdued and muddy.

Her heart fell.

"Here's the thing," he said softly. "I'm not charming like Nick and Baptiste. I'm not a flirt. It takes a fair amount of courage for me to admit something like that to you. Maybe you shouldn't be so quick to dismiss it."

She opened her mouth. Floundered.

Ultimately decided to meet his honesty with her own difficult confession.

"Men don't lose their heads about me, Anthony. I'm not that girl."

His gaze never wavered.

"Let me assure you. You are *absolutely* that girl."

She felt the sudden and unexpected flicker of hope.

They watched each other in a wary silence for a couple of beats. She wished he'd stop bulldozing through every wall she tried to erect between them, then *really* wished she could tamp down some of her surging excitement.

He seemed to *glow* when he looked at her.

"You're going home to London tonight," she reminded him. "I'm not sleeping with you before that. And we have no idea when we'll see each other again. Maybe you should pump the brakes once or twice and stop looking at me like that. Just to be smart."

His eyes crinkled at the corners. One brow eased up. "Smart?"

"Smart."

"Prudent advice. Too bad the door for, ah, pumping the

brakes and being *smart* slammed shut when Baptiste first sent me your information." He shot her a probing look. "Unless I'm misreading the chemistry between us? It's been known to happen."

Melody veered straight into deer-in-headlights mode, her words disappearing on her again. A plausible denial never even entered the room.

"Right, then," he said with a gleam of triumph, reaching for a bagel now that he'd handily won that round. "Where were we?"

She felt a wild swoop of relief to be released from all that intensity. And she could breathe again, so that was also a plus. But then it hit her.

"Hang on. How come *you* can look *me* up, but *I* can't look *you* up?"

Anthony smirked. "Unfair, I admit, but rules are rules. And you *did* agree. So would you be interested in volunteering? We always need surgeons in the field."

"Oh, my God." She pressed a hand to her heart. "I'd *love* to. And you should also speak to my plastic surgeon and mentor, Dr. Muhammed. She's the best doctor I've ever worked with. She's on staff at my hospital."

"I'll do that."

"I'm so excited! I've always wanted to do something like this. But I haven't had much of a chance yet with my training and all."

"Yes, I believe you've earned the distinction of having chosen one of the most difficult fields in medicine? With something like nine years of training *after* medical school?"

"I'm a glutton for punishment."

"But you must love it."

"I *do* love it. Don't you love your career?"

He blinked. Made a face. "*Love* is a bit strong."

"Oh. Well, what would you like to do?"

"I'm committed to this," he said wryly. "What I'd like to do is irrelevant."

She blinked. Having known what she wanted to do ever since she was little, she couldn't quite get her head around his fatalism. What the hell did he do all day? What was life like when your every thought, wish and dream wasn't tied up in your dream career or a family?

"What about practicing law?"

He flapped a hand. "Not sure that's still an option. It's been awhile."

"So you're no longer interested?"

He opened his mouth. Closed it without answering.

"Well, you should think about it."

"*Think about it?* It's not that easy with my current duties."

She gaped at him. She didn't handle ambivalence well, especially other people's.

"I'm not telling you to build a rocket and fly to the moon. Didn't you just say you have a law degree from NYU? Don't you know some people you could talk to about it? What's the big deal? You'll never have a great career unless you get started. You're burning daylight."

"Burning daylight?" He seemed disconcerted. "Now you sound like my father."

She shrugged. "Smart man."

Anthony scowled and looked down at his bagel, his eyes sliding out of focus. He showed all the signs of a man who was stuck between what he wanted to do and what he thought he should do.

Maybe it was time for a bit of motivation.

"You know what's really sexy?" she said, taking great care with spreading the cream cheese on her bagel. "A smart man who works hard and engineers the life he wants. *Noth-*

ing's a bigger turn-on than that. You didn't bring any jam, did you?"

His attention snapped back to her face.

She channeled all the limpid innocence she could.

"Are you *challenging* me?" he asked gruffly.

"Is it working?"

He thought it over. "I believe it is."

She felt an immense wave of satisfaction. A man like this could rule the world if he wanted to. She knew it. "Good."

"You're quite a piece of work, Dr. Harrison," he said, eyeing her with a wary new respect. "And don't try to get me off topic. The question has to do with you working for my foundation."

"Right. So should I fill out an application, or…?"

"Absolutely not. You're hired."

Her heart leapt. "Are you serious? Easiest interview of my life!"

"Yes," He grimaced at her list as she picked it up again for a quick perusal. "If only I could say the same. How am I coming on your questions? And what is the precise position I'm under consideration for?"

"Potential recipient of my affections."

He laughed. "Sounds delightful. Fire away."

"So do you have brothers and sisters?"

"Just me. You?"

"An older sister. Carmen lives in the city. And my parents live in Chicago now. All doctors."

He looked aghast. "What, *all*?"

"All."

"What a collection of overachievers! I think my father took a page from their book. My whole life, he's pressed me to work harder and do *more*. Whatever *that* is. No accomplishment is ever good enough."

"Is that why you and he don't get along?"

His expression darkened. "It's in the top ten reasons, yes."

"And your mother?" she asked, determined to steer the conversation back into waters that didn't make him look so severe.

Wrong move. A storm cloud drifted over his face and settled in.

"They split when I was ten. Then she was, ah, killed. When I was thirteen." His lips thinned. "Bad fall while skiing."

"Oh, no." She pressed a hand to her chest. "I'm so sorry to hear that."

He nodded, making a game attempt at a smile even though his attention seemed far away. "She introduced me to the work with the medical foundation. Took me to Africa when I was twelve. Life-changing experience—"

"Well, well, well," said a sardonic male voice with a French accent. "What have we here?"

Startled, Melody and Anthony glanced around to discover Baptiste and Samira standing there watching them with identical expressions of stunned delight.

10

Samira and Baptiste both looked very chipper this morning, their faces alight with keen interest to discover Melody and Anthony together and, unless Melody was much mistaken, excitement about something else.

Anthony quickly stood to shake Baptiste's hand, then kissed Samira. "You're looking much better today."

"I'm feeling much better." Samira gave Melody a veiled *what the hell is going on and why didn't you tell me?* look as she leaned down for a quick hug. Melody tried not to blush too hard, but that was like trying not to get a sunburn when you lay out on a Bermuda beach all day. "And what're *you* two fine folks up to?"

"I would say they're on a date," Baptiste said, now all but levitating with mischief as he gave Melody a double-cheeked kiss. "That's what it looks like to me."

"Just a quick breakfast." Melody, who wasn't quite ready to define or discuss her blossoming relationship with Anthony with anyone, decided that the best defense was a good offense. "And what are *you* two doing here?"

Baptiste and Samira exchanged a shifty look.

"Nothing," Samira said quickly. "I just had a quick checkup to, ah, make sure everything's okay. With my stomach."

"If I didn't know any better," Melody said without thinking, reaching for one of the Danish, "I'd think you were pregnant and had an ultrasound appointment or something."

Her little joke was met with wide-eyed astonishment from Baptiste and Samira. Melody put the Danish down, a growing suspicion now crawling over her nape. Baptiste turned to Samira. Gave her a silent beseeching look. Samira sighed, rolled her eyes and nodded.

Melody's bottom jaw clanged to the table.

Anthony looked up from peeling open his yogurt, frowning.

"What's going on?" he asked carefully.

"We *are* pregnant!" Beaming, Baptiste whipped a glossy strip of ultrasound photos out of his pocket and flashed them in their faces. "*Look* at this! The baby has a very strong and loud heartbeat! I think it's a boy."

"Let's get one thing cleared up," Samira said. "*We* are not pregnant." She pointed back and forth between herself and Baptiste before jerking her thumb at herself. "*I* am pregnant. Never say that again."

"*I* am also partially pregnant," Baptiste said quietly, with more than a tinge of defiance.

"No, you're not," Samira and Melody both said.

They all laughed as Melody and Anthony surged to their feet to hug and kiss the parents-to-be.

"Oh, my *God,*" Melody said, her mind effectively blown. "I can't even… I can't even…"

"Neither can we!" Samira said.

"*I* can," Baptiste said. "Remember, Melody? At the Halloween bonfire?"

"Are you releasing me from my vow of silence?" Melody asked.

"Proceed," Baptiste said with smug smile and a benevolent bow of his head.

"Baptiste had a panic attack that night," Melody told Samira, who was all ears. "He saw that house on the hill, Howard's Folly, and he was sort of overwhelmed because he said he could picture the two of you there with kids and stuff. A family. It was pretty intense."

Samira looked a little startled as she turned to Baptiste, who cocked an *I told you so* brow at her. Then she laughed, blinking back a tear or two. "Stop trying to make the pregnant woman cry, you two. I'm already on the edge as it is."

More laughter on all sides. Melody took the opportunity to grab Samira's hand before turning to the menfolk.

"Excuse us for a minute, fellas. I need to grill Samira about all the gory details. I'm sure you understand."

With that, she towed Samira to a love seat out of earshot several feet away, where they plunked themselves down and leaned in for some girl talk.

"Oh, my God," Melody cried. "What the *hell*?"

Samira swiped her eyes. "I know, I know. My head is still spinning."

"How does a responsible thirty-something woman wind up pregnant? Do I need to have the safe sex talk with you?"

"Evidently. I wasn't on the pill at the time. We used condoms, but we were a little exuberant that first night and didn't, ah…Well, you get the picture."

"I'm not sure I do, but who cares? You've both carried on about what an extraordinary night *that* was, so I can't wait to see this gorgeous baby! So at the gala when you weren't feeling well? That was, what, nausea?"

"I had some cramping. No bleeding. And my OB was very encouraging just now."

"How do you feel about this turn of events? And to think you were so worried at the gala because Baptiste hadn't talked about the future of your relationship. What did I tell you, you silly rabbit?"

"He seems very excited," Samira said, blushing.

They both looked around at Baptiste, quickly discovering what an understatement *that* was. Deep in an animated conversation with Anthony, his mile-wide grin telegraphed his incandescent happiness.

"He loves you like crazy, Sami," Melody said.

"I'm not sure how I got this lucky." Samira wiped her eyes again, possibly remembering how she'd just come off a broken engagement when she met Baptiste. "Okay, and that's enough about me. What the hell's going on with you and Anthony? I *knew* you had chemistry!"

It was Melody's turn to blush. "I'm not really sure. We got stuck on the elevator together and…I don't know. He's a very interesting person."

"He's a very *sexy* person." Samira shot him a surreptitious glance over Melody's shoulder. "He hasn't stopped looking at you this whole time. So what now?"

"I wish I knew. We've texted a couple of times, then he brought breakfast so we could spend a little time together. But he's going back to London tonight."

"Yeah, he's riding with Baptiste again. So when will Anthony be back this way?"

"I keep telling you, I don't know. I don't see what could happen anyway. He lives in London."

Samira, who was now deep into her unlikely fairy-tale romance with a French citizen who lived in Paris, gave her an exasperated look.

"*Really?* Have I taught you nothing?"

"Oh, please. Don't pretend you have all the answers all of the sudden. Like you and Baptiste are some old married couple. Two days ago, *you* were high up on that ledge, ready to throw yourself off because *you* weren't sure where *your* relationship was going. *I'm* the one who had to talk *you* down."

"Ancient history," Samira said breezily, flapping a hand.

They both laughed.

"But you like him?" Samira asked, all dewy-eyed hope and as sentimental as a Hallmark store. "You see potential?"

Melody ducked her head and fidgeted with her ponytail, not quite ready to admit, even to herself, that Anthony had occupied most of her non-work-related waking thoughts since she met him. And there was no way to describe the unreasonable vibrancy in her skin and blood when she was with him.

When he looked at her.

When he touched her.

Which was why she was determined to keep her expectations low.

"He's got some potential," she said lightly.

"Have you looked him up online yet?"

"No. We're getting to know each other as people without all that."

Blank look from Samira. "Is that wise?"

"We shall see."

Samira pulled out her phone. "Well, *I* can look him up—"

Melody snatched the phone and tossed it aside. "No, you can't."

"Turnabout's fair play." With a serene smile, Samira retrieved her phone and started tapping on it. "I seem to recall that *you* were the person who tipped me off about Baptiste being a billionaire playboy."

"You know what? Look him up all you want. Just don't tell me about it unless it turns out he's on the FBI's Most Wanted list or something."

"But…"

"Thank you for your compliance," Melody said, not quite sure why it felt so important to keep her word with Anthony. But she was determined to live up to her end of the agreement.

Samira blinked.

Melody whipped out her own phone and pulled something up. "You know who else has some potential? This guy from Doctor Love dot com who wants to match with me. *Look.* Jerome Ayers, forty-five. Internist. And he's right here in town. I can't believe I've never met him before."

Samira frowned down at the man's handsome face, then up at Melody. "You're still doing that?"

"Why would you even ask me that? *You* were the one who ignored my vow of spinsterhood and insisted on setting up my profile. We're trying to get together for drinks as soon as our schedules line up."

Samira gave her a thin-lipped look.

"What?"

"I just think you should give Anthony a real chance," Samira said. "Assuming, you know, that he's not secretly a pedophile or something."

"Well, we'll see. But I'm not losing my head about dating *anyone.* I doubt there's a prince out there for me. That's why I'm focusing on my career."

"*Anthony* could be your prince, is all I'm saying. You never know."

Melody shrugged and fidgeted with her earring, this whole topic making her agitated for reasons she didn't care to explore right now. Or, possibly, ever.

Samira gave her a shrewd once-over. "So are you going to give him some before he goes back?"

"What?" Melody tried to look shocked by the very idea, which maxed out her limited acting skills. As though this burning question wasn't melting her from the inside out. As though she hadn't been fantasizing about the weight and strain of Anthony's tall body as he thrust inside her, his sweat-slicked chest hard against her pebbled nipples. *"No.* I'm done with casual sex and friends with benefits scenarios. They never get you anywhere and just leave you feeling like roadkill in the end."

"Okay, but I'd like to point out that *my* relationship started out with casual sex, and look at me now," Samira said, using both hands to point at her belly.

"Yeah." Melody sadly shook her head. "An unmarried black woman with a baby on the way. Just another statistic."

They burst into laughter as Samira smacked her arm.

"Oh, and listen. We're keeping this quiet until I pass the three-month mark. So if you run into my parents—"

"Of course," Melody said quickly.

"Let's go see what the menfolk are talking about."

They walked back to the table, where Baptiste had made himself at home with the food and was finishing off the other egg sandwich and reaching for a scone. Anthony, who'd been sipping his coffee, lowered his cup and sat up straighter, his attention zeroing in on Melody's face and hanging on tight.

If any other man had hit her with this level of intensity, it would have made her fidgety and desperate to hide the ruined side of her face. With Anthony? It made her lips want to smile and electric butterflies swoop low in her belly. It made her stand up straighter and hold her head up high. It made her think that maybe her scar was the very last thing he noticed about her.

"So have you finished talking about us?" Baptiste asked happily as he stood, slung an arm around Samira's waist and reeled her in. "Is everyone straight on all the gory details?"

"We're straight," Samira told him, reaching for one of the bagels. "And we should get out of their hair. We're interrupting their *getting to know you time*."

"Not at all." Anthony blinked, breaking the spell with Melody, and gestured at all the extra food like a gracious host. "Help yourself. We'll never eat it all."

"Thanks." Standing, Baptiste carefully selected a raisin bagel and slid it into one pocket of his leather jacket, then wrapped his scone in a napkin and slipped it in the other. "I'd like to borrow Melody for a second before we go."

"Oh." A little startled, Melody let him take her hand and steer her back to that same love seat, sparing Anthony a quick and bemused look over her shoulder as she went. "Okay. What's up?"

Some of Baptiste's radiant joy receded in favor of worry lines grooving down his forehead as they sat. "I have to go back to Paris tonight for some meetings I've been putting off. It's killing me to leave Samira just now, when she's still so worried about the baby, but I don't have a choice."

Melody began to see where this was going. She nodded. "I'll keep an eye on her while you're gone. Don't worry."

Baptiste sagged with relief. "I knew I could count on you. You may have your hands full, though. She insists she's not slowing down. And she doesn't want me hovering over her. To no one's surprise."

"That's our Samira," she said, and they both laughed.

Baptiste glanced over her shoulder, beaming absolute adoration in Samira's direction as she said something to Anthony. "I didn't know I had all these dreams inside me. And if I had, I never would have thought they'd come true."

"You're such a good guy," Melody said, playfully patting his cheek while he ducked his head and fought back a tear or two. "You see? *This* is why I always tried to help you out."

Baptiste hastily wiped his eyes, cleared his throat and reverted to mischief maker in chief. "You know who is an even better guy than me? *Anthony*."

Melody rolled her eyes. She tried to look, at best, only mildly interested in this information, but her jackhammering heartbeat was probably audible all the way up to the top levels of the atrium.

"Is *that* so?"

"Yes. Among the three of us? Me, Nick and Anthony? Anthony was always the most serious student. He was the honorable military man. The most reliable friend. The best person. No question whatsoever. No one ever despaired of his future the way they did for me and Nick. *We* were better for knowing *him*. Not the other way around."

"Really?" Melody soaked this information up like a dried sponge tossed into the after-dinner dishwater. So much for appearing nonchalant. "I mean...come on. You have to say that. You're each other's wingmen."

"Wingmen?" Baptiste laughed. "Maybe in the old days. But now my first loyalty is to Samira. You are her best friend, so my loyalty goes to you by extension. It's my duty to inform you that if Nick ever approaches you, you should run away unless all you want is an hour of his time and a basket of flowers the next morning, never to see him again. But *Anthony*? Another story altogether."

"Hmmm." Melody smoothed her lab coat and hoped that the rising heat in her face wasn't as incandescently bright as it felt. "So why is this paragon of virtue still single, pray tell?"

"Well, he dates. He's had some girlfriends. But no one special. And of course he has to choose carefully. Because of his, ah, family." There was a pause while Baptiste eyed her closely. "Has he told you much about it?"

"Well, I met his father last night at the gala. *He'll* make someone a colorful father-in-law one day, won't he?"

"Indeed," Baptiste said, something speculative glimmering in his green eyes. Along with the ongoing amusement. "Anthony seems very—what's the word?—*smitten* with you."

"It was that fancy red dress," she said, trying to get a deflection out there as soon as possible. "That's why it was so expensive—"

"All right, enough's enough." Anthony appeared, looming over them with a glower directed at Baptiste. "I had to wait thirty-six hours for a bit of Melody's time, and now here you are eating into most of it with your personal melodramas. Time for you to be on your way."

"Nobody ever liked him very much," Baptiste told Melody, jerking a thumb at Anthony. "Fair warning."

They all laughed as Samira joined them. "Might be fun to get together for dinner one of these days, don't you think?"

Melody shot her a *what the hell?* look. The last thing she needed was for Anthony to think she'd put *that* bug in Samira's ear and decide that Melody was too clingy for him. But he nodded eagerly, much to her surprise.

"We'd love to," he said. Samira beamed with satisfaction and a flash of triumph in Melody's direction. "I'll be back from London a week from Friday. Maybe then?"

Melody's ears perked. He *would*? He *was*?

Then she gave herself a swift mental kick in the ass.

"Hang on," she told Anthony, her spinning (swooning?) head making her all the more determined to keep her feet on the ground. "Don't you think you and I need to have a few more conversations before you start speaking for me and making plans weeks in the future?"

"No," he said, his smooth voice thick with repressed laughter. "Is it the date you object to, or the part about seeing me again so soon?"

She opened her mouth, praying a snappy retort was on the way while the three of them waited with raised brows and open interest.

"Don't you wish you had a bowl of popcorn right now?" Baptiste said to Samira in a stage whisper.

"I *do*," Samira said gleefully.

Frowning, Melody redoubled her efforts to—

Her pager went off.

Oh, thank God.

Melody all but sagged with relief at the timely interruption. But then she checked the display and her heart crashed through the floor.

"Oh, no."

Anthony tensed and put a hand on her arm. "Not your little car accident girl?"

She nodded helplessly. "Gotta go."

And she took off at a dead run.

11

It was just after five that evening when Melody walked back through the atrium in her street clothes, purse and jacket in hand. A blazing ruby sunset created patches of shadows throughout the space, but her brain was full of the fine technical points of the surgical procedure that had abruptly ended when the cutest little five-year-old girl known to humankind bled out on her table. Also taking up brain space? The long walk from the OR to the waiting area, during which she tried to think of something to say to mitigate the parents' pending pain. And the biggie? The parents' inconceivable devastation. So she wasn't paying much attention to her surroundings and had no idea Anthony was still there until she heard him.

"Melody."

Startled, she looked around in time to see him emerge from behind the same pillar they'd sat near that morning. A closer examination revealed that he'd set the space up as office central, with a briefcase, laptop and paperwork spread all over the table they'd used for breakfast.

He was all somber eyes and open concern. He was, in that dark moment, the best thing she'd seen all day.

"How is she?" he asked quietly.

Melody shook her head.

His face fell. "I'm so sorry."

She nodded.

He studied her long and hard.

She let him because this was her life and the career she'd chosen. He needed to know before their budding relationship went one step further. If he didn't understand *this* about her, then he could never know her at all.

She was a doctor who put her heart into every patient she treated.

Sometimes her heart got ripped out.

"You're dead on your feet," he finally said.

She shrugged with complete indifference about her exhaustion level. Even if a bed appeared right in front of her and she dove into it, she probably wouldn't be able to close her eyes.

"Another day at the office."

His jaw tightened. "Doubtful."

There was a pause.

"Anthony. What are you doing here?" she asked quietly.

His direct gaze never wavered.

"You can probably hazard a good guess."

The knowledge that this man had scuttled his entire day just so he would be here if and when she eventually reappeared threw her for a serious loop. Funny how he insisted on stealing her breath every time she saw him.

She thought it over, trying to make sense of him.

"But...I thought you were going kayaking again?"

He shrugged and shoved his hands deep into his pockets. "I decided against it. It's quite cold today. And I wouldn't want to push my luck. The odds of my tipping over and drowning myself in the Hudson were unreasonably high."

That unlikely image broke through some of the gloom over her head and made her grin.

He watched her, arrested.

The moment stretched. The sudden rush of her blood sounded like the ocean roaring in her ears.

He opened his mouth. Seemed to encounter a fair amount of unexpected difficulty getting his voice to work.

"I got a lot of paperwork done instead," he finally said, glancing around at the atrium. "It's a lovely space."

"It is," she said, noticing it again for the first time in a long time. "It's easy to stop paying attention when you're here every day."

"And when you're dead on your feet. Come on. I'll take you home. I don't like you driving like this."

The one thing that could snap her entirely out of her exhausted stupor, other than discovering that he'd been there all day waiting to see her again, was the renewed suggestion that she couldn't safely get herself from Point A to Point B.

She frowned. "Didn't we cover this last night? I can drive myself."

Exasperated sigh. "Yes, of course you can, Superwoman. But why not let someone else take care of *you* for a couple of hours? Haven't you earned that after your nightmare shift?"

Her tendency to bristle struggled with her growing desire to surrender to this time with him and let someone else take the reins for a while.

"First of all, I prefer *Wonder Woman,*" she said. "She's way more powerful. No one really knows who Superwoman is."

His lips twitched. "A thousand pardons."

"Second, you have a way of barking out orders and

making decisions for both of us that's a little heavy-handed." She crossed her arms and frowned. "Maybe that worked with your men in Afghanistan, but do I look like one of your soldiers?"

He gave her a bemused yet heated once-over that stripped away her jeans and long-sleeved tee and left her all woman.

"I'm well aware of who you are," he said silkily. "Let me assure you."

Melody shivered involuntarily. If only that voice didn't dance over her skin like that.

"Great." Her voice sounded husky, so she had to clear it. "So maybe we should try this whole thing again with a different approach?"

Unmistakable respect gleamed bright in those eyes.

"Let me rephrase, Dr. Harrison. It would be my great pleasure to do this one small thing for you—and perhaps cook you dinner—before I leave late tonight. I want to spend more time with you. You know that."

Still no *please* or even a request in there, but the sincerity went a long way toward mollifying her. As did his absolute focus while he waited for her answer.

Even so, she was no dummy and this wasn't her first rodeo.

"It's too soon for us to have sex. You know that, right?"

She'd expected a wheedle or a negotiation, something to get that door cracked open just a bit.

What she did *not* expect?

"Absolutely," he said with a finality that far exceeded hers. "When we make love for the first time, the event will own that day. It won't be a secondary distraction to something else that happened. Or the result of anything other than us wanting to fuck each other into oblivion. Don't you agree?"

12

Melody ushered Anthony into her apartment a little while later.

He tried not to behave like a shepherd from the Scottish Highlands visiting London's glittering West End for the first time, but it was hard.

Her building overlooked the river. He felt certain that the view on the other side of the sheer panels covering her windows would be breathtaking in the daytime. But he hadn't come for the view. He'd come to learn anything he could about the beautiful and fascinating Dr. Melody Harrison.

And the doctor had been on spectacular display today, hadn't she? The scrubs. The lab coat. The ferocious dedication to her patients. The heartbreak when she couldn't save one of them.

The sight of her in her natural habitat at the hospital this morning had damn near given him a hard-on. As did the sight of her here in her apartment.

As did pretty much everything about her that he'd discovered thus far, come to that.

She led him through the foyer, clicking on lights as she

went, and into the vaulted living room that flowed into a high-end and spotless kitchen. He noted everything with greedy interest, skimming over the furniture (black and gray, straight out of some decorating magazine) and zeroing in on the things that said *Melody* lived there.

A basket full of medical journals on a side table. A bookshelf full of popular fiction including, he saw with great interest, several of his favorite John Grisham legal thrillers. A pair of fuzzy slippers placed side-by-side under the coffee table. A bag of pretzels, neatly sealed with a clip, within easy reach of the television remote. A Taurus mug with a dangling tea bag (English breakfast, sure enough) and a framed Eleanor Roosevelt quote on the wall: "Do one thing every day that scares you." A half-burned candle on the mantel explained the faint outdoorsy scent, and several logs, neatly stacked in the hearth, promised a fire later.

It was the sort of place that invited you to come and stay for a while without worrying whether you scuffed the hardwood floors with your shoe or dropped a crumb or two on the sofa.

He *loved* it.

"Very nice," he told her.

The light in her eyes brightened, but they were still far too shadowed this evening.

"Thanks. And thanks for bringing me home."

He whistled.

"Wonder Woman stands down. How long d'you suppose *that* will last?"

"You can still be ejected." She shot a warning look over her shoulder as she headed for the kitchen, washed her hands and peered into the refrigerator. "Choose your words carefully. What would you like to drink? Do you feel like some pinot grigio?"

"I would love some pinot grigio. But I'll get it." He washed his own hands and nudged her out of the way so he could take inventory. "What have you got here? You actually have a well-stocked fridge for someone who works all the time, don't you? I was expecting a bottle of sour pomegranate juice and a carton of expired eggs."

"I'm full of surprises."

"You *certainly* are," he said.

There was something in his tone (a purr of satisfaction, to be honest) that snagged her attention.

She cocked her head and eyed him closely, not bothering to hide her bemusement.

"Are you making fun of me?"

He stared her in the face.

"Not at all. I'm a great admirer of all your surprises. I can't wait for the next one."

It was always a rare and thrilling moment when he successfully pulled off a flirtatious comment, so he allowed himself a beat or two to enjoy the sudden rush of color as it streaked across her cheeks. Even better? The way her gaze dropped to his mouth and returned, brighter now, to his eyes.

"I thought you said you weren't a flirt," she said, raising a brow.

"*I* can also manage an occasional surprise."

"Yes, you can," she said with a lovely blush.

He felt the hard kick of something powerful in his chest in that delicious moment. Even more powerful was his urge to reach for her.

"Melody…"

She caught herself and reined in her smile as best she could.

"Why don't we just get something delivered and watch a movie? You don't have to cook for me."

"I'm trying to impress you. Obviously. It's a male thing. If I can cook one good meal, I figure I'm already head and shoulders above the competition."

"Interesting." She watched him from the other side of the fridge door while trying to manage that lingering smile, a move that only emphasized her dimples. "And how do you know I'm not already impressed? Maybe this is all wasted effort. Ever think of that?"

"Why risk it?"

Laughter chased away a few more of her shadows as she sat on one of the bar stools at the counter. "Maybe *I* should be worried about impressing *you*. This will be the second meal you've served me today. I feel like I'm way behind."

"If I were any more impressed, my head would explode clear off my shoulders. Trust me," he said wryly. "At this point, I'm just hoping for a sign that you're a real person. You've got the brains and the looks, and you're a successful surgeon to boot—"

To his horror, she made a choked sound. Her features twisted into an expression of despair.

"No, I'm not," she said sharply, pressing her hand to her heart. "You *know* that's not true!"

A flare of panic made his brain blank out for a millisecond, but then it hit him.

Ah, there it was. The delayed reaction he'd known had to be in there somewhere. He'd seen it a million times overseas, both with his men and himself. People endured a trauma, they blocked it for a time and then it inevitably caught up with them. That was the way it worked.

As a Brit, he spent a great deal of time pretending he had no emotions and then ignoring them when they occasionally insisted on breaking through his barriers. These things had their own protocols, as most things did. When another man broke down, you quietly left the room to give him his privacy or, if worse came to worst, you put a hand on his shoulder. In the direst of circumstances, you squeezed the shoulder.

The thing you did *not* do was allow yourself to get swept up in the loss of control until it felt like the other person's pain—a pain that often had nothing to do with you—felt as though it would tear half your heart out by the roots.

Yet in that startling moment, a primal something awoke inside him. And that thing, whatever it was, was fiercely determined to do anything—*anything*—necessary to erase that unhappiness from her face.

That being the case, there was no hesitation. He let the fridge door slam shut and hurried over, reaching for her.

"Melody—"

She batted him away with a snarl.

"Don't touch me! You'll only make it worse!"

He hesitated.

Her watery expression turned murderous.

"Okay, *okay*." Stung, he held up his hands and retreated. "But you can't think that—"

"I just…" Repressed sobs thickened her voice and made her shoulders shake. "I just need…one minute. That's all."

The sight of those spectacular eyes swimming in tears rocked him to his soul. He'd never felt more helpless.

"You have as long as you need," he said quietly.

She didn't need his permission, of course, but it seemed to comfort her.

Nodding, she rested her arms on the bar and dropped her head into the little shield of privacy they afforded. Then she wept…and wept…and wept…taking years off his life during a period that, perversely, only lasted about a minute.

Around the forty-five-second-ish mark, she began to take deep breaths and whimper herself into a calmer state. From there it was no time at all before she raised her head, snatched a tissue from the box on the counter, blew her nose and wiped her eyes dry.

With that, she faced him again with grim satisfaction. She looked almost as good as new. But for the redness in her eyes and nose, he'd never have known she'd just been crying.

He, meanwhile, needed a vodka tonic, a Valium or three and a long nap with the shades pulled and soft music playing in the background.

"You're finished?" he asked, incredulous. "Just like that?"

She nodded. "I told you I only needed a minute."

He gaped at her. "That's remarkable. Does Greenwich know about this? They have trouble keeping the time, from what I hear."

She snorted.

"I've had a lot of practice. When you treat cute little kids, there's always an opportunity to get your heart broken. Even if it's only when they get well and leave the hospital and you can't see them every day anymore."

"Yes, but a *minute*? On the dot?"

A shrug. "That's about all the time residents have to duck into a supply closet or toilet stall and cry it out before someone's looking for them. Why are you looking at me like that? It's *your* fault for insisting on coming over tonight. You *know* I'm wrung out and exhausted."

"Yes, but I'd foolishly had a second of being grateful that you're human like me because you shed a few tears. Now I discover that you're doubly amazing. Imagine my dismay."

She rolled her eyes, which had begun to sparkle again.

"Technically, I'm *not* human like you. *You* had a panic attack. *I* had a crying jag. When you think about it, you'll see that a crying jag is far less of a humiliation."

They laughed long and hard together, and the advent of

this renewed burst of sunshine into his life made him lose his head a little. Taking her face in his hands, he leaned down to kiss her. Once. Twice. Three tastes of heaven were all he allowed himself lest his surging blood make him forget what he wanted to tell her.

So he rested his lips on her forehead instead, stroking the sides of her face with his thumbs. Not as tempting as kissing her mouth, but he damn sure wasn't ready to let her go yet.

"Where's my wine?" He felt the apples of her cheeks plump with a smile as she spoke. "I was promised pinot grigio."

"In a minute. I have a question for you." Dropping his hands, he eased back enough to be able to see her face. "Could anything have saved your little girl today?"

A pause before she answered, although he had the distinct impression that she knew the answer right away.

"No," she said, exhaling. "Not once she started bleeding again."

"You don't blame yourself, then, do you?"

A longer hesitation this time.

"I don't blame myself—"

He breathed easier.

"—but that doesn't stop me from running through all the *what ifs* in my mind. What if I'd done *this* instead of *that*. What if I'd let the team continue with the CPR for another five minutes before I'd called it? That sort of thing."

"The *what ifs* are bloody torture, aren't they?" He hesitated, running his hands over the top of his head, then plowed ahead because they had a lot of things in common and there were a lot of things they needed to know about each other. "Half the time, I'm drowning in *what ifs*. I mean…What if the convoy had left a bit sooner or a bit later that day? What if we'd had more air support or ground support on a particular day?"

She looked startled.

"*What ifs* marching into infinity. They're exhausting, aren't they?"

"Yeah." The faint hint of a smile softened her eyes. "They're exhausting."

The quiet understanding stretched between them, swelling into something that felt significant. Almost like a turning point. That was unprecedented enough. But then he felt a withering flash of the loneliness he knew he'd feel later, when he flew thousands of miles away from her to go back to London. Where he couldn't see this face every day the way he wanted to, much less for a good chunk of every day.

Anthony's head spun with all of *this,* whatever *this* was.

When Melody was in the room? His head couldn't seem to spin hard enough.

His throat tightened down with a sudden wave of nerves. He didn't know what was going on here with this woman he'd just met. Only that he needed a moment or two alone to process it and get his burning face back under control.

Trying to be as nonchalant about it as possible, he gave her another forehead kiss, then went back to the fridge and pulled out the bottle.

"Let me pour you some wine for you to take with you."

"Take with me? Are you evicting me from my own apartment?"

"You'll feel better after your shower." He opened cupboards, looking for the glasses. "And when you come back, I'll have dinner ready."

She hopped down and regarded him with bright interest. "What're you cooking for me?"

He frowned over at her. "Don't be nosy. You'll find out soon enough."

He opened the wine and poured her a glass. Watched her accept it with a smile before disappearing down the hall for her shower. Then downed his own glass and doubled up with his hands braced on his thighs, giving himself a minute to figure out what the bloody hell he thought he was doing here.

Well, he was having the time of his life swimming in water way over his head, that's what.

Trying not to drown on the one hand.

Desperately trying to figure out when he could come back and swim again on the other.

Might as well work on dinner while he tried to formulate a plan, he decided, reaching for the chicken.

How he thought he'd manage a long-distance relationship with Melody, he had no idea. And that whole bit about being back in a couple of weeks and therefore available for a double date with Samira and Baptiste? Where he'd breezily made it sound as though he had a preplanned business trip back to the States and would just happen to pop by Journey's End for a visit?

Yeah, no.

Complete fabrication.

And one likely to cause him a fair bit of grief with his private secretary, who might need to shuffle some meetings on Anthony's behalf.

But what was Anthony supposed to do? Leave town with no further plans in place to see Melody again? No way. Admit that he was already so smitten with her that he'd happily rearrange his schedule to accommodate a visit? Probably a bad idea. Ask Melody to visit him in London, then pay for her ticket? Probably a worse idea. She might have decided that he wasn't the complete arse she'd once feared, but he couldn't quite picture her going to such lengths—or accepting such a gift—from a man she'd just met.

Nor did he think she'd be comfortable knowing that *he* was going to such lengths for her just yet.

So, a little white lie it was.

That got him back here the next time.

But what about the time after that?

And, more to the point, how the hell was he going to survive two weeks before he saw her again?

Frowning, he chopped some vegetables, then found a frying pan and some olive oil.

It was no good trying to be logical about the whole thing; he'd already tried it. The logical part of him—a good 80 to 90 percent—liked to send calm reminders that it was early yet. That he and Melody didn't know each other well. They might quickly uncover irreconcilable differences that made them despise each other and therefore render this whole situation moot.

Yet the instinctual part of him—the quiet but insistent 10 to 20 percent that had kept him alive while overseas, usually with little more than a prickle along the back of his neck—insisted that whatever his relationship with Melody turned out to be, short-lived wasn't it.

And what if—his pulse quickened at the thought as he poured himself another glass of wine before beginning to sauté the vegetables—what if he and Melody made love this next time he came to town? What then, genius?

He had no idea how he'd go home again after that. The mere thought made his stomach clench.

Insane, right? He lived in London. London was his *home*. Not some remote outpost from the center of the universe.

And then he had a flash of true insanity.

Maybe…

Maybe he should mention Melody to Granny.

The old girl often had practical advice for him, didn't she?

God, he was cracking up.

He lost himself in his cooking, throwing together the go-to meal that had saved him from many a bowl of cereal for dinner over the years. And he was so engrossed with plating the food and getting the presentation just right that he didn't realize Melody had returned until he heard an astonished voice behind him.

"Oh, my God! How did you *do* this?"

Startled, he turned and discovered that this woman could, in fact, unravel him more than she already had. Honestly, he had zero chance with her, which hardly seemed fair. Spending time with this siren was like planning a field trip to the sun: fraught with peril and likely to leave him burned and forever changed. Someone should have sat him down to explain the dangers and have him sign a waiver of liability before ushering him into her presence and making the introductions.

At least then he'd have had some idea what he was coming up against.

He stared at her while his wits packed their bags and left the building.

First thing? Her scent. She'd anointed herself with all those secret perfumes, lotions and potions women liked to use, resulting in a fragrant cloud of X-rated flowers that surrounded her as she came closer. Her hair? Wild and free, exactly the way he liked it. Her face? Clean and luminous, with only a little gloss to make her lips even more tempting than they already were.

And then there was her body.

Her body. Her body. Her *body*.

Acres of golden skin, glowing with that light that only *she* seemed to capture. With her strappy little black yoga top, a nice portion of her baps were on overflowing display. Narrow waist. Wide hips and toned legs nicely displayed in her nylon shorts. An arse that wouldn't quit. Bare feet with pretty pink polish.

All in all? The package of a woman with many natural gifts who took spectacular care of herself. An athletic woman with a healthy dose of bombshell thrown in for good measure.

The package of his dream girl.

13

Wait, what?

His *dream* girl? Had he actually just produced such a sickly-sweet thought? Had he been catapulted into some fairy tale without his own knowledge?

Quite possibly.

The lovely Dr. Harrison had just shaken him up like one of Bond's martinis. That was for sure.

Given the emptied-out status of his head, it was a damn good thing that she was preoccupied with the dinner because he was more than preoccupied with her. And being here with her like this…seeing where and how she lived…coming into face-to-face contact with how much he wanted her and how much he longed to stay for a while yet—it all added another thick layer to his sweet misery.

Leaving her to go back home for nearly two weeks—*fourteen* bloody days!—would slice a clean year off his life. No doubt.

But she'd asked him a question, hadn't she?

He squinted at her, trying to focus.

Yes. She definitely had that bright-eyed air of expectancy about her. There was a question on the table.

"I, ah…" He scratched his head as heat flooded his face, wishing his brain worked better. Or at all. Probably best to just come clean. "Sorry. I don't think you should expect me to be an intelligent conversationalist when you parade around in that body."

An incredulous snort of laughter from Melody.

"*Parade around—?* What are you talking about?"

"This whole…" His helpless wave encompassed her from head to toe. "What you're working with."

More laughter.

"*What I'm working with?* Are you picking up slang from American teenagers? Never say that again."

"Glad I amuse. And how do you keep yourself in such exceptional shape, pray?"

Melody hesitated, her hand going to her hair to make sure it covered the side of her face.

Without thinking, he intercepted her hand, lowered it and brushed her hair back from her face.

"Don't do that," he said quietly, his words scripted by an entity that seemed to have nothing to do with the working remnants of his brain. "You don't need to hide anything from me. Ever."

She flushed scarlet. Looked down.

He couldn't have that either.

So he tapped her under the chin.

"You're stunning, darling. Hold your head up high."

She looked at the floor. Her feet. Anything but him.

"Anthony…"

He waited in silence.

She blew out a breath. Raised her head, cheeks pink and

eyes shining. Steadily met his gaze while she tucked that same hair behind her ear.

He felt a tremendous surge of satisfaction.

"*There*. That's better, isn't it?"

"I'm not sure," she said, dimpling at him. "I feel a little shaky with you, to be honest."

He opened his mouth with no real idea of what to say. Only the absolute certainty that more of the right words were on the way.

"We're just having a quiet dinner together. Nothing to feel shaky about." He paused, feeling more than a little shaky himself. "And you were about to tell me how you stay in such fantastic shape."

"I, ah…" She blinked and seemed to get her thoughts together. "Spinning. Weight lifting. A little yoga."

"Where on earth do you find the time?"

"I have to make the time. It helps me decompress and stay sane, so I do what works."

"It's also working very well for me, if it ever comes to a vote."

"Stop flirting. My delicious dinner is getting cold." She looked at the plates. "What is this?"

He blinked, taking an embarrassingly long beat or two to shift gears. This thing between him and Melody was damn intense.

"This is, ah, sautéed chicken and vegetables with spaghetti sauce and pasta. Sometimes, when I'm feeling wildly adventurous, I make it with pesto instead. Or it can become Mexican with salsa and rice. Or homestyle with gravy and mashed potatoes. I'm a renaissance man. Exactly like DaVinci."

"You look like a genius from where I'm standing right now, that's for sure. Thank you so much."

He somehow resisted the urge to puff his chest and strut about like a hormonally-charged peacock during mating season, a difficult feat with her beaming at him like that.

"My pleasure." He handed her a plate and fork. "Shall we—"

His phone chirped.

"Sorry." He pulled it out with a quick glance at the display. "I meant to turn this off—oh, it's my father."

His heart sank. He felt his expression turn sour.

"Everything okay?" she asked quickly. "Go ahead and take it. I don't mind."

The thing was, he didn't want to take it. Wasn't one dose of his father in the last few days enough to last him for at least a month?

Even so, he hesitated, compelled by unknown and unwelcome forces to do the right thing.

"I don't mean to be rude…"

"It's your *father*."

With a sigh, he hit the button. "Hello?"

"I don't like the way we left things the other day," the old man said in his craggy twang. "Don't like it at all."

"It wasn't good," Anthony agreed, willing to suspend his raging suspicions of everything his father said and did for a few seconds, just to see where this was headed.

"Seems like the two of us should be able to share a drink every now and then without drawing weapons."

"That's a wildly ambitious goal," Anthony said, watching Melody take their plates to the table and pour more wine.

"I think we should try it again. When will you be back this way?"

Anthony's attention split in half, divided by his longing to see Melody again as soon as possible and his growing unease at the vulnerability in his father's voice. The old man didn't do vulnerable, and he damn sure didn't do needy.

Surly, controlling and intransigent? Tony had those covered. Anthony knew how to deal with them.

But *this*?

Anthony was as outside his element with this softer side of his father as he was with his growing feelings for Melody.

"In a couple of weeks," Anthony said reluctantly.

"Great. So maybe we could—"

"Sorry, but what would be the point?" Anthony crossed his arms and leaned against the counter, hunching in on himself the way he had when his father yelled at him for his daily infractions (being bad at football and soccer and too good at studying and reading quietly on the sofa came to mind) back when he was a kid. He caught himself doing it and straightened up again. "What are you going for here?"

Melody, who'd been making a valiant effort to give him a modicum of privacy, caught his gaze across the table, her expression troubled.

The old man, meanwhile, paused before finally snorting out a disbelieving laugh.

"It's the oldest story in the book, AJ."

Anthony winced at the use of his childhood nickname, short for Anthony Junior. The sound of it tugged on heartstrings he hadn't realized he still possessed and wished he could cut out and throw away.

"I might be facing down the end of my life." Tony cleared his hoarse throat. "It would be nice if my tombstone said something other than *Selfish SOB*. It doesn't matter what your grandmother or any of my business colleagues or drinking buddies think about me. But what *you* think? *That* matters."

"I'm surprised to hear that," Anthony said.

"Not as surprised as I am to say it."

Anthony snorted. Well, there it was. The hidden agenda. This latest attempt at amnesty was, of course, all about his father and his selfish motives, and Anthony was just foolish enough to be surprised. Having evidently given up convincing Anthony move to Houston as a lost cause, Tony had progressed to wanting to make sure his slate was clean if and when he found himself ringing the doorbell at the pearly gates. He didn't truly want any meaningful involvement in Anthony's life or to be a good father. Perish the thought. What he wanted was Anthony's good opinion—to win the room over the way he did with everyone else in the world except for Anthony and his grandmother. Bottom line? Tony didn't want any asterisks by his name or record when it came time to meet his maker.

Anthony should have known better than to think otherwise, even for two seconds.

"Do you have a sincere bone in your body?" Anthony said.

"Do you have a forgiving one in yours?" Tony asked quietly.

Well, the old guy had him there.

Anthony fumed in silence for a moment, wondering which was worse:

Dying with regrets on your soul, or living with bitterness in it?

Either way, Anthony didn't want any part of that dysfunctional equation.

Not when the air was ripe with possibilities and new beginnings.

He watched Melody get up and go back to the kitchen to work on the dirty pan, her gaze averted, giving him zero clue as to what she might be thinking.

Anthony scrunched up his face. Rubbed his forehead. Took a deep breath.

"For the record, I think this is a terrible idea. But I'm willing to try it again. See what happens."

"Excellent," Tony boomed. "You call me when you get back to town, y'hear?"

"Yes," Anthony said sourly.

"How's your pretty little Miss Melody? You're with her right now, aren't you?"

Anthony bristled. "I don't see how that's any of your—"

"Put her on. I want to talk to her."

"Christ."

"Do it."

Anthony shot her an apologetic look and, without a word, passed her the phone.

Looking startled, she pointed to herself.

Me?

He nodded grimly.

"Hello?" she said with vague alarm.

Tony said something that he couldn't quite catch.

Melody listened, her color rising as she tried to repress a smile.

"I'm immune to your would-be charms, Tony."

Tony's booming laugh came through loud and clear. Then Melody listened again.

"You have to say that. You're his father." More listening, then she laughed. "Oh, so when you say he's a *paragon of virtue,* you actually mean it as an insult? I see. Got it. Well, I can make up my own mind about Anthony, anyway. I'm a pretty good judge of character. So I'll decide for myself."

Here, she nailed Anthony with a secretive female smile that made nerve endings tingle to life across his belly.

More listening, her smile fading.

"Oh. Oh, I'm sorry to hear that," she said quietly. "Sounds like you've had a good recovery, though, right? … Of course I'll keep you in my thoughts and prayers." She looked at Anthony, her expression shadowed as she listened again. "No, I'm not putting in any words for you. Forget it. He's *your* son. If you don't like the bed you made for yourself, then fix it. Don't come to me for—don't even try it. Your sweet talk won't work with me, Tony…No, I'm not calling you *Pop*. *No*. Forget it."

Laughing again, she held the phone out to Anthony, brows raised.

Anthony studied her carefully, then took the phone.

"What embarrassing things have you said to her?" he asked his father. "If you've ruined my chances—"

"I didn't ruin a thing, boy. I told her you were a goddamn paragon of virtue. You should thank me for being your wingman. I'm trying to help you out. Know why? 'Cause that girl is far out of your league. She's got beauty, brains and a backbone. The three Bs. You'd better watch yourself with her. You might find yourself proposing before dessert tonight."

He might indeed, Anthony thought grimly as he hung up, scrunched his face and rubbed his forehead.

A moment passed while he and Melody watched each other in the kind of awkward silence they hadn't experienced since their first couple of interactions.

"So…" she finally said. "Are we supposed to pretend he never called?"

"The idea has some merit."

"I'm sorry to hear he's had heart issues."

He nodded. His tight throat began to burn, much to his dismay.

She studied him closely.

"You okay? You have to help me out here. Do you prefer

to sulk by yourself, or should I pick a fight so you can blow off some steam? Or I could just find an old plate and you could smash it on the floor."

He wanted to smile, but his mouth suddenly couldn't seem to remember all the steps.

"We, ah…" He ran a hand over the top of his head. "We don't get along. Never have. I'm far too British for him. Like to make an occasional decision by myself, without considering whatever order he's barked at me. He and my mother had a nasty divorce. The nastiest. That took up the last few years of her life. She was free of him for about thirty seconds before she died in her skiing accident." He studied the tips of his shoes, trying not to sound too bitter or too whiny. He was a grown man, for God's sake. Decades had gone by. Wasn't that time enough for these old wounds to heal? "I blame him for making her life miserable. I suppose he blames me for looking like her. We've happily hated each other for all these years, but now he's gone and got himself a heart condition. Mucked up the natural order of things."

Her expression cleared. "Ah. Now he wants to be a good father."

"Correction: now he'd like the credit for being a good father."

She tipped her head to the side while she thought that over.

"He's scared about being sick. Plus, it's probably scary reaching out to you. You've got that—" she swirled a hand at his face— "great horned owl thing going."

"I do *not*—"

"And I'm guessing he's a pretty proud and stubborn guy. This can't be easy for him."

"Can't be easy for *him*? *I'm* the poor bloke who had to grow up under that yoke of tyranny. You weren't there when he forced me to play American football when I was little, then heckled me from the sidelines. You weren't there when he took me hunting when I was *six* and killed a wild boar, then field cleaned it in front of me. You weren't there when—"

"You're right. You're right," she said quickly, holding up her hands and retreating a step. "I'm sure he's Satan. Can we eat before our food gets any colder?"

Her twinkling eyes got him.

He started to grin. Caught himself.

"He *is* Satan."

"I'm taking your word for it, because none of this is *any* of my business. Whatsoever. At *all*."

He waited, his entire body primed to hear the rest.

"But…it does seem to me that you have to live with yourself. If he's a bad father, that's something he has to live with. He's earned that guilt. But I'd hate for *you* to ever feel bad or regret anything *you've* done."

"So I'm supposed to give him my best while he gives me his worst?" Anthony demanded, flaring up at the inherent unfairness of being expected to good-naturedly tolerate his father's ongoing disdain and disapproval. "I'm supposed to forgive him his nastiness and neglect?"

"No," she said gently. "You're supposed to do what your conscience tells you to do. And never do anything you can't live with later. So if any part of you thinks he could change, maybe you could think about giving him the benefit of the doubt. That's all I'm saying."

The words slowly sank in, leaving him uneasy because he knew she was right. Painful experience overseas had taught him that he could live with almost anything except the nagging certainty that he'd left stones unturned, or that the entire situation could have turned out better if only he'd put his back into working a bit harder.

And the truth was that while Tony had been a poor father, Anthony had never been much of a son, either. Did he call? No. Did he observe birthdays or holidays? No. Did he even remember he had a father most days, or do anything other than nurse old slights and grudges? No.

So when Melody held up her mirror and forced him to look into it, it wasn't that hard to see that he was his father's son after all.

He nodded, turning away to take his seat at the table, and she was kind enough to give him a moment to compose his features.

"Who thought popcorn was a good idea?" she asked later, after they'd eaten and cleaned up the kitchen. He sat on the sofa and she handed him the giant bowl. "Can you even eat after all that delicious chicken and pasta we just had?"

"'Course I can eat. What's the point of watching a movie with no popcorn?"

"True."

Standing just to the side of him, between the sofa and the coffee table, she found the remote and clicked on the TV, which was mounted over her mantel. A fire crackled. A candle flickered on a side table. Their refilled glasses of pinot grigio already sat on the coffee table. And if Anthony had ever spent a happier or more contented evening in his life (notwithstanding his father's call), he couldn't remember it now.

Funny, wasn't it?

He'd insisted on coming tonight because he'd wanted to

take care of her after her difficult day. He'd thought a quiet dinner together might be just the thing she needed. Little had he realized how much *he* also needed this little slice of paradise.

"But I still think *Skyfall* is the best Bond movie," she said.

"Agreed. But we have to start with *Casino Royale* and suffer through *Quantum of Solace* first."

She shot him an incredulous look over her shoulder. "We're not going to make it through all that tonight."

"I'm hoping you'll invite me back."

"Oh, you are?"

"You know I am."

Blushing prettily, she turned back to the remote and calling up the movie.

Which allowed him the opportunity to note her plump arse. The toned thighs and calves. The smooth golden skin within easy reach of his eager hands.

His heart thumped into overdrive. Why? Because he rode the horns of a dilemma.

On the one hand, they'd agreed they wouldn't make love tonight. And he knew it was too soon. Best for them to get to know each other better first.

On the other hand? He'd behaved like a perfect gentleman all night. Could anyone *really* fault him if the reins of his control slipped out of his grasp for a minute or two?

"No comment?" he asked, setting the popcorn on the coffee table. "I blatantly angle for an invitation, and you leave me hanging?"

She pursed her lips, still not looking at him. "You might forget all about me once you get back to London and the Annabella Carmichaels of the world."

If only she knew. If only he could tell her he had a better chance of forgetting to breathe or to blink.

"Unlikely," he said quietly, succumbing to temptation.

Leaning forward, he ran his fingers up one of her calves, across the sensitive back of her knee and around to the petal-soft inside of her thigh, stopping only when he reached the lower edge of her shorts.

She let out a long and serrated breath. A shudder rippled through her as her head fell back, shifting the heavy tumble of her hair lower.

"Anthony..."

"Shh," he said. "Give me the remote."

She turned to look at him, a question in her eyes.

The heat of his desire and intentions burned his face, so he could only imagine that he was looking at her the way a starving wolf regards a grilled steak dinner. He tried to smile. To dial back some of his intensity.

But this was *his* woman—they both knew it—and he couldn't wait to touch her.

"Trust me," he said, taking the remote and setting it on the side table. "It's only for a minute."

Her lips curled. "A minute is all it would take."

"Not for what I have in mind for you when that glorious day comes. But you can come here. Just for a minute."

She hesitated. But not for long. Her glittering gaze held his as she took his hand and he drew her closer. She took her time about straddling him and settling her knees on either side of his hips. Then she stared down at him, waiting to see what he would do.

He filled his hands with the hair on either side of her neck and tugged just enough to bring her head down. Until her mouth came within range.

Then he kissed her.

Slowly at first. Just a few lingering brushes so he could adjust to the voluptuous feel of her the way a man needs a moment to dip his toe in and adjust to the thrilling heat of his steaming bathwater. And he meant to leave it at that. He really did. They'd already had a spectacular evening together, and now he'd had the added pleasure of touching her leg and kissing her. Best to leave well enough alone.

But then she emitted a tiny sound, one of those helpless mewls that women make when their blood runs hot and they teeter on the edge of their control. And of course there was no real way of controlling the surging lust between them any more than a scientist could flip a switch and stop a smoke-spewing volcano from erupting.

He broke the kiss and stared into her face for one startled moment, trying to wrap his mind around all these new developments as they hit him with the power of a fire hose.

This woman existed in the world. He'd never imagined a woman like her was out there, let alone hoped he could find such a creature and somehow interest her in *him*. Yet Melody was here now. In his arms.

Flustered, he opened his mouth and tried to convey some of what he felt. But there were too many questions jockeying for position for him to manage anything coherent.

Did she feel this too?

Could she possibly care for a chap like him?

And the biggie:

Would she remember him once he left town?

"You can't forget me when I'm gone," he said hoarsely, tightening his grip on her hair, but not enough to hurt. "Don't you forget me."

She looked incredulous.

"No," she said, kissing him again.

This time there was no pretext of caution or moderation. They were just two people driven temporarily insane by the feel of each other. Her eager mouth tasted tart, like the wine, and met his at every turn, gliding through endless positions as they explored all the ways their lips and tongues could fit together.

She ran her hands through his hair, pulling it in her unrestrained efforts to get closer to him.

The prickling pain across his scalp drove him higher. He couldn't breathe with her body this warm and solid against his. Couldn't think with her fragrance in his nostrils and her taste in his mouth.

And the *feel* of her…

Planting his hands on her flexing arse, he toppled her to one side and rose up over her, an animalistic sound rumbling in his chest. She quickly scooted up, laid her head on the armrest, spread her thighs and opened her arms to receive him.

But before he settled his weight on her, he yanked his sweater off over his head, dropped it to the floor, and yanked up the bottom of her shirt, revealing heaving breasts encased in some sort of a sports bra.

He had to have the skin-to-skin contact, even if it was only a little bit.

Had to.

And she was more than ready for him.

Those glittering eyes, heavy lidded now, tracked his every move. Her lips, swollen and tender from his kisses, turned up in a half-smile. And feverish color highlighted every inch of her skin.

Utter disbelief made him shake his head.

He didn't get this lucky.

It just didn't happen.

And then he dove in, kissing her again. Kneading her silky thighs as he urged her to wrap them around his waist and then, when she'd done that, to wrap them tighter. He ran his hands up and down her sides, savoring that smooth flesh and the feel of her soft belly against his. He wove his fingers through her hair and kissed her harder. Deeper. Longer.

His hips, now entirely outside his control, thrust against her.

She cried out.

That was it for him. He had to make her come tonight. *Had* to.

He reminded himself of a couple things in a half-hearted fumble for self-control.

They weren't teenagers messing around in the back of a parent's car, for one thing. There would be no satisfaction for him tonight—not like this, not unless he wanted to do the drive of shame back to his hotel with a sticky wet spot at the front of his trousers—for another.

But he'd found a driving rhythm that seemed to have taken the rest of Melody's breath away, and her face twisted with gathering ecstasy. His hands were full of her bare thighs and shorts-covered arse, and the concrete length of his cock was right at home against her sweet spot.

Bottom line?

He wasn't leaving here tonight until the lovely Dr. Melody Harrison came for him.

Oh no, he was *not*.

So he surged harder. Sharper.

More of her cries. Louder. Unabashed. Maybe with an incoherent attempt at his name thrown in.

He dipped his head, kissing and nuzzling her until she arched into him. He would have kissed her lips again, but he wanted her mouth free to make all the sensual sounds she could possibly produce for him.

And he had so much to tell her.

He ran his lips around to her ear. "Don't you forget me while I'm gone."

She said something he didn't catch.

He nipped her lobe just hard enough to make her shudder.

"*Melody*. Don't forget me while I'm gone."

Dazed, she cracked her lids open and watched him with eyes that shimmered like the finest brown crystal.

"I won't," she said.

"Promise."

"I *won't*," she said, scratching her nails up his bare back and generating the most exquisite pain imaginable. "I won't forget—"

He shifted around without breaking the contact between their hips, running his mouth over her baps until he found the beaded point of a nipple. He nuzzled it through her little bra. Scraped gently with his teeth.

And held her tight while she called his name and flew apart in his arms.

He greedily watched it all, splicing together a home movie he could binge on tonight when he finished himself off in the shower before he and Baptiste flew back to London later, and then again tomorrow and every day and night between now and when he had her like this again.

The way her features tensed and then slackened into a smile of purest rapture. The way her labored breath evened out. The vivid color that crept across the tops of her breasts, up her neck and across her cheeks. The haywire curls surrounding her head in a gleaming halo.

All of that was the best reward imaginable for his unselfish act and helped ease the insistent ache in his bollocks that would remain blue until he could get himself into that shower.

But not yet.

For now, there was only her. *This.*

He sprawled out, half on and half off her, and pressed his face to her fragrant neck so he could wallow in this perfection for another minute or two.

"What about you?" she asked drowsily when she'd caught her breath. "I don't want to leave you like this."

"Like what?" he asked, running his hand up and down her thigh, which still held him tight about the waist. "Feeling like the king of the world?"

Sultry laughter from Melody.

"*When* did you say you're coming back again?"

"A week from Friday," he told her, now circling her nipple with his thumb for the thrill of feeling the way her hips jackknifed against him. "So you make sure you don't forget me."

14

Back in London two afternoons later, Anthony arrived ten minutes early for tea with his grandmother and was ushered into the sitting room of her private apartments by ancient Mrs. Brompton, a woman who had, he felt certain, also been a retainer for Anne Boleyn.

He unbuttoned his suit jacket and sat on one of the pale green silk sofas in the room that never changed (green damask wallpaper, priceless paintings of the hunt in gilt frames, framed family photos, fresh flowers), eyeballing the elaborate tea service and cakes while Mrs. Brompton fussed over it.

"You didn't put the salmon sandwiches on rye bread again, did you?" he asked. "You know I can't stand rye bread. The whole operation will be ruined if I see any rye bread anywhere. And if and when I get to be in charge around here, I'll make it my first day's work to get you fired."

Mrs. Brompton, who had never smiled in living memory and might not, as far as anyone knew, possess teeth, remained, as ever, unruffled. "Then it's a good thing you'll never be in charge, isn't it, sir? You've got several cousins to take that burden from your back, don't you? And if you don't care for rye bread, you'd best take it up with your grandmother. That's all she eats."

"I know," he said glumly.

"Touch nothing. She should be here any moment."

"Won't you stay and bless me with your sparkling personality until she arrives?" he asked brightly.

Mrs. Brompton stiffened. *"No."*

With a final severe looked aimed at the dead center of his face, she creaked off toward one of the mirrored doors, but not before he caught a glimpse of a dimple.

"You're twinkling at me, Mrs. Brompton," he called after her. "One of these days, you're going to slip up and smile. The whole thing. With teeth and everything."

"Unlikely," she replied, swinging the door shut as she went.

He waited a good five seconds before, propelled by his rumbling belly, he reached for a smoked salmon sandwich.

On rye.

Scowling, he popped it into his mouth, then hastily rearranged the remaining sandwiches to hide the empty space. It looked pretty good, he thought.

"I told you to touch nothing," Mrs. Brompton called from the other room.

"Sorry! Accident!" he said.

Grumbling reply from the other side of the door.

Chuckling, he reached for his phone and settled in to wait.

No response from Melody yet, he saw with a tiny stab of disappointment. He'd texted her this morning already:

Get out of my head. I'm trying to work.

Of course, she was six hours behind now, so she hadn't been awake yet. And of course she had work. Dr. Harrison was a delightfully accomplished and busy woman. But she'd get back to him soon, he knew. She always did.

Grinning to himself, he scrolled back through some of the other texts they'd exchanged so far. It was an impressive batch considering he hadn't been gone that long.

Anthony: What should I bring you back from London?

Melody: I get a souvenir??? Yay! How about a crown jewel? Not all of them. Just one. Two at the most.

The irony of that one made him chuckle. Still did, as a matter of fact. If only she knew.

He'd thought about his reply. Then,

Anthony: Since you're determined not to help a bloke out, I'll figure something out on my own.

Melody: Don't you have strange and delightful candies over there? Bring me some. But nothing with nougat. I hate nougat. And no fruitcake. Americans hate fruitcake.

Anthony: This relationship is over. I cannot proceed with someone who doesn't appreciate the hearty deliciousness of fruitcake.

Melody: That's a shame. You were beginning to grow on me. Farewell!

Anthony: I was??? Kindly do not toy with my emotions.

Melody: YOU'VE BEEN BLOCKED.

Anthony scrolled through several other messages, still grinning. Ah, here was one he liked:

Anthony: What are you doing? Send me a pic.

Melody: Just out of the shower. Getting ready to brush my teeth.

Anthony: SEND ME A PIC!!!

And she'd sent him a picture of a toothbrush with tooth-paste on it.

And later,

Melody: I'm thinking about getting a dog. I love dogs.

Anthony: Oh, yeah? What kind?

Melody: Not sure. Something smallish and manageable in an apartment. Do you have dogs?

Anthony: No, but I like them. My father has owned several border collies and my grandmother loves dogs.

Melody: Tell me about her.

Anthony, again appreciating the irony: She's a force of nature. Very no-nonsense and smart. Knows how to command the room. There's no one like her.

Melody: She sounds scary!

Anthony, laughing to himself: You've no idea.

Melody: Hope you have a good visit with her.

Anthony, hesitating because he understood the enormity of what he was about to say: I'd love for you to meet her one of these times when you visit me in London.

Melody, after a longer pause than usual: Don't say things you don't mean.

Anthony, heart thumping: Funny you should say that because I thought twice before I sent that message. And I still wanted to send it.

And Melody had replied with a smiling face—

His phone rang, startling him. He turned it off, grateful it hadn't happened during tea with his grandmother, and was about to put it away when he saw the display and realized it was Melody wanting to video chat.

He quickly checked the time. Two minutes. He had *two* minutes.

"Hey," he said as the picture resolved into a lab coat wearing Melody sitting behind the desk in her hospital office with a steaming mug in hand. And her *smile*. Honestly, her smile carried enough wattage to light the entire city on this rainy London day. God knew it lit him from the inside out. "It's great to see you. What're you doing?"

"Taking a quick break between patients. Thinking about what movie to watch tonight."

"It'd damn well better not be *Casino Royale*. Or any of the Bond movies, come to that."

She laughed. "Well, it's on my mind because I didn't get to see it when you were here, did I?"

"We can see it the next time. Watch something else."

"And how was your tea?"

"Just about to have it."

"Oh! Sorry! I thought tea was at four."

"Normally it is. Granny takes hers a little later sometimes."

"So you're at her house?" Melody's gaze scanned his surroundings. "What a gorgeous room."

Again: the irony.

"I'm at her house," he said, struggling hard to keep his grin on lockdown.

"I'll let you go. Have a scone for me. With clotted cream and all that."

As always, it made his heart ache to tell her good-bye.

"I will, darling."

She grinned at him. "I love the *darling*."

"You don't have a nickname for me, I've noticed," he said sourly.

"I'll have to think of one."

"It needs to be something affectionate and/or dignified—"

The mirrored door swung open.

Bloody hell.

Anthony leapt to his feet and snapped to attention.

"Gotta go," he whispered to Melody. "Call you later. Bye."

And he hung up on Melody's startled face just as the herd of beagles swarmed into the room, tails wagging.

"Hello, guys," he said, putting his phone up and shooing them away from the tea tray on the coffee table. "No, you don't want to eat Granny's cakes. She won't like that."

"She certainly will not." His grandmother, the Queen of England, strode in and brought that crisp air of authority and unmistakable voice along with her. Today's twinset was a foamy green colored one that rather matched the silk-covered walls, and her pearl necklace was the lustrous three-stranded one she usually favored. Evidently she'd had no public engagements this afternoon, because she wore plaid trousers and flat little shoes rather than the skirt and chunky black heels she usually chose. "You're *late,* AJ," she said, offering him her hand.

"Your Majesty." He took it and gave her a kiss on each cheek before nodding sharply and kissing her hand. "I'm not late. I'm never late."

"You were late for tea when you were eleven."

"Yes, and you cured me of that, didn't you? Fed all my treats to your nasty little beagles and made me watch. I've never been late since, have I?"

"Cover your ears, boys," Granny called down to the dogs as she sat on the sofa and reached for the teapot. The dogs collapsed in a heap about her feet, their eager little faces turned up and on the scent of the cakes. "He doesn't mean it."

"Oh, I meant it, boys," he assured the beagles.

Anthony sat beside his grandmother. They grinned at each other.

"You've done something with your hair," he said, pointing at her head.

Her hair, like his lateness, was a running joke between them. She'd worn her sandy brown hair in the same bun (he remained silently convinced that she'd taken one of the portraits of Queen Victoria off the wall around here some-where, shown it to her stylist and demanded the same look) since good old Henry VIII beheaded that second wife.

She patted the bun and made a show of primping. Her blue eyes, so like his own, sparkled like a young girl's, and her English rose complexion, lined now with her seventy-plus years, went a lovely shade of pink in the cheeks.

"Do you like it?"

"I do."

She splashed a little cream, just the way he liked it, and handed him a cup of her special Queen's Brew blend. Then she caught sight of the tiered tea tray and frowned.

"You haven't eaten one of my salmon sandwiches, have you? I'm one short."

He stifled a sigh. He doubted Mrs. Brompton had ratted him out. Ergo, he *still* hadn't been able to fool his grand-mother any better than he had that time when he was six and hid her handbag under a seat cushion. She'd eyeballed the askew pillow, retrieved her bag and given him the rough edge of her thinned lips and raised brow.

No, you couldn't put one over on the old girl.

Which left his lifelong score something like Granny: 496 —Anthony: 0.

"Yes, I choked one of your nasty sandwiches down. Wish you wouldn't put them on rye bread. I *hate* rye."

Granny shivered with satisfaction as she raised her own sandwich. "Why do you think I choose it? More for me."

"Next time I'll have to choke all of them down. Just to punish you."

They laughed. She handed him one of her heavy cloth napkins, which he smoothed across his lap. They selected their various cakes and sandwiches. Munched happily.

God, it was good to be there. Nothing relaxed and grounded him like spending time with his grandmother. In an ever-shifting world where mothers died far too young, overseas wars were fought and fathers disappeared and reappeared, forgetting you were there one moment, then turning up again and demanding a relationship with you the next, this one woman had been his constant.

They were each other's favorites, he and his grandmother. Oh, she'd deny it if questioned, probably giving a politically correct answer about loving all her grandchildren equally, but death had bonded them into an unshakeable team. She had scraped him up off the ground when his mother died, setting aside her grief over the loss of her daughter to make sure that he got out of bed, showered and went to school in the mornings. She had held his head in her lap, night after night, and wiped away his orphan's tears until finally those tears eased a bit and he remembered what it was to smile again.

And he had returned the favor when his grandfather had a massive stroke just as he graduated from NYU Law, forgoing the bar exam so he could return to London and sit quietly by Granny's side during those shell-shocked days when she planned the funeral and led the country through its mourning period without ever letting her spine bend or her shoulders droop. Granny never cried, but Anthony had been there within arm's reach that time or two when her steps faltered or she blindly reached out for a hand to hold.

When the dust had settled and she'd asked him to return to London and stand in for her on some of her appearances, he'd happily agreed. Not because she was his monarch, but because she was the brokenhearted blue-eyed grandmother he adored and she needed him in a way no one else ever had.

It had been both his duty and his honor to slide into the role.

That arrangement had quickly segued into a full-time schedule for him. If a royal body was needed at a ribbon cutting, ship christening or board meeting and all the senior members of the family were already booked? Well, then, by God, Anthony Scott was your man.

Was it a thrilling career? No. But anything for Granny.

"Nice of you to visit your old Granny, Bubba," she finally said, using the childhood nickname she'd given him when teasing him about his Texan roots. "Make sure I'm still alive."

"Well, if you'd keeled over, it probably would have made the papers," he said, carefully selecting a slice of date bread.

"Hmm." She sipped delicately, her straight spine never touching the back of the sofa. "I hear your wretched father's had a heart attack. Imagine my surprise upon discovering he has a *heart*."

Anthony rolled his eyes. Of course she'd heard. And now here it came. Never took long.

"Is that concern I hear in your voice? Planning to send him a card, are you?"

A sharp bark of laughter from Granny, much like her little dogs.

"Speaking of keeling over. A card from *me* would finish him off for sure, wouldn't it? Poor man would die of shock. So how is he?"

Anthony shrugged.

His grandmother treated his face to that same slow inspection she'd employed back when she'd caught him and one of his cousins filching strawberries from her garden and, unbeknownst to them, they'd had red rings around their mouths.

"I imagine he's feeling his mortality now," she said, pursing her lips. "Probably regrets he's wasted so much time with you. As well he should."

Anthony shrugged again, his ears beginning to burn. Leave it to Granny to get to the heart of any matter in two or three short sentences over tea and a biscuit.

"I'm not his greatest fan, obviously," she said, clipping her words as though she had a pair of shears. "Never have been. But he's the only father you have and you're his only child. He needs you. You'll give him a chance."

Well, there it was, Anthony thought dismally.

The royal order.

"Don't scowl at me," she said. "Your mother would tell you the same if she were still here. God rest my precious daughter. You know I'm right."

He supposed he did.

The mention of his mother made a sweet ache of loss tighten around his heart. Angry as his grandmother had been at Tony following the collapse of their marriage, she'd only ever encouraged Anthony to love his father. It was Anthony who'd gone off script by hating the man's guts for the repeated infidelities and making his mother so miserable. If only Mummy were still alive. She'd know what to say to help Anthony get past some of his anger. He knew she would. She wouldn't have wanted Anthony to spend his life mired in bitterness about past events.

And then there was Melody, he thought moodily, selecting a scone and putting it on his plate. Her advice to give his father a chance had resonated with him, of course, but it was easy to try to talk himself out of making a real go of it with his father. Excuses always abounded. For example? Why waste time on a person who would likely never appreciate Anthony's effort and would probably never change anyway?

But here, finally, was a directive.

One did not ignore one's sovereign.

Or granny.

Still, he didn't have to be gracious about it.

"Why is everyone taking up for that man lately?" he grumbled.

"Who do you mean?" she asked, her keen gaze sharpening. "The young woman you were making cow eyes with when I walked into the room?"

"I was not making *cow eyes,*" he said as severely as he could, knowing all along that the general effect was ruined by the sudden heat burning his ears. "And you should stop spying on people all the time. It's beneath you."

She hiked up her chin, looking absolutely unrepentant. "How else am I to find out what's going on in the real world?"

He had to laugh.

"We'll get back to your young lady in a minute," she said. "But first, it's time."

He froze. *This* was what he'd been afraid of when she insisted on tea.

"Time?" he asked, stalling while he got his thoughts together.

"Yes. *Time.* T-I-M-E. You're to be the Earl of Stockbridge. You'll be thirty-five next year. We've put it off long enough."

He slumped back against the cushions and felt his shoulders begin to hunch. "I don't see the point, to be honest. Why is this necessary? My mother didn't care about the title."

"Your mother acceded to your bullying father's wishes when you were born." She scoffed. "*He* wanted you to be a *regular boy*. Whatever *that* means."

It probably didn't mean growing up in a palace like Buckingham, the one in which they currently sat, with nearly eight hundred rooms and a thousand servants, Anthony thought glumly, keeping his commentary to himself.

"So we did *not* give you the title when you were born and we did *not* give it to you when you turned eighteen or twenty-one. We didn't even give it to you when you became a war hero."

"I'm not a—"

She silenced him with a glare.

"I'd made up my mind long ago. We'd either do it when you married or when you turned thirty-five. And now the time has come."

"Yes, but what are we accomplishing here? I don't need the estate or the income from the lands. I'll have my trust fund soon. I'm not a farmer. I have no desire to supervise tenants. I just don't see the point."

"You *do* understand that this is a tremendous honor and not a punishment?" she asked icily. "And that several of your ancestors went to the Tower and sacrificed their heads for much less than an earldom."

Anthony's voice rose with frustration.

"And *this* earldom will come with the sacrifice of my relative anonymity. Right now, I'm keeping my head down with my boring little engagements and flying under the radar—"

"You are *deluding* yourself."

Anthony had never had any idea how she accomplished it,

but his grandmother had a knack for making her voice boom throughout the room without ever speaking a decibel higher. She also did this thing where her entire face turned to stone— starting with her forehead, lingering with her eyes and ending with her rigid lips and squared jaw—that had always scared the hell out of him and everyone else who ever beheld the phenomenon.

And Melody thought that *he* had an intimidating expression.

Wait'll she got a load of *this* routine.

Just to make sure she really had his attention now, the old girl remained perfectly still and stared him down for several seconds. Until his whole head burned along with his ears. Until he shifted uncomfortably. Until he ducked his head, unable to maintain eye contact.

Until he wished he'd never been born.

"Let me see if I understand you," she said with that deathly calm of hers. "You are flouting my wishes, your entire heritage and who you are. Why not run off and join the circus and have done with it if you're so determined to be someone else?"

Frustration got the best of him.

"But who *am* I, Granny?" He hoped she would forgive the yelling, just the once, but for God's sake, did she think *he* knew what his lifelong ambivalence was all about? "I'm British and American, but I'm not quite British *or* American enough. Am I a Texan? A Londoner? Would I do better in a place like New York? Do I have a career other than marching about being a figurehead to my charities? Am I doing any good there at all? Am I a lawyer if I'm not licensed? I'm not in the military anymore. I know *that* much. But I've damn well still got the guilt and the panic attacks to go along with it. What the hell am I supposed to do with myself? And how am I to know whether people like *me* or want anything to do with *me* as a person if I've got a fancy new title and my face suddenly splashed all over the tabloids?"

She absorbed his entire tirade with nary a blink or eyelid twitch.

And when he paused to catch his breath and his voice stopped ringing off the silk-covered walls, he had a serious *oh, shit!* moment.

Had he just said all that? To his *grandmother*?

Bloody hell.

"Are you quite finished?" she asked when he'd worn himself out.

"Yes," he said dully, thinking that this would have been the moment, back in the day, when guards with swords would have shuttled him down to the river, where a barge would have escorted him to a nice room in said Tower of London to await the block and the ax.

"And what do you have to say to me, sir?"

He paused to straighten his tie. At times like this, it was hard to remember that he was a grown man.

"I'm sorry for yelling."

"And?"

He thought it over. "For being an ungrateful arse."

"Very good." She thawed out, reached for the teapot and poured again. "Have some more tea and a cookie, Bubba. You must be parched and famished after that disgraceful display."

He snorted out a laugh and took a gingerbread cookie.

She selected a cucumber sandwich. On rye.

"What's this all about, AJ?" she asked briskly.

He opened his mouth, but no answers came to him for several long and embarrassing seconds.

"I'm tired of being half this and half that," he finally

managed. "I want to belong somewhere. I want to know who I am and what I'm supposed to be doing."

She took her time about finishing off her sandwich, dabbing her mouth with her napkin and clasping her hands in her lap. Her rigid posture straightened even more, if that was possible, and he half wished he had a textbook to balance on her head just to see how long she could keep it there. Probably for life, he was guessing.

He braced himself. Here it came.

"Let me help you out of your existential crisis, young Hamlet…"

He winced.

"You're supposed to be keeping your word and helping take some of the burden off *my* shoulders."

Anthony bit back a despairing sound. What were you supposed to do when your beloved elderly grandmother and monarch, who *still* worked more than the rest of the family combined, played the duty card?

"*You* are the future Earl of Stockbridge. All your cousins have their titles, and you shall have yours. There will be a small blip on your radar when I bestow the title, and then I'm certain everyone will forget all about you and leave you to your anonymous woolgathering. I'm sure you'll be delighted."

He snorted. That was the thing about Granny. She had a biting sense of humor.

"Yes, well, this isn't exactly the most opportune time for me." He ran a finger under his starched collar, which now felt hot enough to singe his fingertips. He wasn't at all sure he should get into it this early, but what choice did he have? Plus, he'd already told Melody he wanted her to meet Granny, hadn't he? "I, ah…I seem to have met someone. It might be easier if the news of my earldom didn't drop just yet."

She'd reached for a scone and begun breaking off bits to feed to the tail-wagging assemblage, but now she paused, one brow up.

He coughed. Fidgeted with his collar again.

"She's a, ah, pediatric surgeon in, ah, Journey's End. New York. Harvard-trained. Brilliant. Beautiful. Very funny and kind. An extraordinary woman."

He'd meant to leave it at that—he had the growing suspicion that he'd lapsed into babbling—but Granny kept watching. And waiting. And of course he'd never mentioned a woman to her before, so the conversation had already crossed into unprecedented territory.

"Her name's Melody Harrison. I just met her, so it's all very new. And I obviously don't have a crystal ball to know where all this will end up. It's far too soon to talk about anything serious. Like, ah, marriage."

Christ. Had he just said the M-word? *Him?*

Granny's other brow went up.

Yes. Evidently he had.

"So I'm sure you'll understand that now is not the time for the press to become interested in me or anyone I might be dating. We don't need the drama or pressure when we're just getting to know each other."

Granny stared at him, her face entirely motionless.

He smoothed his trousers, trying to remain composed.

Damn her! She had a way of stripping away his layers until only the barest parts of his soul remained. A ten-minute tea with Granny was like an MI6 interrogation—no possibility of escape until you'd answered all the questions, and you were likely to have a nervous breakdown before it was all over.

"I have not, technically, told her who I am. We've agreed to, ah, hold off on researching each other online just yet. Well, actually, that's not entirely true. I *might* have looked her up online when my friend mentioned her to me, and then, once I saw how beautiful and accomplished she was, I *might* have insisted on an introduction. But *she* hasn't looked *me* up, and I haven't had the chance to tell her who I am. So she doesn't, ah, know about my father's fortune or my inheritance. And she definitely doesn't know about *you*. I can get away with it—for a little while, anyway—because people in the States don't know or care much about what most of the family gets up to over here."

Granny stared at him.

"The funny thing is, though, that she's so busy with her own life, I don't think she'll give a rat's arse about mine. She doesn't seem like the type to get her head turned by my social or financial status. Speaking of which, if your friend Mrs. Carmichael tries to pawn her underage daughter off on me again, I'm going to lose my bloody mind."

Dead silence. One beat passed…two beats…

When the wait became unbearable, he snatched up his tea.

Had be babbled?

He'd definitely babbled.

Ah, well. Bottoms up.

"Is that wise, dear?" she finally asked.

He put down his cup and saucer, frowning. "What?"

"Lying to this girl you seem to care about."

He tried to hide a sudden wave of guilt behind his outrage.

"I'm not *lying*—"

Dear God, those brows of hers again.

He snapped his jaws shut, let his eyes roll closed and rubbed his forehead.

"Has it occurred to you that your plan is completely illogical?" she said idly.

He reluctantly opened his eyes to discover her tossing bits of scone to each dog in turn.

"What d'you mean?" he asked, scowling.

"I mean that you want her to want *you* for *you,* yet you don't give the poor girl enough information to know who *you* are. You don't want her to find out from someone else, do you? If you've chosen well, she'll love you if you're a prince, and she'll love you if you're a pauper."

"Love?" he spluttered, the word hitting him like a cream pie to the face. "Who said anything about *love*?"

The Queen of England didn't roll her eyes, but his grandmother came pretty close that time.

Meanwhile, her silence spoke volumes, leading to more verbal diarrhea from him.

"Yes, well, maybe I'm not ready to start testing my choice just yet. It's all very soon to throw this at her. Why not give her a minute to adjust to dating a new man who lives on another continent before we smother her with all the family that goes with him. And I'm not officially a *prince*."

"Oh, for God's sake." Granny finished distributing the scone, dusted off her hands and stood, tossing her napkin onto the tray. Anthony leapt to his feet. "You are *delusional*. Come, dogs. Let's go."

She turned toward the door, hesitated and turned back.

"You will tell this girl who you are."

"I plan to."

"Right away."

"Fine," he said around his clenched jaw.

"And you will decide what you want to do with your life. If you want, I don't know, a hobby to take you away from your duties for me, you will pick one. Why not play polo again?"

"Because it's a bloody dangerous sport, in case you've forgot that time I fell and broke my arm and collarbone into a million pieces. If I wanted to take my life in my hands all the time, I'd head back to Afghanistan."

Granny's lips thinned.

"Most of all, you will *stop whining*. If I were this young girl, I'd want nothing to do with you in this state. Look at you moping about your circumstances as though you live in a one-room hovel with a leaking toilet. I've never seen such a disaster. Get yourself sorted out. Keep your chin up. We don't complain."

She pointed to a framed black-and-white picture on her little writing desk in the corner. It depicted London during the Blitz, with demolished buildings in the background. In the foreground? A pile of rubble, atop which sat a woman serenely sipping her tea with a cigarette dangling from her free hand.

This badly-needed dose of perspective made him smile. Granny always made him feel better. Well, *first* she always raked him over the coals until his eyebrows singed. *Then* she always made him feel better.

"Love you, Granny."

She dimpled fondly, coming back to pat him on the cheek. "There's that emotional American side of you peeking through again. You must beat it back. Come, dogs."

She and her furry entourage swept off through her mirrored doors, leaving him to finish off the cakes and try to figure out how best to inform Melody about *all* the parts of his life.

15

Melody's phone rang just before seven that Saturday night, as she walked down DeGroot Avenue, Journey's End's main street, toward the pub. She'd been enjoying the garlands, wreaths and twinkling white lights in every direction—oh and look at the gorgeous menorah in the bookstore window!—and thinking about how nice it would be if Anthony could see her little town dressed in its holiday finest.

Her belly swooped at the possibility that it might be him calling.

But a quick glance at the screen told her it was Samira wanting to video chat. She felt a tiny stab of disappointment, but told herself not to be foolish. She'd struggled through thirty-something years of life without tying her moods to the frequency with which Anthony Scott communicated with her, and she wasn't going to start now. Plus, she and Samira had been playing phone tag all day and Melody wanted to make sure she still felt okay. So she hastily veered over to the nearest bench, dodging a couple passersby, sat and plugged in her earbuds.

"Hey," she said. Samira appeared stirring something on

the stove and had evidently propped her phone against a shelf. "What's going on? Are you cooking something?"

"Yeah. Mushroom risotto. Why don't you come for dinner? You know Baptiste is still out of town, and I'm never going to eat all this food."

"Can't. I'm about to have drinks with Jerry."

Samira stopped stirring and frowned. "Who?"

"Jerry. The primary care physician from Doctor Love dot com? I mentioned him the other day. He's a nice widower and his kids are out of the house. Plus, he's really handsome. I showed you his picture. Our schedules finally lined up."

"Oh." Samira's face fell. "Right. I wish I'd never had the brilliant idea of signing you up for that site. Why didn't you tell me *no*?"

Melody gaped at her. "You cannot be serious. You got me into this in the first place! You *knew* I'd resigned myself to being a spinster!"

"Yeah. Sorry."

"Unbelievable."

"It's just that I thought things were going well with Anthony," Samira said, now wiping her damp brow with the back of her hand. "You said you've talked to him every day since he's been gone and all."

"Yeah? So?"

"*So?* So, why don't you give *him* a chance? Why get yourself jammed up talking to two guys at once? If you really like Anthony, then why waste someone else's time?"

Because she *really* liked Anthony. That was why.

The past several days since he left town had been the worst kind of exquisite torture. She hadn't stopped thinking about him for one waking or sleeping second of that time. Nonstop questions scrolled through her mind:

Where was Anthony?

Who was he with and what were they doing?

Did he think about Melody a millionth as much as she thought about him?

Would he call or text her again soon, like he'd said he would?

Or would he hook up with some beautiful English rose and forget poor Melody over on this side of the pond?

And the one question that ruled them all:

How on earth did she think they could cobble together any semblance of a relationship when he lived in London —London!—and she lived here? Wasn't it already hard enough to get men to act right when they lived in the same town as you? Think of all the opportunities for sketchy behavior when the man lived thousands of miles away!

The questions had seemed especially pointed today, because Anthony had been quieter than usual.

Melody tried to keep that fact in perspective. No big deal, right? Maybe he'd had a busy day.

Or maybe he was gearing up to ghost her.

The latter thought made her belly cramp. Which in turn only renewed her determination not to lose her head over some guy she barely knew.

What did she think this was? Some fairy tale?

Did she *look* like Cinderella?

"I'm not wasting someone else's time. I'm keeping my options open," she told Samira. "We covered this already. *What?* Stop looking at me like that. Men play the field all the time."

"And why bother with a guy who's already done with kids when you know you want them?"

"We're going for drinks, Sami! We're not eloping to Vegas. Plus, his profile said he's open on kids."

"Fine. I'm sure you know best." Samira sprinkled salt on

the risotto. "I'm sure you know *all* about the best way to find your prince."

Something about the sudden smugness of Samira's tone made Melody suspicious. She squinted at Samira's image on the screen and discovered that, sure enough, there was a glimmer of mischief in her eyes.

"What's up?" Melody demanded. "You look like you know something."

Samira's grin widened into Cheshire Cat territory.

"Nope. I know *nothing*. It's none of my business, anyway."

"Hang on," Melody said, snapping her fingers as a sudden certainty came to her. "You looked Anthony up online, didn't you? You nosy witch!"

Samara laughed and shrugged. "Don't get snippy. You looked Baptiste up online, so I can look Anthony up. You knew karma was coming for you on that one."

"Well, what'd you find out?"

Samira, who was a very poor actress, tried to look appalled and clutched the invisible pearls around her neck. "I thought you wanted to get to know him the old-fashioned way. Are you going back on your word?"

Melody's heart sank. She'd made a promise to Anthony and she wasn't going to break it.

"No. I'm going to keep my word. No thanks to *you* and your evil temptations."

"You are a true woman of integrity. And there's nothing bad about him, so don't worry. I'd never let you fall for someone with a criminal record or five baby mamas or anything."

A wave of relief swooped through Melody. Thank God for good friends.

"Appreciate that. Gotta go." She stood and swung her bag over her shoulder. "Jerry might be waiting for me."

"Want me to send you an emergency text in a few minutes? So you can pretend it's the hospital and get out of there if he's a dud?" Samira asked.

"Nah. I'll just sneak out the bathroom window. Love you."

"Bye," Samira said, laughing as she hung up.

Melody adjusted her scarf against the wicked chill and started to take the buds out of her ears—

Her phone rang again, startling her.

Anthony's image popped up.

Anthony!

Her heart did a funny little flittering thing. Half of it wanted to leap for joy (today wouldn't be the day he ghosted her, after all!), but the other half wanted to cringe with guilt (not *now*! What if Jerry chose this moment to appear?). But then she reminded herself that she and Anthony hadn't even slept together yet, much less had any discussions about exclusivity.

She was a grown woman and a free agent. She did what she wanted.

That being the case, she had nothing to feel guilty about. Even if her belly insisted on squirming when she answered.

"Hey!" There was a slight delay while Anthony's picture resolved to reveal his face looking very handsome as he sat in his car. "How are you?"

"Much better now that I'm seeing your lovely smile." As always, he beamed at the sight of her, making her feel as powerful and important as the Queen of England. "Oh, but you look very busy. Where are you off to?"

Another guilty conscience squirm.

"I'm just, ah…" She gestured vaguely over her shoulder,

where the lights of the pub blazed through the mullioned windows. "Just going to Pub 221B."

"Trying the fish and chips, are you?"

"I think I might. What're you up to tonight? It's midnight there."

"Not much," he said, his dimples deepening. "So listen, I'll be up for a bit yet. Just ring me when you get home."

"I will." As always, she felt that ache of sadness at their *good-byes*. There were far too many of them, and never enough *hellos*. "Talk to you soon."

"Very soon," he said, and hung up.

In a pathetic sign of how far gone she was, she actually had to resist the urge to kiss the screen where his face had just been. Had to massage away the throb of loneliness in her chest.

If only she were meeting *Anthony* tonight for drinks.

If only they didn't live so far apart.

The distance only compounded her yearning for him.

It was one thing to not see him every day. Even if he lived here in town, her career kept her too busy to see anyone every day. Unless she lived with him.

But not only wouldn't she see Anthony today, tomorrow or the next day, but he was across the Atlantic Ocean from her.

The. Atlantic. Ocean.

God.

How on earth did people make long-distance relationships work?

Well, this was why she needed to keep busy, wasn't it? A perfect illustration of why she needed to get out a bit and not become obsessed with one guy in particular, especially the guy who lived *thousands of miles away.*

Energized, she hurried the last several feet down the sidewalk and went into the wood-paneled pub, which bustled with activity. People stood all up and down the thirty-foot bar, enjoying their drinks, and the tufted leather booths were mostly full. She scanned the crowd, looking for…ah. There he was in the back.

Thank God Jerry hadn't edited his profile picture into something that bore no resemblance to the real man. A good-looking guy of forty-something, he had a brown-skinned face with smiling eyes. Salt-and-pepper hair. A nice sports jacket over a dress shirt and jeans. He sat in a booth with a bouquet of sunflowers in front of him and had that tense, *waiting for someone* air of expectancy that was always a dead giveaway.

"Hi, Jerry," she said, hooking her game face firmly over her ears as she approached the table and held out a hand. "I'm Melody. How are you?"

He did a double-take that seemed to encompass and quickly dismiss her scar, his face flooding with color. Then he launched into the kind of delighted grin that Jennifer Lopez probably received wherever she went.

"*Hi.* I'm Jerome Ayers. Call me Jerry. Well, you just did, didn't you?" He leapt to his feet, started to shake, then looked back to the sunflowers on the table. Hastily shook her hand, leaned in to kiss her cheek, then passed her the flowers. "These are for you. I hope they're not too much."

Poor thing. At this rate, he'd start to hyperventilate in a minute.

And she'd thought *Anthony* was awkward.

"They're *beautiful,*" she said, trying to set him at ease. "You're so thoughtful. You didn't have to do this."

"This dating thing is a whole new world, since I married my wife back when dinosaurs roamed the earth. I don't know what the rules are anymore. I've been stumbling through."

"Who hasn't?" she asked, putting the flowers on the table, her bag on the seat and taking off her coat.

He laughed, then waved at the open bottle of wine and two giant goblets on the table. "Have a seat. I'm not much of a drinker, but I took a chance and ordered a bottle of merlot. Feel free to order something else. What are you in the mood for?"

What was she in the mood for?

The question hit her hard as she put her coat down, slid into the booth and reached for the menu.

She was in the mood for going home, taking a shower, pouring herself a glass of wine and video chatting with Anthony. Better yet? She was in the mood for Anthony to come back because she'd seriously begun to doubt whether she could wait another week before seeing him again. Assuming he actually turned up like he'd said he would.

What she *wasn't* in the mood for?

Dredging up the necessary energy for a pleasant blind date experience with a man who didn't feel like her type.

Still…

Jerry seemed like a decent guy, even if he didn't make her hormones sing, and it wasn't *his* fault her heart wasn't in it.

"Merlot sounds perfect. Thanks."

He poured and passed her a glass, then raised his own in a toast.

"To new friends," he said.

"To new friends."

They clinked. Sipped.

"This is delicious," she said, deciding to make more of an effort. "Good choice. So how's your day been so far?"

Jerry's appreciative gaze skimmed her face. "My day has taken a big turn for the better. You never know what you're going to get when the moment of truth finally comes, do you?

I'm convinced that the last woman I met had some other person pose for her photo, because she looked nothing like her profile."

"I know, right? I was on another dating site awhile back. A lot of these people are imposters, or else they all have advanced degrees in photo editing."

They laughed together as the ice was officially broken between them.

He raised his glass again. "To truth in advertising."

"Absolutely—"

Her peripheral vision snagged on a figure looming over their table just as an icy male voice spoke.

With a posh British accent.

"Hate to interrupt…"

Anthony?

A wild surge of joy caused Melody's heart to careen into cardiac arrest territory. She risked a severe case of whiplash spinning her head around to make sure it was him.

Then she saw the expression on his face and remembered that she was on a date.

With. Another. Man.

Shit.

A great horned owl could be intimidating, yeah, but at least it might occasionally blink or turn its head around to the back to look for a mouse. The look Anthony gave her now? With those chilling blue eyes, hardened cheekbones and squared chin?

Great horned owl that had been stuffed and mounted on a mantel. All-seeing, with no warmth and no soul.

Her smile turned brittle as sudden horror rooted her to the spot.

Oh, God. *Anthony.* Who'd come all this way to surprise her.

She saw it all through his eyes—the wine, the flowers, her sexy shoulder-baring cashmere sweater—and wished she could crawl under the table and hide. Since she couldn't do that, a cringe would have to suffice.

"...But I just wanted to say hello. I found myself unexpectedly in town for the weekend." When his scathing disdain had frozen most of Melody's flesh solid, Anthony turned, held out his hand and leveled all his frigidity on poor Jerry, whose only mistake had been clicking on Melody's profile. "Anthony Scott. And you are...?"

Jerry hastily stood and shook. "Dr. Jerry Ayers. Great to meet you."

"And you," Anthony said, but he didn't look like anything was *great*. In fact, he regarded Jerry like some noxious substance he'd discovered clogging his toilet. "From Doctor Love dot com, I presume?"

A shadow began to fall across Jerry's face.

"Ah...yes," he said, his narrowing gaze swinging between her and Anthony.

"Brilliant," Anthony said.

By some miracle, Melody squared her shoulders and got her voice working. She was not a criminal here, and she would not stand by while Anthony treated her like one.

"Anthony—"

"Well, don't let me keep you from your *date*." Anthony zeroed in on her again, his voice roughening. Difficult as it was to keep her chin up and meet his gaze through the obvious anger, she caught a flash of something profoundly hurt. Bewildered. "Have a lovely evening."

They stared at each other for one excruciating second.

Desperate for something to say that would take *that* look off his face and restore the glittering warmth she'd seen when they laughed together, or when they lay together on the sofa, she opened her mouth.

Floundered.

Wished she'd never been born.

His lips curled into a sneer as he muttered something indistinct and strode off, sucking all the room's air with him as he'd done the night they met.

The sight of him walking away kicked her out of her paralysis and her ass into high gear.

He'd made a tremendous effort to come back early. To see *her*. And his reward for his effort?

Discovering her out with some other guy.

She surged to her feet with a helpless glance at Jerry, who was now doing a remarkable imitation of Anthony's frosty disdain, and tried to smile as she grabbed her coat and bag.

"Would you excuse—"

He flapped one hand at her and used the other to top off his wine.

"Go," he said bitterly.

"I'm really sorry, Jerry. You seem like such a—"

"A nice guy, yeah, I know. But you're the second woman who's walked out on a date with me to chase some other guy. Hard to miss the message there."

He toasted her, then drank deeply.

"I'm sorry," she said again.

Dashing off without bothering to put on her coat turned out to be a mistake, as did running around in heels. But she wove her way through the crowd loitering near the door, raced outside with a blast of arctic air to her cheeks and looked wildly up one end of the sidewalk and down the other—

There he was!

She hurried after him, doing her best to catch up with his long strides.

"Anthony!"

He kept going.

Cursing, she sped up

Luckily, he'd reached his rental, some sort of dark SUV parked at the curb. His fob *beep-beeped* and the lights came on just as she met up with him at the driver's side door, which he swung open.

She scrambled back, out of the way.

"Anthony."

He paused without looking at her, one hand on top of the door and a muscle pulsing in his temple.

She stood on the door's other side, wondering how she'd landed herself in this mess and telling herself he had no right to be upset when she knew in her heart that he did.

His single quick and angry glance at her face made her recoil as though he'd scraped the business side of a potato peeler across her forehead.

"So glad we had that discussion about you not forgetting me." His words were rapid-fire and clipped, like bullets fired from a pistol, and the steam from his breath was like smoke. "Made all the difference, don't you think?"

"I *didn't* forget you—"

"All evidence to the contrary, you mean?"

Melody stared at him, wanting to kick her own ass for landing in this terrible situation. Wanting to cry for hurting him like this, and over something that, in the end, had meant absolutely nothing to her.

"What are you doing here?" she asked.

His gaze shifted away, focusing on something over her shoulder. "Making a fool of myself, apparently."

"I didn't know you were coming."

"That much is obvious."

"Why didn't you—?"

"Baptiste made a last-minute decision to come back and see Samira today because he couldn't wait to see her. I hopped a ride on his jet because I couldn't wait to see you. Anything else?"

His chill and the night's chill combined to make her shiver. She wrapped her arms around herself and huddled miserably inside her sweater.

"You can't even look at me?" she asked.

He hesitated. Then his gaze swept her up and down, barely touching her eyes, and that was somehow worse than his cold stare.

"You should put your jacket on," he finally said. "You'll catch your death without it."

"I'm fine. Can I just explain?"

"No point."

"Anthony..." Rising frustration—or maybe it was despair —pitched her voice higher. "You can't just shut me out like—"

"If and when you decide you'd like to pursue a real relationship, you know how to reach me."

"If you'll just—"

But there was no reasoning with a brick wall, and she wasn't breaking through his stony attitude unless she discovered a jackhammer in her back pocket. So she backed up a few steps (in this mood, he'd probably run her over and not think twice about it) and watched helplessly as he climbed in, shut the door, started the engine and, with a final narrowed glare aimed at the dead center of her face, zoomed off.

She watched helplessly as he disappeared around the corner.

Even his flashing red taillights seemed to rebuke her.

16

Melody cycled through several emotions during the time it took her to walk back to her car and head home.

Disbelief.

Frustration.

Guilt.

And finally and most powerfully?

Anger.

First of all, she hadn't done anything wrong.

Second, the arrogant SOB had just cut her out of his life without giving her a chance. Just given her the relationship equivalent of the death penalty without deigning to listen to her side of the story.

Controlling, much? Yeah. Possessive, much? Hell, yeah.

Was that fair and just when she was only doing what twenty-first century women did in the dating world?

No, it was not.

And how had she even landed herself in this situation when she'd so recently resigned herself to spinsterhood?

Fuming and running on autopilot, she made it almost all

the way home before her car turned itself around and headed for Journey's End's one big hotel, which was the place where they'd had the gala the night she met Anthony and was presumably where he planned to stay tonight.

By the time she'd parked, marched through the lobby, waited for the elevator (oh, God, it was the same elevator that had trapped them together the night they met) and pulled out her phone to dial his number, she'd worked herself into a royal snit.

Mr. High and Mighty didn't get to walk out on her without listening to her side of the story.

Oh, no, he did *not*.

"Yes?" he said in that cool accent, water running in the background.

"I want to talk to you," she said, grateful that the elevator car was empty when it finally arrived. "I'm on my way up. What room are you in?"

Long pause.

"*On your way up?* You're full of surprises tonight, Dr. Harrison, aren't you?"

"I'd say we both are," she said flatly. "Are you going to tell me your room number, or should I just go to the top floor and start knocking on doors until I find you?"

Another pause. "Seven-eighteen."

Was that a touch of amusement in his voice?

"Are you *laughing* at me?" she demanded, punching the button for his floor.

"Wouldn't dream of it. But I'd hate for us to waste more of each other's time when we're so clearly not on the same page."

"You're back in town, so you apparently care a little bit about me. Seems like you could give me a few minutes after going to all this trouble."

A rumble of dissent from Anthony. "Maybe it's time for me to start cutting my losses."

"Well, you're going to hear me out. That's only fair, don't you think?"

"Perhaps, but I'm not in a very fair mood at the moment."

"Sucks to be you," she said, and hung up.

She'd waited too long to press the button, so she did, in fact, ride to the top floor and have to come back down again. When she finally arrived, got out and checked the room number sign to see which way she should go, she only had time to take a step or two in the right direction before a door way at the end of the hallway flew open and Anthony hurried out. Now wearing one of the hotel's fluffy white robes, he jammed his hands on his hips, shot an impatient glance in her direction and froze at the sight of her.

They stared at each other in a seething silence.

"Did you get lost?" he demanded.

"Your indecision forced me to ride all the way to the top."

He made a disparaging sound that didn't help her equilibrium any as she headed toward him.

She felt like a dead woman walking.

She squared her shoulders and kept her chin up as she came closer, a difficult task under his unrelenting attention. When she finally arrived at his door, he stepped aside and let her in, treating her to a whiff of his just-showered scent and fresh shampoo. He looked and smelled delicious, much to her current dismay, with his strong calves and nice feet in flip flops visible below the bottom of the robe.

Her pulse rate kicked pleasantly higher—he probably wore nothing underneath, and what a sexy thought *that* was— but she still wanted to hit him.

She walked inside his giant suite, noting the edgy furniture, his overnight bag sitting at one end of the sofa, the Thurgood Marshall biography on the coffee table, the open briefcase and paperwork atop the desk and the massive king-sized bed framed by the doorway into the bedroom. Tossing her jacket and bag onto the sofa, she turned to face him.

He leaned against the desk and crossed his arms, his expression as dark and impenetrable as an Amazonian rain-forest at midnight.

She cleared her throat and tried to gather her wits. It was one thing to fantasize about cursing him out when she was safely in her car. A whole different story when confronted with that unblinking and merciless stare.

"You should have told me you were coming," she said.

Irritable shrug. "I wanted to surprise you."

"I can't believe it," she said, running a shaky hand through her hair.

"Why do you sound so shocked?"

"Why?" Melody spluttered, her words slipping away from her like Jell-O through her fingers. "Because we just met and that's a lot of effort."

"Evidently my imagination's run away with me," he said, his voice like razor blades, rusty nails and glass shards in a velvet pouch. "Because I thought we had a great deal of chemistry and a lot in common. I thought we were getting to know each other better by talking and texting while I was gone. I was hoping to speed that process along by coming back to see you again."

"But..." She rubbed her temple, trying to *think*. Men didn't go to this sort of effort for her. Ever. Especially sexy and fascinating men like *this*. Oh, sure, they might flirt a little and pretend her scar didn't bother them, but they didn't follow through. They never followed through. "You can't just show up out of the blue, Anthony. What if I'd been out of town or something? You would have wasted your time."

"I knew you'd be here. You'd already mentioned that you were planning a quiet weekend. I foolishly thought you'd be glad to see me—"

"I *am* glad to see you."

"—because you'd said you missed me."

"I *did* miss you."

"Not too much, apparently," he said coolly. "Or maybe you missed me as much as I missed you, but you have the gift of getting over it by substituting someone else in my place. Amounts to the same thing from where I'm standing."

"Can I just expl—"

"I'm not a fan of your approach."

"And I'm not a fan of your little temper tantrum," she said, something coming over her. Maybe she'd messed up tonight, but what did he expect? This was all new to her. They were new to each other. And she would not be bullied or talked over. She had as much a right to say her piece as he did.

His eyes flashed. "My *what*?"

"*Temper. Tantrum.* You picked up your toys and went home without giving me a chance to tell you what I'm thinking."

He hesitated, frowning. Cracked his knuckles.

Crack-crack-crack.

Then he caught himself doing it and lowered his hands.

"I was angry." His face flooded with color as he swallowed with a rough bob of his Adam's apple. "I was hurt."

"You froze me out. And *that* hurts."

They stared at each other, the air full of reproach and sudden vulnerability.

He started to speak. Faltered. Crossed his ankles and cleared his throat.

"The floor is yours," he said with a mocking little sweeping gesture. "I'm all ears. I can hardly wait."

Melody opened her mouth to tell him her side of the story, but first she had to master the lingering urge to hit him.

He had the remarkable ability to nail her with those ice-hot blue eyes one minute, as though the fate of humanity hung on whatever she said next, and then sound terse and bored the next, as though he'd rather be trimming nose hairs than talking to her right now.

"There you go being an arse again," she said quietly.

He winced. "Sorry."

Mollified, she took a deep breath.

"I wasn't aware that spending a little time together and exchanging some texts and phone calls equaled an exclusive relationship," she said.

"Indeed." His lips flattened. "And here I'd thought that if one had a special person in one's life, one wouldn't *want* to be with anyone else. At least, that's how it worked for me this week. Oh, and I mentioned you to my grandmother. Something I've never done in my life before."

Her breath caught.

"I thought you were also feeling something along those lines." He snorted. "Clearly not, based on the way you and your date were laughing together."

What? She and Jerry may have laughed, but they weren't *laughing together*. Why did Anthony have to make it sound like she and Jerry had been caught doing advanced positions from the *Kama Sutra* on the table next to their glasses of merlot?

Outrage took over her body and her words. "Okay, not that it's any of your business—"

He made a low noise that sounded dangerously like a growl.

"—but that was just a blind date that was never going to go anywhere. I already told you that Samira signed me up for Doctor Love dot com. Jerry turned up as a match. I thought, *why not meet him and see what happens*? I've got nothing better to do on my rare night off. But he was a little old for me and he wasn't really my type anyway. If he'd asked me to stay for dinner, I would have ducked out."

"*I* am obviously your man for *seeing what happens*." Anthony said. "Not some bloke from a dating website. Did you ever think of *that*?"

Of *course* she'd thought of that.

It scared her how much she'd thought of that in the last several days.

Not that she planned to admit it.

"A girl has to be smart, Anthony." Her voice rose. "I can't lose my head for some guy who lives on the other side of the Atlantic from me on the basis of a little chemistry. You can't seriously blame me for that."

His lips twisted. "None of my business? *Some* guy? *A little* chemistry?"

"You know what I mean!"

"Sadly, I don't. Maybe you can enlighten me by answering a question or two. Let's see if we can't get on the same page."

"Fine," she said warily.

Anthony squared off with her, nostrils flaring. "You're on this dating website in the hopes of finding someone to connect and have fun with. Perhaps build a relationship—"

"I'm not trying to *build a relationship*," she said in a knee-jerk reaction to the R-word, which always made her squirmy. "My career is—"

"Yes, yes, your career is the most important thing. You're a nun for your career. Your career is your one great love. But if you accidentally ran into someone you could enjoy spending time with, you wouldn't run screaming in the other direction. Correct?"

She folded her arms and glared at him for putting her on the hot seat like this. "Anthony…"

"Humor me."

She thought it over but couldn't detect any fatal traps. "Correct."

The light in his eyes intensified with unmistakable satisfaction. "You and I get along very well, have a lot in common and have tremendous chemistry. Not *a little* chemistry."

"It's…pretty good chemistry. I'll give you that."

"In fact, we like each other quite well, don't we?"

Melody hesitated. Fiddled with an earring. "I don't *hate* you, if that's what you mean."

He stared at her, as compromising as the razor wire-topped brick wall surrounding a maximum-security prison. "Quite. Well."

"Yeah, whatever," she said, unable to meet his gaze head-on. There was too much to see in his expression, and she had far too much to hide in hers. "We like each other. Somewhat. What's your point?"

"My point is that the logical response to all that, according to you, is for you to spend your limited free time meeting men off some dating website who may or may not be your type and with whom you may or may not even want to have dinner. Am I getting this right? You applied your formidable Harvard-trained brain to our situation and decided that your best course of action is to play the field?"

"Don't you stand there with your posh accent looking down your aristocratic nose at me like I'm crazy," she snapped.

He recoiled.

"You can't expect me to sit around in suspended animation waiting for you to appear when we've never discussed *anything* beyond your coming back next week. How am I supposed to know what you're thinking? Do I look psychic to you? Do you see a crystal ball anywhere on me? If we're going to be *anything* to each other, you can't freeze me out and walk off in a *snit*—"

He got in her face. "A *snit*?"

"—because I can't read all your hidden thoughts or see behind those owl eyes. And, by the way? I was *very* glad to see you tonight. Now I just really want to hit you."

A glimmer of amusement lit his expression.

"Are you always this direct?"

"Samira complains that I am. I believe in being open with my feelings, yes."

"You seem to be open enough with your feelings for both you *and* me."

"If you're not good with being open with your feelings, you know what you should do? *Practice*."

His lips twisted. "Silly me. And here I'd thought that my actions in flying several thousand miles to see you again spoke loud and clear."

Melody's pulse went haywire.

A tense stare-off followed, during which she felt fairly certain that they'd stumbled onto another thing they had in common: an overwhelming mutual desire to hit—or maybe fuck—each other. But after a beat or two, he blinked and locked away some of that intensity.

"Now that I think about it, you make a fair point," he said. "Why don't I start practicing right now?"

His voice resonated with a silky undercurrent that made the fine hairs all up and down her arms and across her scalp stand at attention.

"Why don't you?" she said breathlessly.

"I'd thought it was all perfectly obvious, but I've left some gray areas." He paused. "Won't happen again. I don't want us to have any misunderstandings."

"Neither do I."

The air shifted between them until it seemed to sizzle with possibilities, all of them thrilling. Melody felt her thumping heartbeat all the way up in her throat.

He opened his mouth, but quickly seemed to hit a snag. A rush of color flooded his cheeks. He closed his mouth, looking away. Ran a hand across the top of his head, making his hair stand up in spikes.

"What's wrong?" she asked.

He glanced back at her, trying for a rueful smile that never quite appeared.

"Funny how you talk about the way I can be intimidating when I look at you." He swallowed hard. "When you look at me? I don't know if you've noticed, but I can't think straight."

He *what*?

"That can't be true," she said.

Those eyes crinkled at the corners, heating her up as quickly as he'd frozen her out a minute ago.

"Dr. Harrison. You know it's true."

Yeah, she kinda did know.

Deep in her heart? When he looked at her with *that* rapt attention?

She absolutely *did* know.

Much as she didn't want to simper or lapse into foolish behavior, she couldn't turn down the flame on her overheated face, which had to be glowing like a stoplight in the dead of night.

"This practice session is off to a pretty good start," she

said lightly. "Is there anything else you want to tell me about your feelings? I want you to get really good at sharing them."

"Oh, you do?"

"I do."

He nodded. Took a deep breath.

"The thing is…I spend a lot of time feeling unsure about things. I'm not sure whether I'm mostly British or mostly American. Whether I belong with my father's family or my mother's. Whether I'm doing a good job with any of my charitable work or if it would make more sense for me to move in another direction. My grandmother called me Hamlet the other day." Shaky laugh. "I have a million questions and no answers."

She held her breath.

"But…" He hesitated, cheeks flushing. "The second I saw you? I just…You're *amazing*. In every possible way. There's no one else like you. So I'm willing to rearrange my life to make room for you. See where this can go. There's nothing halfway here. I'm at a hundred percent. There are no questions. Just one loud answer. *Yes.*"

Relief and happiness soared straight through her, making her lightheaded. Her feet walked her toward him with no real thought beyond the overwhelming desire to touch him again.

She opened her arms. *"Anthony—"*

He stiffened and held up a hand, stopping her before she came any closer.

"What now?" she said, backing up a step.

"I've already told you." That edge reappeared in his voice and eyes. "I can't take any mixed messages from you. Don't kiss me or touch me unless you want me to fall crazy in love with you. I'm not dabbling in this. The stakes feel too high. We can build something here, but it's never going to work if we can't trust each other while we're apart. It's bad enough being thousands of miles away from you. I discovered that this week. You can't expect me to go back to London and lie awake because of missing you and also wonder who you might be with when I'm gone." He paused. "How will we work out the distance thing? No idea. What I *do* know is that we can work out any details if we're committed to being together. So if you don't feel the same way, best we say our good-byes now."

Melody stared at him, absolutely incapable of speech.

He frowned. *"What?"*

"Didn't you just claim you're not good at expressing your feelings? You made my heart ache." She laughed shakily and rubbed her chest. "You're like Shakespeare."

"No, I'm not," he said flatly. "I'm just a man who wants what he wants. No compromising this time. So this is your warning. Think about what I said."

He was right. This was a big deal, not a snap decision.

She slowed down, thoughts swirling around her like winter's first snowflakes caught in a stiff wind, and tried to give his feelings the consideration they deserved.

Were there areas of concern here? Sure. This thing between them was brand new. They didn't know each other well, and their relationship would probably strain the term *long distance* to the breaking point. It wasn't like he lived a couple hours away in Manhattan. Wasn't like she created her own schedule and could hop a plane to see him whenever the urge hit.

Would loneliness play a part here? Yes. Uncertainty? You betcha.

Trust would be crucial, and it probably wasn't the greatest idea in the world to put a huge amount of faith in a guy she'd just met.

Plus…

Her scar throbbed, reminding her of its presence. She rubbed it, trying to find a little comfort. But there was no comfort, and there never would be. Because she still stuck out like a broken and bloodied thumb. Still drew second glances for all the wrong reasons. Still caused small children to huddle closer to their parents whenever she showed up in the room.

And she was no psychiatric genius, but she was pretty sure that an insecure woman in an ultra-long-distance relationship with the sexiest man in the world was a recipe for a disaster of *Titanic*-sized proportions. Did they have a fighting chance here? Probably not. Would her wounded and vulnerable heart go down in flames? Most likely.

On the other hand…

She met his gaze, so steady and patient, while her heart stuttered on every other beat.

On the other hand, this man fascinated her. Excited her. Challenged her.

Thrilled her.

Would she trade a champagne-filled steak dinner with Jerry for ten minutes on the phone with Anthony?

Every day and twice on Sundays.

Where could a relationship between her and Anthony possibly go?

Nowhere, probably.

But they didn't need to figure it out right now. They just had to agree to give it a shot.

Besides. A woman could only ever have one great love in her life, and hers was her career.

So how much could Anthony really hurt her if she only ever gave him a tiny corner of her heart and her life?

Not that much. She wouldn't let him.

She thought of her mantra.

He can't hurt you, Mel. Nothing can hurt you if you don't let it.

And wasn't she entitled to a little fun where she could find it? She hadn't had sex in *six months.*

He remained utterly still, a shadow slowly crossing his face as he watched her.

"It's okay." He sounded hoarse. "You don't have to—"

"I'm in."

"—let me down gently. I'm a big boy—*what* did you say?"

"You heard me."

A light clicked on in his expression, making his blue eyes glow with sudden intensity as he reached for her. "Come here."

Joyous laughter bubbled up as she—

"No, wait." He held out a hand to stop her before she came any closer. She froze, her smile sliding away as she watched him slump onto the sofa, rest his elbows on his knees and rub the top of his head with enough vigor to scalp himself. "Let's give it a minute."

"*What,* Anthony?" she cried, frustration pitching her voice higher. "What *is it*?"

He raised his head and, unsmiling, ran that scorching gaze up and down her body. When his attention settled on her face, there was no mistaking his X-rated intentions.

The heat of her responsive desire threatened to melt the clothes off her body. Hell, he wouldn't even have to undress her tonight—she was *that* hot for him.

She waited to see what he would do, her chest heaving with breathless anticipation.

"I want you" he said, his voice rough. "I know we talked about taking things slowly, but slow isn't on the menu for tonight. Just so you understand."

Well, thank God for that. She needed a lot of things from him right now, but *slow* wasn't on the list.

"Good."

He blinked. "So no regrets tomorrow."

"Okay…?"

"Just so we're clear. Because I don't want—"

"Oh, for God's sake," she said, kicking off her heels because he showed every sign of launching into another set of rules and concerns. "And to think I encouraged you to talk more."

"What're you…" He cleared his throat and tracked her every movement as she swept her sweater over her head, tossed it aside and went to work on her jeans. "What're you doing?"

She used a lot of hip action to wriggle her way out of her jeans. The upshot? A muttered curse from Anthony as he turned away so he didn't have to look at her, rested his elbow on the back of the sofa and used his shaky hand to rub a forehead that was beginning to look a little sweaty.

Naked now except for her black bra and bikinis, both of which were sheer scraps of air decorated with pretty little satin bows, she walked the rest of the way and came to a stop right in front of him.

"We've done enough talking for tonight," she said.

"Yes, but I still need to tell you more about my family," he said, staring at the far wall.

"I think that can wait till tomorrow," she said, brushing her hair back so he could see *all* of her breasts. "Don't you?"

His breath hissed as he turned back and drank his fill of her from bottom to top, his eyes purest blue flame now. Her calves and thighs. The little ribbons where they sat on the widest points of her hips. The bare cleft between her legs, easily visible to his view. Her flat belly and torso. Her full breasts, with special attention given to jutting nipples that needed his mouth.

And then, finally, that bright gaze flicked up to her face.

She had to wonder, with a wild thrill of excitement, what kind of animal she'd just invited out to play. Because *this* Anthony right here? He wasn't shy or awkward at all. She'd stake her life on it.

"Is this regulation pediatric surgeon lingerie you're wearing?" he asked, his voice thick.

She couldn't quite smile. Not with him looking at her like that. "Not technically, no."

He narrowed his eyes. Skimmed her up and down again. Rubbed his lips.

"You wore it for a date with some other man." Taking all the time in the world, he reached out and stroked his long fingers across her belly, right where her bikinis ended, making her flesh leap. "What do you have to say for yourself?"

It took her a second to catch her breath enough to say *anything*.

"I wore it for myself," she told him. "But I thought about *you* when I put it on."

There was a long pause.

"Good answer," he said, eyes flashing.

Without another word, he surged, caught her around the waist and tumbled her, squealing with surprise and delight, to the sofa beneath him.

17

Melody had thought she'd learned a few things about Anthony in the last several days. How deep and resonant his voice could get, for example, or how intensely he could focus on her. She'd thought she'd had some idea of what she might be getting herself into after their interlude on the last sofa they'd shared together.

She'd thought wrong.

She had a single breathless moment to get her mind right while she wrapped her arms around his neck and ran her fingers through the warm strands of his hair. He settled his sinewy body against hers (even with most of his weight settled on his flexing arms, he was *heavy*) and the insistent bulge of his erection against her sweet spot as she opened her legs for him. And there was one suspended moment out of time where she looked up into his face and saw it all. Those heavy brows, silky to her touch and so much darker than the hair on his head. The ruddy flush of his tan skin, the sharp slope of his nose and unyielding planes of his cheekbones, prickly now with five o'clock shadow. The tender and velvety curves of his lush mouth as she ran her thumb over his lips.

His eyes…his eyes…his *eyes*.

They'd turned a fiery indigo now, shot through with shifting white striations and dark flecks, rimmed in a startling black and showcased with the kind of thick mahogany lashes for which women booked expensive salon appointments.

Her smile faded.

If only she had a thousand years or so to lose herself in these *eyes*.

She didn't think he'd mind. Not with the way he stared back at her.

His gaze flicked down to her mouth.

Back up again.

"Last chance," he warned softly.

Was he serious?

"I don't want any chances."

She wrapped her legs around his waist, savoring the downy brush of his velour robe against her inner thighs, and tightened her hold on his face to bring him in for her kiss.

His entire body tensed.

There was a final millisecond of clarity when she thought, *oh God, we're really going to do this,* and the moment to prepare herself ended.

With a low growl, he cupped her face in his hands and lowered his head.

And she quickly discovered she wasn't ready at all.

Anthony started out with deceptive politeness, working his way across her lips in maddening little exploratory kisses while they got the feel of each other again. But those nibbles heated her blood to boiling. It wasn't long before her hips began to thrust involuntarily against him and she mewled for more like a starving kitten.

He took that as his cue.

His mouth slanted over hers, settling into place and

demanding entry with a relentlessness that stole her breath. And suddenly his voluptuous tongue was deep inside her, possessing her with slick and skilled sweeps that left no corner of her mouth unexplored. There was nothing for her to do and nowhere for her to go; his strong and possessive hands on either side of her face, gripping her hair, saw to that. Her only job in life was to receive and to *feel*. For a strong and powerful woman like her, who marched through her day trying to control every aspect of her life—career, finances, home, weight, romance—the surrender he demanded was an unspeakable relief.

He broke away, giving her the chance to try to catch her breath and to murmur his name. Sliding lower, he found every delicious nerve ending on both sides of her neck (including the scarred area!) and nuzzled them. Bit the sensitive tendons where neck met shoulder until she cried out with the exquisite pain. Stroked her skin until she was fooled into thinking it was over and she'd survived, only to shift to another, more tender spot and start the onslaught all over again. She squirmed and pleaded incoherently, trying to get away one second and surging to get closer the next.

Then it was her breasts' turn.

He didn't bother stripping her out of her bra and it didn't matter. Not when he was blessed with hands that knew to start at the outer curves, gently stroking and circling inward rather than immediately grabbing and squeezing as though he was kneading pizza dough. He took it slow and easy with his feathery touches, pretending she didn't have nipples that ached for his attention until her restless and overheated body couldn't take it for another second. With a growl of frustration, she flattened her hands over his, forcing him to manhandle her. Hissed an unabashed *yesss* when he finally squeezed her nipples.

Arched to give him access when his mouth followed his hands.

Ignored his dark laughter and murmured "All you had to do was ask," before he latched on and suckled.

"Anthony."

She couldn't keep the anguish out of her voice. How could she when she'd simultaneously realized both that her body could feel like *this* and that she'd been having Utilitarian Sex 101 with fumbling bozos all these years?

And it wasn't that she didn't know what an orgasm was.

It was just that she'd never known that the pleasure could consume her entire body until even her hair follicles felt like they were singing.

All that time spent focused on her career and grabbing *friends with benefits* quickies here and there on those rare occasions when she had both the time and energy.

And the whole time, there'd been a man like *this* in the world.

What a freaking waste.

He took his time, giving both breasts the same loving treatment. Then he drifted lower, gripping her torso while he rubbed his prickly cheeks over her belly. While his tongue swirled in her navel, making her hips jackknife. While he slid to the floor and scraped his teeth over the meaty part of one of her thighs when she was still trying to recover from the thrill of the navel thing. While his silky hair and hot breath tickled her until she squirmed. While she belatedly registered his intentions.

Somehow she got her heavy lids open and her eyes to focus as she stared down the length of her body at him. Past her heaving breasts still encased in that sheer black bra, with her jutting nipples perfectly visible. Past her quivering belly and the top of her bikinis. And she watched as he raised his head and frowned with unmistakable concentration as he stared at her pussy, experimentally stroking a finger over her engorged folds.

Her flesh leapt.

He reached beneath her panties to stroke her perineum with lazy curls of his fingers.

She twisted and made a strangled sound, then gathered enough breath to form a coherent word.

"Anthony…"

He raised his head, nailing her with that unrelenting and vaguely disgruntled gaze. Evidently he didn't like being interrupted.

"Yes, darling?" he asked conversationally, curling and uncurling those fingers, every glancing touch making her a bit more insane. "Did you say something?"

Well, she'd *meant* to.

It was just that she couldn't get her thoughts to cooperate with her words.

"I just think…" she began, panting, wanting to tell him that she wasn't a selfish person and she knew there were protocols in place here. He worked on her a little bit, then she worked on him, then everybody finished up with the foreplay and they commenced with the screwing. That was life in the civilized world. "You have to stop. I haven't even…I haven't even had the chance to touch *you*."

"I see." He paused, those fingers still stroking. "Anything else?"

She wriggled, trying to break free of that unyielding hand on her hip. "No, but I— "

There was a rumble of impatience and a flash of blue. Amused. Wicked.

Then he lowered his head again, rhythmically using his mouth on her in new and wondrous ways. Leaving her nothing to do but let her eyes roll closed, stretch her arms overhead as she clung to the armrest and accept his gift.

She laughed with surprise and gathering ecstasy. She pleaded. She chanted his name like the mindless fool he'd turned her into. She might have even cried a little. Possibly even sobbed.

Who could say?

Once again, it wasn't like no one had ever gone down on her before.

It was just that none of them had known what the hell they were doing.

When she came it was on a long and high note of astonishment as her body seized up, riding a wave of rippling spasms that seemed to stretch into infinity. Nothing much pierced her consciousness in that unprecedented moment, but she was dimly aware of Anthony resting his head on her belly, his words and hands soothing as he caressed the outside of her thigh and nuzzled her a final time.

He disappeared for a second, leaving her body to melt into the cushions like hot caramel. She murmured a weak protest, turning her head to see where he'd gone and to register her complaint at his loss, but he'd only reached for his overnight bag at the end of the sofa.

And then he was back, kneeling in front of her holding a string of condoms, his glittering gaze skimming over her reclining body from head to toe. Slowly, almost reverently, he ran his fingers down her arm, which was still overhead. Through her hair as it trailed over the side of the sofa. Down the damaged side of her neck. Across the tops of her breasts. Down her torso and between her thighs, to the place he now owned. All the way down her legs, to her toes.

By this time, she'd recovered enough for her body to cool and her cheeks to heat. To wonder what had just happened and worry about her loss of control. She didn't just serve herself up to men on a silver platter or lose her freaking mind like this. Oh, sure, she slept with the occasional one, but those were strictly utilitarian fucks to address her body's needs when she couldn't face another date night alone with her vibrator and a glass of pinot grigio.

A lot like sneezing when her nose itched.

But *this*…

"Is this a normal first time for you?" she asked.

He paused, looking incredulous.

"How could anything be normal about being with the most extraordinary woman I've ever met?" he asked, sounding honestly puzzled.

That answer went a long way toward quieting the doubts that had begun popping up in her head like jacks-in-the-box. She was a little freaked out, yeah, but so was he.

And maybe that was okay.

Meanwhile, they weren't finished here.

Not by a long shot.

So she stood, a real challenge to her jellied knees, and offered a hand to pull him up. Staring up into his face—God, he was tall—she reached for his robe's belt. Untied it. Pushed the two halves apart.

Stared at him, losing a bit more of her mind.

He had a lean torso, tan and dusted with cornsilk. Ladder-rung abs and zero fat on his belly. A thick patch of golden hair and a ruddy erection that made her a very lucky woman. Muscular thighs narrowing to shapely calves. Nice feet.

Easing closer, she pressed her mouth to the divot between his collarbones and gave herself a moment to revel in the warmth of his smooth skin. Trailed her hand low across his belly and savored the slow hiss of his breath. Reached for his heavy length and closed her fingers around him, one by one, until his pounding heartbeat told her that he approved of her firm grip.

Then she began to pump him. Up and down. Harder. Faster.

A shaky laugh from Anthony.

She looked up at his face again, savoring his utter stillness and rapt attention as he stared down at her.

"I'm really glad this is all for me," she said.

"Is that so?" he said on an uneven breath.

"Yeah. So make sure you don't share it with anyone else."

A disbelieving laugh this time. "Don't worry."

Pleased, she let him go, put both hands on his shoulders and pushed him down to the sofa. Straddled him when he sat and watched her with a wary new respect. Held his eye contact as he hastily ripped one of the foil packs open with his teeth and rolled on a condom. Guided him to her slick core, nudging aside her panties' edge to help him.

Then she stayed where she was for a pregnant moment, poised over his plump head, and savored her bird's-eye view of his handsome face, now damp with sweat, and glazed eyes. He also seemed to take a moment to brace for impact, taking a handful of her hair on one side and a handful of her ass on the other.

She glanced down at his mouth and surrendered to the irresistible urge to lick his delicious lips. He eagerly opened for her. She kissed him hard and deep. For one second.

Then she pulled back, ignoring his groaned protest.

"I want to see you come for me," she said, and impaled herself on his huge dick.

They both cried out with the shock of the connection. Watched each other, their mouths agape. She'd thought that this time would be for him—she'd already had her head-exploding orgasm for the night, thanks—but she hadn't counted on the exquisite friction between them, or the way one of his sneaky thumbs found its way to her clit and lingered there with a steady pressure.

His head fell back against the cushions and his lids drooped to half-mast, but he seemed as determined as she was not to miss a second of their first time together.

And what a time it was.

Working him as hard as she could, she braced her hands on either side of his head and rose and fell. Swiveled. Pivoted. Kissed him in little nips and nuzzles. Teased him by withdrawing her mouth until he frowned and tugged her hair to bring her back again. Anything to milk him for every hiss, gasp and moan he was worth. He met her thrust for thrust, grinding against her until they were both sweat-slicked and abandoned and her wild hair hung in her face. Even better? He talked to her the whole time, half-formed words of encouragement, or telling her how tight she was or that she'd found the exact right spot and should never stop.

Through it all, the pleasure spiraled tighter and lower inside her, crystallizing around the point that his thumb now possessed. How he knew things about her body that she hadn't learned in thirty-plus years, she had no idea. All she knew was that there was no controlling the gathering orgasm that was so determined to roar through her.

She was right.

It overcame her, forcing her head to fall back, her back to arch and her mouth to moan, long and loud. Only his strong hand on her hip kept her from keeling over backward and knocking herself out on the coffee table. Honest to God, she'd never had the slightest inkling her body could do *this* under the right circumstances. It was like the pleasure chased her down and tackled her to the ground, refusing to release her until every part of her body shimmered like a handful of diamonds in the noontime sun.

Anthony stiffened. Shouted her name as he thrust a final time.

And when she'd ridden it out and managed to right herself and brace her hands on the back of the sofa again, he surprised her by taking handfuls of her hair on either side of her head and shaking her just enough to make sure he had her attention.

His face and chest were damp. His eyes were bright and glazed. His chest heaved. And his expression was equally bewildered and determined.

"You're probably it for me," he said hoarsely. "You *know* that?"

The words stopped her heart, then shattered it like a fastball through a plate glass window.

Men spouted sweet words and meaningless promises in the heat of the moment. Everyone knew that.

It was the woman's job to know that such promises only lasted as long as the orgasmic aftershocks pulsed through his body. It was a woman's job to keep her head on straight. And it was *her* job to remind herself that a man like this, who could have any London-based model or actress he smiled at, would never truly commit to an ultra-long-distance relationship with a woman whose childhood playground nickname had been *Scarface*. He might think he would, but he wouldn't. He might show up for a while, but then he'd stop. And it was no good telling herself that Samira's long-distance relationship with Baptiste was chugging along just fine. That was *Samira*. Who, in addition to being special, had a beautiful and unscarred face. That could never be Melody.

"You *know* that?" Anthony murmured again, his glowing gaze grazing over her features.

One of the jagged shards of Melody's heart cracked and smashed on the floor.

If only he meant it. If only fairy-tale endings were possible.

She helplessly shook her head.

"Shhh," she said, kissing the hard plane of his perfect cheek, wrapping her arms around his neck and keeping a firm grip on her reality. "You don't have to say that."

"*Yes,* I do."

She shook her head again and held on tight, reminding herself that he couldn't hurt her if she didn't let him. And they might have explosive sex, but that didn't mean she planned to give him an opening into her heart.

18

A nthony knew he was living on borrowed time, but he didn't care.

He borrowed it during the night, as he woke Melody up to make love when her body was warm and supple in his arms and she cooed like a dove. Then again as the morning's first light tried to break through the blackout drapes and he couldn't believe the good fortune that had brought her into his life and his bed.

He borrowed it as they brushed their teeth and she complained about the way he squeezed the tube from the sides rather than rolling and flattening it from the bottom. He borrowed the hell out of it as they showered together, dressed in their matching white robes and argued over what to order for their room service breakfast, with Melody laughing and expressing utter disbelief that a proper English breakfast fry-up included baked beans and grilled tomatoes.

But by nine o'clock, their breakfast had arrived and been set up on his dining table. They had their coffee and tea poured and their toast buttered.

And he was out of excuses.

He'd begun to fear that he'd handled things all wrong and that he should have given her a complete family tree and résumé right when they met. But he'd been so enthralled with her. So intoxicated with the thrill of meeting someone who didn't treat him any differently than any other bloke and the possibility that such an extraordinary woman might get to know and like him for *him*.

And now he was all caught up in the thrilling whirlwind of their relationship. So drunk on her glorious smile and laughter and the touch of her skin within easy reach that he couldn't stand the idea of rocking their fledgling boat with the news that he hadn't been open with her and, worse, that he came as part of a monstrous package deal with his family.

A shadow crept over his heart.

Fear tightened his throat.

And he knew he was out of time.

"So, listen." He tried to keep his voice light, but it wound up sounding ominous, even to his own ears. "We should talk about my family for a minute. I need to tell you a bit more about my father's side. And my, ah, grandmother—my mother's mother— specifically."

She glanced up from salting her eggs, her makeup-free skin absolutely luminous in the morning light. Her hair, still wet from the shower, was piled on top of her head with only a few corkscrew strands trailing down the sides of her neck, and her robe gaped open just a bit in front, showing the curves at the tops of her baps.

And he thought it would be hard enough to leave her when he had to go back to London tonight. Damn near impossible to go if she were angry with him or worse.

"Okay…?" she said. "No one's in prison, are they?"

"What? No. Nothing like that."

She set down the salt. "Well, why do you look so grim?"

He sighed. That settled it.

His acting skills were far more dreadful than he'd feared.

He cleared his throat, then took a sip of water, searching for the right words.

"It's just that…I hope you can understand that…"

She took a bite of eggs, looking puzzled.

He rapped his knuckles on the table, realized he was doing it and tried to use the same hand in an offhand wave.

Her frown deepened, losing a lot of its bemusement.

"The thing is…it was very important to me for us to get to know each other a bit. Just as people. You know. That's why I asked you not to look me up online. And things have progressed so smoothly and so quickly. It wasn't that I never planned to tell you at *all*. That would be unthinkable…"

She put her fork down and folded her arms.

"But when you're in my position, you never quite know who you can—"

"Spit it out," she snapped, startling him.

Right, then.

Spit it out, Anthony Scott, billionaire and future Earl of Stockbridge.

He closed his eyes, raked his hands through his hair, opened his eyes and said a silent prayer to let God know that tomorrow he'd happily be twice as awkward as normal if only God gave him a bit of divine grace right now.

"My father's family is the, ah, *Scott* behind GeoScottCo Petroleum."

She blinked, her expression sliding into incredulity.

"My, ah, grandfather was George Scott. And of course *geo* also means earth. And so he put the names together…"

She made a sputtering noise of disbelief. "Are you talking about the GeoScottCo that has a gas station every two blocks everywhere in the United States? The Starbucks of gas stations? The GeoScottCo that goes with the red, white and blue gas card in my wallet right now? *That* GeoScottCo?"

"That would be the one."

His fidgety hands wanted to rap on the table again, so he laced his fingers and put them in his lap.

One leg, meanwhile, began to jiggle.

"But…" Melody tried to laugh. "I didn't really think anyone *owned* it anymore. I thought it was a huge, multinational publicly-traded company."

"It is." Putting a Herculean effort into it, he tensed his muscles and stopped his leg from jiggling. "It went public twenty-odd years ago. Just before my parents split. So my father, ah, made some money—"

"*Some* money?"

She sounded strangled now.

"It was, ah, one of the largest initial public offerings at the time, yes. But bad timing for my father, who was a cheating rat bastard and had to hand over a good chunk of it to my mother in the divorce. And when she died…"

"You inherited it. As the only child."

"Right," he said, shifting uncomfortably in his chair. "Which is lucky for me, I suppose, because if it was up to my father, I'm sure he would have cut me off without a penny for having the temerity to think for myself on occasion. But my father is still the largest shareholder. And my inheritance is, ah, held in trust for me at the moment."

She gaped at him.

"So, ah…" More from a desire to have a project for his restless hands than anything else, he poured himself another cup of coffee. "That's my, ah, father's side of my family."

More gaping.

He picked up his steaming cup and forced down a sip.

Still nothing from Melody.

"Now might be a good time for you to say something," he told her. "Just... you know. To keep the conversation moving."

She closed her mouth. Tipped her head to one side and studied him closely.

"I'm trying not to be tacky here, but...You basically have more money than God, is what you're saying."

Like that, the suffocating band of pressure that had been constricting his lungs for the past several moments loosened enough for him to manage a complete breath.

They'd cleared the first hurdle, then.

And she didn't seem particularly upset if she was making jokes about it.

"Sadly, *I* don't have more money than God, no. Not until I come into my inheritance. Right now, I'm only living on a small portion of the interest." He sipped again. "But I did hear that my father once extended God a line of credit."

He thought it was a pretty funny line, but she only managed a weak smile.

He supposed it might be a *bit* soon for jokes.

"You know that *I* don't have any money, right? I mean, I'm starting to do very well at the hospital, but my balance sheet isn't balancing at the moment because I still have some med school debt left. Harvard ain't cheap."

He very well knew that Harvard wasn't cheap, and he planned to eradicate her debt situation the second an opportunity presented itself. What kind of man would allow his girlfriend to struggle with student loans when he had more than enough money in the bank for both of them?

But now wasn't that time. He had bigger fish to try at the moment.

"Understood," he said gravely. "I'd planned to ask you for

a short-term loan after breakfast, but now I've thought better of it."

She managed a real laugh this time. Shaky, but definitely real.

Only it was gone much too soon.

"Thank you for telling me," she said, sobering. "I guess you've lifted the ban on me looking you up online now, huh?"

"I'm glad you gave me this little grace period about that. I just felt that—what's wrong, darling? Why do you look so troubled?"

She picked up her tea, frowning as she stared down at the contents. Then she put it down and ran her hands up and down her upper arms, as though she'd caught a chill.

"I think I need a minute." Rueful smile. "I feel like you're not the guy I thought you were. Like I don't know you as well as I thought I did. Which is silly, because we haven't even known each other for two weeks yet, have we? So why would I think I knew much about you at all?"

The first feelings of dread prickled up his spine.

"*I* feel like we're getting to know each other quite well," he said softly. "And I'm exactly the same man I was ten minutes ago."

"You're not, though. Ten minutes ago, I though the biggest obstacle to our relationship was that we live thousands of miles apart. I figured you were a guy who probably had a little money, but I thought you were just a guy. And I felt like we at least had the fundamentals in common. And now—"

"I *am* just a guy, and we *do* have the fundamentals in common. And I don't like the term *obstacle*."

Disbelieving look from Melody. "What would *you* call it?"

"Minor details that we will work out if I have anything to say about it," he said flatly.

"Yeah, but—"

"There are no *yeah, buts*. I live in London and you live here. It's an easy flight, and I have the money to get us back and forth to see each other during this *getting to know you* phase. When the time comes, we'll figure out a solution that puts us on the same continent. It's not like I live on Mars and you live at the bottom of the Pacific Ocean. And I don't give a rat's arse about how much money *you* have or don't have. I assume you feel the same…?"

"Well, don't get me wrong. I'd rather date a guy with money than a guy who lives in a van down by the river. But we come from different worlds. I'm old and wise enough now to know that stuff like that matters. How much can we really understand each other?"

His stubborn gene flared to life. "As far as I'm concerned? Sky's the limit."

He held her gaze, willing her to see every ounce of his sincerity.

And maybe she did, because the tightness in her expression eased enough to allow a hint of a smile to crinkle the corners of her eyes.

"Well…it's not like you just got out on probation," she said, perking up and reaching for her toast again. "I need to keep this in perspective, right? You have some money. That's a *good* thing. It's a blessing."

Oh, how he wanted to freeze time in that moment.

But he'd come too far to turn back now.

"I'm glad you feel that way. Because there's more."

"What?" She tossed the toast back onto her plate, dusted off her hands and leaned back to glare at him. "I thought we

were having a fun morning-after breakfast here. How many other shoes are you planning to drop?"

"Just the one."

"Well, go ahead and hit me with it so I can eat my eggs while they're still lukewarm and not stone cold. And don't give me all that build-up again. Just tell me."

Famous last words.

"Fine. My grandmother's the Queen."

Blank look from Melody. Absolutely no reaction whatsoever.

In fact, she went so blank that he had the strong urge to snap his fingers in front of her face to make sure she was still with him.

She stirred after several long beats.

"The...*queen*?" she asked weakly.

"Yes."

"Of what?"

What a wildly optimistic question. As though there were some chance he'd say that his grandmother was the queen of used autos in the metropolitan Detroit area or some such.

"England, darling. My grandmother is the Queen of England."

Melody made a game attempt at a dismissive laugh. "You expect me to believe that?"

He bowed his head and said nothing.

"*Your* grandmother. Is the Queen of England. Queen Anna. Who rides around in carriages and opens Parliament and, I don't know, does the royal wave." Melody raised her hand and did a credible imitation of the royal wrist flick. "*That's* your grandmother."

Since this showed every sign of continuing all morning, Anthony decided it was time to move things along.

He'd tossed his billfold on the table last night along with

his watch and phone. He reached for it now, pulled out one of the bright orange pound notes that featured his tiara-clad granny wearing her Mona Lisa smile and handed it to Melody.

"*This* is my grandmother."

While she stared blankly down at it, he grabbed his phone and ran an Internet search on himself. After a quick, grimacing glance at what came up below all his most recent charity-related stuff, he handed her the phone.

She blinked up at him, then warily down at the phone.

Then she began to scroll, her face flooding with color and disbelief.

"Oh, my God," she murmured, putting a hand over her mouth. "Oh, my *God*."

He saw it all in his mind's eye.

The family picnics with plaid blankets spread on the ground, perfectly normal if you ignored the Scottish castle, Balmoral, in the background.

The whole family's obligatory Buckingham Palace balcony pictures from his oldest cousin's monster wedding a few years back.

Granny passing him as she inspected the troops, making pointed comments about the sad decline in the quality of the officers while he stood there in his uniform and tried to swallow his laughter and keep his chin up.

There were probably also several photos of him and his various girlfriends over the years, starting with his school crushes, progressing to his phase with a couple of aristocratic women who were basically older versions of Annabella Carmichael, through the various models and actresses and culminating with his most recent ex, a London bank executive.

Melody took her time about perusing, blissfully unaware

that he was mining her shuttered expression for clues or that every second she delayed giving him a reaction shaved a year off his life.

"I don't understand this," she said finally, putting his phone down and rubbing her forehead. "I know about Prince Thomas and his brother Prince Arthur. I saw part of Prince Thomas's son's royal wedding on TV a few years ago. Why haven't I ever heard of *you*?"

"Granny has five children—"

"Granny." There was a hysterical tinge to her strained laughter. *"*You call the Queen of England *Granny*."

"We've got to call her something," he said quietly.

She flapped a hand. "Go on."

"Granny had five children: Thomas, the Prince of Wales. The heir."

"So he'll be king when your grandmother dies."

"Yes."

"And his son was the one with the big royal wedding on TV a few years ago."

"My cousin, yes. He's second in line to the throne. And he has a couple of kids now, so they're third and fourth in line."

"Got it," she said crisply. "Where do *you* come in?"

"When it comes to most Americans, I don't think they know or care anything about the family beyond that. Which is one of the reasons it's so great here. One can fly under the radar. But Granny had four other children besides Thomas: Edmund, Frederick, Alice and Louisa, the youngest. Louisa was my mother. I was her only child."

"But she died when you were a teenager, you said."

"Yes."

Melody cocked her head. Frowned. "So your father, the American oil tycoon, married a princess."

"Yes. And they both wanted me to have a normal upbringing. So they refused any title for me and moved here when I started primary school. I think that's also about the time their marriage started falling apart. Then they split when I was ten, and my father and I couldn't tolerate each other. So I went back to England for boarding school. That's where I met Baptiste and Nick. And you know the rest about the military, law school and my charity work."

"But you're a *prince,*" she cried.

It was hard to miss the accusatory note in her voice.

"I don't have a title. Yet."

"The grandson of a queen is a prince," she said flatly. "So you're in line for the throne."

"Well, sure, if about thirty of my aunts, uncles and cousins and their children get offed at the same time, leaving me as the sole survivor," he said with a shudder. "Otherwise there's no chance. Thank God."

She eyed him suspiciously. "And what do you mean, *yet?*"

He sighed and pushed away his cold coffee, wishing he had a whisky instead.

"All my cousins have their titles and have done since birth. My grandmother acceded to my parents' wishes about me being a commoner, with the proviso that I'd come into the title upon my thirty-fifth birthday or marriage, whichever comes first. I don't want it. I'd rather keep my relative anonymity. But she's the sovereign, and I can't tell her what to do. And she's determined to do it around my birthday next year. It's also her golden jubilee year."

"So you'll be Prince Anthony?"

"No. Earl of Stockbridge."

She sat quietly, letting that sink in for a moment.

Then she snapped her fingers. "That's why Baptiste and Nick call you *Stocky*."

"Yes."

She nodded, her lips twisting.

"So next year, England's going to be focused on your family. You'll be getting your title. There will probably be some interviews. A lot of interest in who you're dating and who might be your countess. Some tabloid stories. And aren't daily tabloids a big issue for celebrities over there?"

He knew exactly where this was going. He didn't like it, but they had to get there and deal with it.

"Yes," he said bitterly.

She stared at him, her expression just as turbulent.

"Sounds like it's time for you to take your perch in your gilded cage."

"I hope not. Because that's the last thing I want for my life. Especially *now*."

"How do you plan to avoid it? Magic wand?"

"I plan to ride it out, then resume my regularly scheduled life."

The deluge of information seemed to take the wind out of her sails.

As it would anyone, he supposed.

He watched with a sinking heart as she planted her elbows on the table and collapsed her head in her hands, gripping big hanks of her hair on either side.

Maybe that was the moment his creeping anxiety took a running leap into fear.

If this woman decided she couldn't handle the package deal that came along with him...

If she turned her back on him *now*...

"Melody..."

Her head came up, brown eyes flashing with something. Whether it was mostly fear or mostly anger, he couldn't tell.

"What are you doing with *me,* Anthony?"

"Getting to know you better and growing crazier about you by the second." He gave her a pointed once-over. "I thought I'd made that perfectly clear last night. I can do better tonight."

"Doesn't your family expect you to marry some duke's daughter? Lady Something or other? I mean…" She trailed off as a new thought hit her. "Hang on. That's what was going on with the mom and the woman at the gala, wasn't it? What was her name? Annabella?"

"I deal with that kind of nonsense a lot, yes. When people find out who I am, everything becomes an audition for the role of princess or lackey who can become part of my *crew* and ride along to enjoy the perceived rich and famous lifestyle. Or people want to pitch for their charity, as though I dole out million-pound checks to every person whose hand I shake. I'm fairly certain I've never had a true friendship with anyone other than Baptiste and Nick. And that's only because I latched on to them at boarding school. They couldn't get rid of me. I suppose I wore them down. *They* didn't have an agenda. *They* didn't give two fucks about my connections or my money, so they know the real me. And with *you*—"

"You *lied* to me, Anthony."

He knew he'd earned the quiet reproach. That didn't mean he had to like it.

"It wasn't a lie, precisely—"

"Don't bullshit me! You want to call it an omission? An oversight? Does that make you feel better about yourself? You asked me not to look you up online for the sole purpose of keeping me in the dark about who you really are."

"Yes, but who I really am isn't a murderer or a criminal."

More bullshit, and her scowling face told him she took it as such.

"Yeah, but you're not a guy next door, either, are you? Don't pretend you are. And anyone who's with you needs to know what she's getting herself into."

That shut him down. She had him dead to rights, and they both knew it.

They eyed each other, the silence seething and wary.

"Look," he said, rubbing his hands over his face in frustration and praying for the grace, just this once, to get his words right with no awkwardness standing between what he said and what he meant. "I want you to understand me—"

"That's part of the problem," she said, her voice rising. "I thought I was beginning to, but now it's like you're some other guy completely."

Now she'd gone too far. "That's where you're wrong."

The sharp finality in his voice evidently caught her attention, because she cocked her head and went very still.

"Enlighten me, then."

He opened his mouth, but it wasn't that easy to frame it so that he told her what she needed to know without telling her enough to make her take the nearest escape route, never to be seen again.

And what was his whole truth? That the more time he spent with her, the harder it was to conceive of a life without her. That he was fairly certain this woman would one day become his wife. Which meant that he was also fairly certain that life as she'd known it up until now was a thing of her past.

But…

Didn't everyone's old life end the second they met their life partner?

"I saw you online. Before we actually met."

"I know."

"I already mentioned how Baptiste told me that Samira had a surgeon friend who might want to work with my foundation. He gave me your name. I looked you up. I read your bio on the hospital's website."

A gorgeous flush crept up her neck and over her cheeks. "And…?"

"And…" He floundered. How to say it without sounding like a complete fool? "I lost my head a bit. There's no other way to explain it. There was something about your *eyes* and your smile." Shaky laugh. "But I felt like—I *feel* like—you're a special person and I *have* to get to know you. We *have* to get to know *each other*. It feels incredibly important. Don't you agree?"

Melody lowered her gaze without answering.

His heart sank. Maybe she didn't agree.

Or maybe she felt exactly the same way and wasn't willing to concede the point at the moment.

"And when I had the chance to rise or fall on my own merits with you—and I damn near fell the first time I opened my mouth, didn't I?—I couldn't bear the thought of mucking it all up by bringing my family into it. I wanted you to know me as a man before you knew me as a royal or a billionaire."

Her gaze flicked back to him, flinty now. "I *want* to know you as you really are."

"You *do* know me as I really am," he said. "You've seen me at my awkward worst. You've seen me have a *panic attack*. You've laughed *and* cried with me. You've fucked me." Her flush deepened. "What more do you think there is between a man and a woman?"

"Honesty."

There would be no compromising with her on this point, which made him want her all the more.

It also scared him all the more, because he wasn't at all sure he was getting through to her.

"Then let me be completely honest," he said, rising panic making him louder than he'd meant to be. "I grew up in Texas knowing that other kids wanted to come to my house and hang out not because they liked *me,* but because I had the house with the biggest pool and the coolest game room and the best horses to ride. So there's the *rich kid* thing. I went to boarding school knowing that most of *those* kids wanted to hang out with the *prince* and maybe get an invite to some palace or other. So that's the *prince* thing. Then I went into the service, where I did my job like all the other blokes, but now I get the *war hero* thing. And none of that's me. It's three titles that people hang on me. And half the time, I don't give a fuck. People can think what they want."

"Anthony—"

"But with *you*?" He laughed shakily. "I was scared to death that you wouldn't like me when we met, but the thought that you might want me only *because* I'm a prince or *because* I have money is worse. I may be half of a prince and half American, but I'm not going to do anything halfway with you. Either you know me and want me as a regular man, or you don't. And that's it. Now you know everything there is to know about me and you can decide whether you want things to go any further or not."

With that, his pent-up energy overcame him and he could no longer sit still. He got up and paced the length of the room. Then a new thought hit him—the most important thing—so he wheeled around and came right back.

"Actually, that was a lie," he said. "That was only part of what you need to know. Here's the rest: I'm crazy about you. I've been joking about falling for you, but maybe the joke's on me because I'm pretty sure I've already fallen. And if you'll do me the honor of investing in this relationship with me, then I will *always* do everything in my power to smooth the way for you and make sure you have as normal a life as possible. And *that's* everything you need to know about me."

"But this is about more than whether I like you or not, Anthony! On top of the long-distance thing, I'm a black woman! With a scar on my face! You think folks across the pond are going to want their precious prince to marry someone like *me*?"

He flinched. Maybe he had blinders on, but he really hadn't thought of it like that. Wasn't this the twenty-first century? Wouldn't everyone back home immediately see what he saw—that she was an extraordinary person whose spirit was every bit as beautiful as her face?

"Melody—"

"I'm a private person from a sleepy little town, Anthony. I'm a doctor. *That's* what I know. I'm not cut out to have paparazzi taking my picture and digging around in my past or for meeting the Queen. All that sounds terrifying to me."

"Fair enough. But you need to know that the thing that terrifies me is the thought of losing you ten minutes after we've found each other," he said quietly.

Something in her expression softened. She helplessly shook her head. "You're naive."

There was something no one had ever called him before.

"I'm not naive. I'm focused on the big picture."

"And what's that?" she asked tiredly.

Anthony did his best to get a little air into his constricted lungs, knowing that his happiness was on the line here and it had never been more important for him to get his words right.

"You and I are well suited to each other. In every important way."

"Anthony—"

"But if you don't agree with that assessment, then now is your moment to say so."

She blinked. Opened her mouth. Faltered. Shut her mouth. Looked away, her gaze sliding out of focus.

He managed a deeper breath, all but sagging with relief.

"I'm not saying our road will be easy—"

She barked out a humorless laugh.

"—but this relationship shows incredible promise. All the rest are details."

"Details," she said wryly. "Yeah, sure, let's go with that."

He gave her his most withering glance, the one that always worked with his men.

She met it with a hitched brow and steady defiance.

The silence stretched between them, every passing second infusing him with increased certainty. A magnification of the feeling he'd experienced when he'd clicked on Baptiste's link and seen Melody's face— her glorious *eyes*—for the very first time.

Her.

He wanted (needed?) *her.*

No one else.

Joy streaked through him. Quiet. Undeniable.

This one would not be dominated. She could not be bent or twisted. The trauma of her burn and then her medical training after that had molded her into someone with a titanium spine who could handle anything. Nothing that ever happened to her would be worse than *that,* and she knew it.

She would always be herself. This woman sitting right in front of him, ready to take him off at the knees if need be.

His thumping heart swelled until he felt like it reached every far corner of his body.

He doubted Melody even realized how strong she was. But *he* knew.

He tried to picture Annabella Carmichael or any of the women he'd dated occupying Melody's spot right now, staring him down with a steel-infused gaze. He tried to imagine any one of them standing strong in the face of paparazzi fire, or speaking up for herself when confronted with, say, his father or his grandmother.

The idea was so patently ridiculous he could almost laugh.

"I need some time to think about all this," she finally said.

He nodded, happy to give her whatever time she needed.

Because he was smart enough to know that a woman like *this* wouldn't come along twice in his lifetime.

19

"Welcome to Howard's Folly!" Samira sang when she opened the door to her new house for Melody about an hour later. "Enter at your own risk."

"I don't want to enter at all." Melody stood where she was on the threshold, folded her arms and gave her a doleful glare. "I'm not speaking to you *or* your French sidekick. I just came to announce that you're in the doghouse so you'll know I'm ignoring you."

"What did *I* do?" Samira asked, widening her eyes and putting a hand over her heart in a D-list stab at innocence that had the potential to fool no one.

Melody jabbed her index finger at her face. "You know very well what—"

"Melody!" Baptiste appeared beside Samira and threw the door open wider. "You came to see our new house. Come in, come in."

"I don't want to come in," Melody said, splitting her glower between them while also tipping her head to each side so she could receive his double-cheeked kiss. "You're terrible friends and human beings. I only came to tell you how bitterly disappointed in you I am and to write you off forever."

Baptiste shot Samira a sidelong look, brows raised. "That's a lot of drama for this early on a weekend morning. Do we have any clue about—"

"I'll tell you what it's about," Melody snapped. "You two knew all about Anthony's status as a royal, and you didn't say one word about it. Not *one word*."

"That's a complete lie," Samira said. "I tried to tell you, but you were too busy speechifying about how the two of you had taken a blood oath to get to know each other the old-fashioned way. Ringing any bells?"

It rang a bell, but Melody was in no mood to be reasonable about anything. "Thanks for giving a sister a heads-up. That's all I can say."

"Well, say it inside." Samira hooked an arm around Melody's waist, steered her inside her massive foyer and shut the door. "It's freezing out there."

Melody looked around with interest, noting the stately staircase, dusty but beautiful floors and paneling, high-ceilinged rooms spinning off hallways on either side and the spectacular view from the kitchen windows.

"Oh, my God," she said.

Baptiste beamed at her. "You like it?"

Melody took off her jacket and thrust it and her bag at his chest before heading for the kitchen, where a massive fire blazed in an oversized hearth big enough to park a compact car in.

"I'm going to suspend hostilities only long enough to tell you that this house is *amazing*. I can't believe you actually bought it, Baptiste. It's been sitting empty for years."

"Yes, well, as I told you the day of the Halloween bonfire, I had a very strong feeling about this house."

"As well you should. Look at this view! Samira, can you believe this?"

"I cannot." Samira, all but levitating with happiness, joined her at the kitchen sink while they admired the glittering Hudson River in the distance. "It was a wonderful surprise."

"So what kind of work does it need?" Melody asked, eyeballing the swimming pool, which appeared to have caved in on one side, and the kitchen counters, which rightfully belonged in a linoleum museum.

"Everything," Baptiste said cheerfully, pointing to a yellow legal pad and several sheets of its paper already lined with notes. "We're pretty sure we dislocated a family of birds when we lit the fire, so maybe we should start with a fireplace inspection. We've been making a list. It needs windows. HVAC. New kitchen. New bathrooms. New roof. New pool. We'd be better off hiring a demolition expert and blasting the house to smith—ah, what's the word?"

"Smithereens," supplied Melody and Samira.

"Yes! We should blast it to smithereens. But we want to restore the house to its former glory. And it will be fun. Right, Samira?"

"I'm not sure if *fun* is the right word," Samira said darkly. "It'll be an adventure for sure. And that's enough about the house for now. We'll give you a tour in a minute. Right now we want to hear about you and Anthony."

"Yes." Baptiste's grin was pure mischief. "Tell us *everything.*"

"A billionaire *prince*?" Melody cried. "And you two didn't say anything to me? You didn't think I needed to know what I was getting into? Are you *insane*? Well, yes, of course you're insane. Only insane folks would've bought this crazy old house. Why are you grinning at me like that? You should feel guilty."

"Why should *I* feel guilty?" Samira demanded. Still grinning. "*You're* the genius who agreed not to look him up online. *You* knew that could lead to disaster. *You* were the one who looked Baptiste up online and warned *me* about *his* shady past. So you knew how important it was to do your research with a new man."

Baptiste scowled. "My past is not *shady*. If anything, it's a little, ah, colorful."

"Whatever you need to tell yourself to sleep at night." Samira gave him a condescending little pat on the shoulder before focusing on Melody. "So what happened? Baptiste says Anthony hopped a ride with him last night? To surprise you? I thought he wasn't coming back until next weekend."

"He couldn't wait to see our beautiful Melody again," Baptiste said, shooting a fond smile in her direction. "I've never seen him so excited."

Melody's conscience squirmed guiltily. She ducked her head, running a hand through her hair. "He *definitely* surprised me."

Samira's face fell with dawning comprehension. "Hang on. He didn't catch you on your blind date, did he?"

"Sort of…?" Melody said, cheeks burning.

Samira's jaw dropped. She clapped a hand to her forehead. "Oh, my God. I *told* you that stupid blind date was a bad idea."

"A bad idea?" Outrage got the best of Melody. She'd never even have been on the dating site but for Samira. Melody had been happily minding her own business as a spinster and nun to her career. "*You're* the genius who signed me up for—"

"Hang on." Baptiste cocked his head, his expression

sliding into unmistakable horror. "My English isn't very good, clearly, but did you just say that Anthony saw you on a date with another man? After he dropped everything and flew back here from London because he missed you so much?"

Melody's heart sank like the caved-in section of the pool.

"I'm not the bad guy here," she said. "We'd never had *any* discussions about the future."

Baptiste snorted and muttered something in French. Then, "Why not stab the poor man in the heart and be done with it?"

Melody winced.

"So what happened?" Samira said.

Melody told them about their words outside the restaurant last night and how she'd followed him back to the hotel.

"So what was the upshot?" Samira asked.

Another snort from Baptiste. "The upshot? The upshot should be obvious. Look at that mark on her neck."

He pointed.

Cringing and blushing furiously, Melody clapped a hand to that side of her neck. Too late, as it turned out.

"What're you? In high school?" Samira cried gleefully. "You talked about *me* getting pregnant with *my* irresponsible sexual behavior, but look at *you*."

"Get off your high horse," Baptiste said smugly, now pointing to Samira's neck. "You have one, too."

"I do *not*," Samira said.

Melody checked Samira's neck. Smirked. "Yeah. You do."

Samira made an outraged sound and started to smack Baptiste's arm. He laughed and deflected. When the ensuing scuffle was all over, he was leaning against the sink with Samira in his arms in front of him, both facing Melody.

"So you and Anthony are a couple. Judging from the way you blushed just now, you're very happy about it," he told

Melody, pressing a kiss to Samira's temple. "Now you know everything about him. What's the problem? Why are Samira and I in the doghouse?"

"*What?*" Melody said, wishing her face would cool off a little and aghast that anything so obvious required an explanation. "Why did he hide it from me? It's not the crime. It's the coverup."

"You know what? I don't blame him." Baptiste hiked up his chin with a tinge of defiance. "I don't. His whole life, people trip all over themselves, trying to get close to him, but they don't care anything about him. They think he can get them access to his family or his money. I've seen it. It's horrible. They think if *he's* famous and they hang out with him, then *they* will also be famous. They see him as a figure. A tool. The man inside the tool is an afterthought. What would that be like? I get some of that because of my money." He paused, frowning thoughtfully. "And because of my stunning good looks. Let's be honest."

Samira rolled her eyes and whacked him in the belly with the back of her hand.

"But I don't get anything like what he gets," Baptiste continued, repressing his grin. "I wouldn't want to change places with him. I can't fault him for wanting Melody to be interested in him as a person. Not at all."

"I didn't come here to listen to some rousing defense of Anthony," Melody snapped, her heart aching at the thought of what Anthony's life must be like if he had to constantly question the motives of everyone he met. "You're supposed to be on *my* side. Why do you think I came here?"

"Sorry," Baptiste said gravely. "I'll try to stop being so truthful."

"And he's part of the *royal family,*" Melody said, vaguely mollified. "The press follows them around everywhere they go. They have security and no privacy. They can't walk down the street without people gawking at them, much less go to a store to buy groceries. They have rules and protocol. They have to ask the Queen for permission to do everything—"

"That's not technically true," he said, turning Samira loose with a pat on the ass. "And even if it was, she's a lovely person. Very reasonable."

"Wait, what?" the women said, gaping at him.

"You've met the *Queen*?" Samira asked.

"I've met her many times," he said, shrugging. "Anthony would often invite me to spend the holidays with him because my mother was off somewhere with a boyfriend. So I'd go to Sandringham for Christmas."

"As one does," Melody said, brows raised.

Samira sniggered.

"The point is," Baptiste continued, ignoring the interruption with dignity, "that everyone has a family that you have to deal with. And Anthony is a minor royal. There's no chance of him inheriting. Several of his cousins sail under the radar—"

"Fly."

"And the press hardly notices them at all."

"I just don't think it's that easy," Melody said. "This whole thing terrifies me. It was enough to deal with when I thought the biggest obstacle was the fact that he lives in London and I live here. But now... I don't exactly look like Cinderella, do I?"

She slumped against the cabinet, crossed her arms and ankles and studied her shoes, wondering what the hell she'd gotten herself into.

"Then it's simple," Baptiste said, his voice clipped. "Say good-bye to him. Tell him it's over."

Melody's head came up. *"What?"*

"You don't want him? You've decided he's not worth the effort?"

"I never said that!"

Baptiste shrugged, green eyes flashing. "Do him a favor. Let him go before you hurt him any worse. I've known him for over twenty years. I've seen him date many women. All kinds of women. And I've never seen him as excited as he was last night, coming here to see you."

Melody hesitated. "But I'm not sure I could handle his family or the press, Baptiste. And that's assuming we get over the distance hurdle."

"It's not his fault where he was born," Baptiste said fiercely. "He didn't ask to deal with the press. He wants to live his life, just like you and me. And he comes the way he comes. If he came with diabetes, you wouldn't use that against him, would you?"

No, she would not.

Melody floundered, turning to Samira for support, but Samira only shook her head and held her hands up in a *you're not getting any help from me* gesture.

Melody frowned and thought it over, no mean feat with Baptiste's stern profile accusing her in silence as he turned to look out the window.

She thought about the fun she'd had with Anthony. The rapport they'd developed. The things they had in common. Their incredible night together in his suite. She thought about the way he looked at her and the way she'd missed him when he was gone.

She thought about letting him go and either resuming her workaholic ways or launching herself into a search for a life partner on DoctorLove.com. She thought of Anthony winding up with an Annabella.

Her belly clenched in protest.

"I can't do that," she said quietly, shaking her head. "I don't want to let him go."

Baptiste studied her closely for signs of sincerity, then eased back from rabid best friend mode. "Good. Then there's your answer. You can deal with the rest together."

Melody blinked and felt a wild surge of relief.

There was her answer.

Simple.

Actually, it wasn't simple at all—on top of everything else, when would she and Anthony find time to see each other? And what would they say about all this at the hospital if and when it ever came out?—but it would become simpler if she and Anthony focused on getting to know each other and building a strong foundation for their relationship.

Baptiste watched her cycle through a thousand kinds of turmoil, then made a scoffing sound.

"You women. Why all the worry?" he muttered. "Honestly, you do it to yourselves."

Melody rolled her eyes. "Says the guy who freaked out when he saw this house for the first time."

"Whatever," he said, shrugging. "Why not see it as a grand adventure for the two of you to enjoy together?"

She nodded. That made sense.

But there were still shadows over her heart.

"I just feel like…" Melody struggled to put it into words without sounding overwrought. "I thought I'd met a guy with potential. But he's not the guy I thought he was. That's very unsettling."

"Did you think he was a good guy?" Baptiste asked.

"Yeah." Melody tried her best, but there was no killing her smile. "I think he's a *great* guy."

"Then he's exactly who you think he is," he said. "He's a

little bit more, too, but he's *exactly* that guy. And he deserves a chance."

Melody nodded, turning to Samira. "Sami? You've been awfully quiet."

Samira and Baptiste exchanged a long and measured look, at the end of which Baptiste dimpled and gave her a tiny wink. Samira flushed to the roots of her hair, repressed her answering smile and focused on Melody.

"What's that saying? 'Life's what happens when you're busy making other plans'?'" Samira asked.

"Yeah." Melody clicked her fingers. "Who said that? Buddha?"

"John Lennon," Baptiste said.

"I was busy making plans to marry a man who turned out to be gay," Samira continued. "I planned a dress. I planned a wedding and a life. And that was all the wrong plan for me. I didn't plan to fall in love with and get pregnant by a French guy in a Phantom of the Opera costume while I was dressed as Queen Nefertiti. But here I am. And I've never been happier."

"I can see that," Melody said. "You two are pretty much incandescent with joy these days."

The lovebirds made quick goo-goo eyes at each other.

"The point is," Samira continued, "that I'm not so good at making plans for myself. Maybe you're the same way. You planned to devote the rest of your life to your career or maybe to meet a great guy via online dating. Planned for him to be local. Planned for him to be a doctor like you. But what if God or the universe or whoever has a better plan for you? What if your perfect guy is a British royal? The only way for you to find out for sure is to see what happens."

"Wise as well as beautiful," Baptiste said, staring at

Samira with his heart-shaped eyes. "No wonder I'm crazy about her."

"Yeah, okay, lovebirds," Melody said sourly. "I hate it when you talk sense—"

There was a loud knock, then the sound of the front door creaking open and slamming shut and a deep male voice with a posh accent.

"Baptiste? I hope you've got some advice for me because I've royally mucked things up with Melody. You need to help me get my arse out of a sling. And did you know that your front doorbell is hanging by the...hanging by the, ah, wires?"

Anthony arrived at the kitchen threshold and froze at the sight of Melody. His breath hitched. His face turned red and blotchy, as though it belonged to a prizefighter leaving the ring after a particularly difficult round.

"Hi," he said to Melody, his voice softening.

And there was her answer, her last lingering doubts scuttling back into the shadows whence they'd come. The way his eyes lit up when he looked at her; the way her heart thundered when he walked into the room; the way thoughts, words and feelings crowded into her mouth, demanding to be shared with him.

She'd never felt any of this with another man.

Not even close.

And she'd thought her best option might be to cut him loose? Because she wasn't sure about his family or the potential loss of her privacy? *Really?*

No, ma'am.

Not her.

She might be a closet coward, but she wasn't stupid.

"Hi," she said, keeping most of her simper on lockdown.

Anthony dimpled at her, then took a deep breath and surveyed the room.

"So," he said crisply. "I see you've convened the meeting without me."

They all laughed.

"We voted on the future of your relationship with Melody," Baptiste said. "Almost all of us are in favor of it."

More laughter, during which Anthony came over and took Melody's hand, lacing his fingers with hers as he kissed her cheek. A surge of something arced between them the way it always did. Electricity. Rightness. *Belonging*.

"I need to borrow Melody." He glanced around, spied the dining room and tugged her toward it. "Won't be a minute."

"Take your time," Samira said, shooting Melody a veiled *Don't screw this up!* look.

"This is a beautiful house, by the way," Anthony said. "I do hope you plan to patch up the broken cobblestones in the driveway, though. I'd rather not break an ankle."

"Add that to the list," Baptiste quickly told Samira, pointing to the legal pad.

Once they got to the dining room, Anthony turned to face Melody, holding tight to both her hands. "I suppose Baptiste and Samira now know more about our relationship than I do?"

"Sorry about that. I came to talk to Samira, and he was here too. I hope you don't mind."

"It's fine."

"And I hope you weren't coming to discuss all our personal business with Baptiste," she said sternly. "You said something about that when you walked in. You wanted to get your arse out of a sling."

He pulled a confused face. "Not at all. I said my arse would be in a sling if they didn't fix the broken cobblestones in their driveway."

They laughed together, and it was an enormous relief after

the emotional roller coaster of making love all night followed by their tense discussion this morning. Evidently he felt the same way, because he leaned in for a kiss that was hard and urgent.

He broke away when they were both breathless, resting his forehead against hers.

"I'm *sorry*."

"I know," she said.

"I hate that we've spent our limited time today being cross with each other."

"Me too. But we had to talk about it."

"Yes." He straightened and looked down at her with those intense blue eyes. "Baptiste wants to leave around dinnertime. He's got meetings in the morning. So do I. But I can't go with things so unsettled between us." He paused, giving her heart the chance to thump into overdrive. "We have to come to an understanding, you and I."

She took a shaky breath. Nodded.

"I know. But there's something we need to do first."

20

"I have to confess," Anthony said around lunchtime, hanging on to the sticky trunk as they navigated the freshly cut Christmas tree through Melody's foyer and into her living room. "When you said we had something to do first, I was hoping it involved a bed and significantly less clothes for both of us."

"You poor victim. You just suffer through life, don't you?" Melody said.

"I'm glad you've noticed."

"Well, you can't just pop into town and derail *all* my weekend plans. Today's the day for me to pick out my Christmas tree and decorate my place. It's only fair for you to help. And by *help* I mean for you to do all the chopping and heavy lifting."

"It *did* give me the chance to show off my manly muscles. Were you impressed?"

"I was deeply impressed. Let's put it right here for now. I'm so excited. I think we got a good one. I love Fraser firs."

They leaned the tree in a corner near the fireplace, and Melody dusted off her hands with satisfaction.

He headed for the kitchen and washed his hands. "I think you made a grave mistake not going for the blue spruce. I'm not mad. Just bitterly disappointed."

She followed, bumping him aside with her hip so she could wash her own hands.

"That tree was about ten feet tall and ten feet wide. I don't know how big you think my living room is, but it's not *that* big."

"I see that buyer's remorse has set in. You'll just have to live with the terrible consequences of your irresponsible actions."

They both laughed. He greedily noted her dimples and the way the sparkle intensified in her eyes, storing the images away for later, when she wasn't right there within arm's length.

"Do you decorate for the holidays?" she asked.

"No. That's never been very high on my bachelor agenda."

He hesitated before plowing ahead, grateful that the truth was now out and he no longer had to censor his words with her. It took far too much effort when he wanted to tell her everything about himself and his life.

"My father always hired a team of professional decorators to descend on the ranch and turn it into a winter wonderland. And the staff at Sandringham take care of Granny's trees, although she does like to have all the little kids in the family come for tea and decorating. Some years all the decorations are stacked on the bottom branches of the tree. That's as high as they can reach."

Melody laughed.

He looked down at his hands, which still had sap on them. "I'm rather proud of myself. This was my first official Christmas tree chopping."

"Well done," she said, beaming up at him.

His heart contracted, hard.

He hesitated, not trusting himself to be judicious with his words just at the moment. They were all crowded on his tongue, surging forward and demanding to be said.

How much she was growing to mean to him.

How her smile undid him.

How he planned to move heaven and earth to see her as often as he possibly could.

"I don't want to leave," he said helplessly. "You have no idea."

She slowly sobered.

"I don't want you to go," she said, surprising him.

Time for their talk.

"Here," he said, lifting her by the waist and plunking her on the counter. She immediately wrapped her legs around his waist and pulled him closer. "How are we going to handle this?"

"I don't know. I've never had a long-distance relationship before. Maybe we should set some ground rules?"

"Good plan. Rule number one: we're not seeing anyone else."

Disbelieving look from Melody. "Didn't we settle all that last night?"

"The topic can never be *too* settled," he said darkly. "Rule number two: we have to talk every day. *Talk*. With voices and preferably images. Not just texting."

"Agreed."

"We've done a very good job of that so far, don't you think?"

"I do think. But…and I'm not trying to be too clingy or anything, but please don't play games with me."

"What?"

She shifted uncomfortably. "I know it's been fine so far, but a lot of people use texting to play passive-aggressive mind games. It's like they don't want to text too soon, or reply too soon, or act like they're too anxious to hear from the other person—"

A lightbulb went off over his head.

He laughed, incredulous. Maybe he should be grateful that she truly had no idea how bad he had it for her. At least a shred of his dignity remained.

"I *just* flew back here because I couldn't wait to see you. Did you forget already?"

"No, but—"

"You'll be hearing from me. Promptly and often. So spend your time worrying about something more likely to happen." He thought that over. "Like the US deciding to rejoin the UK because they miss having a monarch."

"Good." Her quick laughter faded. "And if you change your mind about wanting to be with me—*what*? Stop glaring at me all the time."

"What else do you expect me to do when you talk such nonsense? Haven't you been listening? I'm looking for ways to spend more time with you. Not ways to get rid of you."

"But if you change your mind—"

"I *won't*."

"Anthony." Her brown eyes flashed with frustration. "Will you please listen to me?"

"Fine," he snapped, struggling with his own frustration.

She didn't get it, this one. She really didn't get it at all.

She took a deep breath. "If you change your mind about wanting to be with me, please just tell me. Just call and tell me. Don't drop off the face of the earth and ghost me. I have this terrible image of you hiding behind, I don't know, your private secretary or the palace or something, and me never hearing from you again. Please don't do that to me. Okay?"

She was dead serious.

"Okay," he said quickly. "You have my word. And I want yours."

"Oh, I have no problems dumping people face-to-face," she said cheerfully.

He had to laugh.

"What else?" she asked.

"I want pictures."

"Pictures?" She gave him a narrowed look. "What kind of pictures?"

"Just what you're up to every day. You in your natural habitat."

"Oh, good. I thought you were going to ask for nude pictures."

"What for?" He frowned at her, honestly puzzled. "We'll be having phone sex every night, so we won't need the pictures, will we?"

"Phone sex?"

"Phone sex. Nonnegotiable."

"We'll see," she said, but he could tell from her speculative gaze and the slight purr in her voice that she found the idea as arousing as he did. "And I want to see pictures of London. You in your apartment."

"That can be arranged."

"And don't glower in them."

"No promises. I'll probably be thinking about how much fun you, Samira and Baptiste will be having here without me."

"I work all the time. How much fun do you think I have?"

"I don't know," he said, smoothing a stray curl away from her temple.

They watched each other for a quiet and wistful moment or two.

"Maybe I'll be like a toddler when Mummy drops him off at nursery school," he finally said. His voice had gone hoarse. "The moment of parting will be difficult, but then I'll stay busy and get into a routine and the time will pass."

"Oh? Out of sight, out of mind? Does that work for you?"

"It didn't work at all this week, no. Did it work for you?"

"No," she said quietly.

His sadness was one thing. Seeing hers felt as though a tiny corner of his heart had been ripped out. He rubbed her sweet lower lip with his thumb. Gently kissed her.

"So, listen." Easing back again, he reached into the pocket of his leather jacket and produced a small rectangular tin tied with a red bow. "I wanted to bring you something from London."

She brightened, beaming up at him. "You did? Thank you! What is it?"

"It's some of my grandmother's favorite tea. Some hearty breakfast blend that she drinks all day. It's what we drank when I saw her for tea this week."

Melody took it with a blank look that quickly turned into an incredulous frown. "Are you telling me that this is your grandmother's personal tea? From her kitchen?"

Every now and then, he experienced moments of profound gratitude that he was who he was. Like at this precise moment, as her expression eased into absolute delight.

"It's from her kitchen," he said. "And she hopes you enjoy it."

Melody practically choked on her tongue.

"The *Queen of England* hopes I enjoy her tea?"

He shrugged, trying not to laugh. "I believe I'd mentioned that I told her about you."

"Oh, my God," she said with a semi-hysterical laugh. "Should I give you a thank-you note for her before you go? I have nice stationery."

This was the woman for him. No question

"I'm sure she'd love that." He kissed her forehead again. "One final thing before I go: Christmas. What're your plans?"

"I'm working most of the week. Probably dinner with Samira and Baptiste since my parents will be in Florida. And then I have the week after off. Scheduled vacation. What about you?"

"I've already committed to Sandringham. We exchange gifts on Christmas Eve. There's church and a luncheon on Christmas Day."

"Ah. What about your father?"

Yeah, he'd been thinking about the old man. Wondering if he should reach out to him over the holidays.

"Not sure about that yet."

"He's your father," she said gently.

"I can see whose side *you're* on."

"I'm on the side of happy families."

"Yes, well, anyway…I was wondering if you might want to go for a little holiday with me. Well, actually, I'll be tacking the holiday onto the back end of a trip for my charity. You said you have the time off."

"A *holiday*?" With his hands on her hips and her legs still wrapped around him, he felt the sudden excitement vibrate through her. "What did you have in mind?"

It was very hard to keep a straight face.

"Have you been to Tanzania?"

There was a pause, followed by a burst of startled laughter.

"Tanzania?" she shrieked. "Yes, I go to Tanzania all the time. I was just there the other weekend. I was hoping you'd choose someplace more exotic."

"I take it that's a *yes*?" he asked, laughing.

"Yes! But I only have a week. Is that okay?"

"We'll figure it out," he said wryly. "My office will make all the arrangements. Do you have your passport?"

"Yes."

"And you'll need some shots."

"I work at a hospital! I know how to get shots! Oh, my God! Oh, my *God*! And we're going to see some animals, right? I don't want some spa vacation where you get mud baths and sit in hot springs. I want to explore and see *everything*."

Overcome by her enthusiasm and his own sudden hot emotion, he kissed her again and did his best to make it powerful enough to last through this week until he saw her again. To convey some of what he felt.

It seemed to work.

When he let her go, her face was flushed, her eyes glazed, her lips dewy and her breath raspy.

"I believe…" *Christ.* He had to clear his throat. "I believe I've mentioned that I seem to be developing strong feelings for you."

"You have mentioned," she said, her lids still at half-mast.

"Spending time with you on vacation in one of my favorite places in the world will probably put me over the top. If I'm not already. Fair warning."

"I'm a big girl," she said, wrapping her arms around his neck and tightening her legs around his waist, bringing his raging erection right up against the sweet spot between her thighs. "Your warnings don't scare me."

"I was hoping you might say that," he murmured, angling her head so he could kiss her again.

Read *EVERYTHING I NEED* Now!

THANK YOU FOR READING *Everything I Need*! I hope you enjoyed watching Anthony and Melody fall in love as much as I enjoyed writing their story!

QUESTION: Hang on! Their story isn't over yet, is it? They haven't even said *I love you*! Is there more?

ANSWER: Yes! Anthony and Melody's romantic saga concludes in *EVERYTHING I NEED*, which is now available!

Here's a teaser:

Long-distance romances never lead to happily-ever-after. Or do they?

The road to true love never runs smooth. Especially when an awkward British billionaire with family issues finds himself smitten with a workaholic pediatric surgeon from small-town Journey's End.

But Anthony Scott refuses to give up on his thrilling new relationship with beautiful but guarded Dr. Melody Harrison. Even when the frequent goodbyes and ongoing loneliness threaten to break both their hearts.

Long-distance love affairs often crash and burn. But not always…

If you love hot and emotional contemporary romance, pick up *EVERYTHING I NEED*, the steamy conclusion to this two-part romantic saga today!

And if you like reading stories about rich and powerful men falling crazy in love, then don't miss my Warner Family series. The first book, ***TENDER SECRETS***, is available for FREE! Download now!

Want to stay up to date on all my news about upcoming book releases and deals? Sign up for my **newsletter** and **Facebook** page.

Finally, thank you in advance for helping me spread the word about my books, including telling friends, mentioning them on your social media and/or leaving reviews on the retailers. Word of mouth sells more books than anything else, and I appreciate your help.

Turn the page for an excerpt from the conclusion to Anthony and Melody's story, *EVERYTHING I NEED*…

Chapter 1

"That's everything, I think." Anthony Scott emerged from the bedroom, passed through the living room to deposit his overnight bag in the foyer by the front door and came back to sit on the sofa in front of the crackling fire. "All packed."

Melody Harrison watched the proceedings from her kitchen, where she poured herself a cup of tea, and tried not to freak out now that they'd reached Sunday evening and the end of their first weekend together as lovers. Easier said than done, especially with an unexpected mass of anxiety tightening her chest and creeping steadily higher. The moody silence, which had grown worse all afternoon after they finished decorating the Christmas tree they'd cut together and returned his rental car, also didn't boost her flagging morale any.

"How much longer until Baptiste picks you up for the airport?" she said.

His best friend, Jean-Baptiste Mercier, a Parisian billionaire with his own plane, had recently begun dating her best friend, Samira Palmer, here in small-town Journey's End in Upstate New York.

Anthony checked his watch. "Fifteen minutes," he said, his upper-class British accent sounding more clipped than ever. Like a pissed-off Benedict Cumberbatch as Sherlock Holmes complaining that Mrs. Hudson had moved his violin.

Her heart sank another couple notches.

"You okay?" she asked brightly, stirring her tea.

He frowned. Avoided eye contact. "'Course."

Melody worked hard to feel reassured. Unfortunately, she never quite managed it beyond about 30 percent. The thing was, he didn't look okay. He didn't look okay at all as he rested his elbows on his knees and absently rubbed his hands together, his grim and downturned profile something that you might see on a man walking the last several steps to the lethal injection chamber.

Do not freak out, Mel, she told herself as she joined him in the living room, settled in the armchair and set her mug on the coffee table. *Do not get clingy. So Anthony's a little sour right now. So what? Do not make a mountain out of a molehill.*

Good advice, but she was pretty sure that the mountain was already there. The longer he didn't look at her, the more she felt as though Kilimanjaro had been inserted into the middle of her living room.

Suddenly he glanced up. They looked at each other long enough for her to feel a jolt of turbulence from his cornflower blue eyes. His jaw tightened. He quickly blinked and turned away, at the setting sun on the other side of her sliding glass doors, but the damage had been done.

She felt profoundly unsettled. As vulnerable as a squealing and furless newborn panda.

And *this,* sports fans, was why she should have stuck to her vow to focus on her status as both a spinster and a pediatric surgeon and to avoid romantic entanglements. Failing that, she should certainly have waited to get to know Anthony better before she leapt into the horizontal boogie with him, but she'd divested herself of both her panties and most of her good sense within a few short days of meeting him, hadn't she?

Yep. She was a regular genius.

Now here she was. With her heart in her throat and no real idea what to expect next as he returned to London and they officially embarked on their committed long-distance relationship.

Desperate for something to do with herself, she reached for her tea. Blew on it. Sipped it. Tried to figure out how she'd wound up here on this glum Sunday night, where the darkness and chill inside far exceeded anything going on outside and this man's moods were now, evidently, at the center of her existence.

Well, actually, she knew exactly how she'd wound up here.

She'd met Anthony several days ago, at a gala celebrating the merger of Baptiste's French winery with one here in Journey's End in the Hudson River Valley. After a rocky initial meeting, she and Anthony had discovered they shared some serious chemistry. They'd spent some time together while he was in town. At the end of last weekend, he'd gone back to his London home. He and Melody had talked and texted religiously while he was there. Then he'd surprised her back here in Journey's End this past Friday. Emphasis on *surprised* because he'd caught her on a blind date with someone she'd met online.

That had gone over well. Not.

A blowup had ensued, followed by some spectacular sex.

Then Anthony had filled Melody in on a pertinent detail or two from his past. Like the fact that his father was a Texas oilman and Anthony had a trust fund in the neighborhood of a billion dollars. Oh, and Anthony's grandmother on his mother's side? The Queen of England. As in, *the* Queen of England. True, he was her youngest grandchild and about as likely to accede to the throne as Melody was, but he was still a prince of England.

Had Melody seen any of that coming? No, she had not. Was she, as a black woman with her own life and career on this side of the pond, prepared for the possibility of press intrusion into their fledgling relationship? Was she prepared for the scrutiny (and public judgment) of her appearance, including the burn scars she bore on her face and neck, which dated from a childhood accident in the kitchen? *Hell* no. The thought made her cringe.

And yet…

Was she prepared to say good-bye to this man? To wish him a great life without her?

She watched him absently crack his knuckles, her innards softening to caramel goo.

Absolutely not.

So she and Anthony had decided to be exclusive and continue seeing each other. See what happened.

And what was happening at this particular moment was that Mr. Anthony Scott looked as cold and forbidding as he'd been when they first met. There was something about seeing him in a sweater, jeans and leather jacket, with his blond hair brushed and shot through with golden streaks, that made her heart ache. This morning, they'd been naked in bed together, her fingers running through that silky hair and his body thrusting deep inside hers. Now he sat over there, a million miles away on her sofa, and she couldn't muster the courage to go sit beside him, much less reach for his hand.

Yet they thought they could make a run at a successful long-distance relationship when they couldn't breach the brick wall that had sprung up between them while they were in the same town and the same room?

Yup. They were off to a *baaaad* start.

She could almost laugh if it wasn't all so doomed to failure.

She and Anthony were going to crash and burn, and they were going to crash and burn *big*.

Guaranteed.

Don't think like that, Mel, said a quiet little voice in the back of her head.

Be brave. Take a chance.

She took a deep breath and decided that she wasn't going to let this whole thing go down in flames on account of her unmitigated cowardice. Hadn't she survived a horrible childhood burn and all the corresponding surgeries, pain and negative attention from staring people? Hadn't she gotten into and then clawed her way through Harvard Med, for God's sake? Couldn't she act like a mature adult and try to reach across their divide?

You bet your ass she could.

She cleared her throat. "You sure you're okay? You've been awfully quiet."

"I'm fine," he snapped, staring down at his hands as he rubbed them.

"Clearly," she muttered, putting her mug back on the coffee table with a distinct *thunk* before moving over to sit beside him on the sofa.

His head came up. He nailed her straight on with those unwavering blue eyes, frosty now.

"Meaning?" he asked aggressively.

That tone made her hackles rise.

She nailed him with her own unyielding stare. Screw it. This relationship had nothing if they didn't master basic honesty and Communication 101.

"Meaning you're starting to remind me of the night we met. When you were being a *jackass.*"

He looked startled.

"And since I'm sure that's not your intent, and I'm pretty sure something's on your mind, why don't we talk about it? Give you a chance to practice talking about your feelings."

Whoa. She hadn't meant to be *quite* that forceful.

Neither of them spoke for several beats. The silence turned brittle.

"You probably wouldn't want to hear every thought that's popped into my head this afternoon." His wry smile never came within a mile of his eyes. "I believe you've complained about my being too blunt with my words at times?"

Fair point, not that she wanted to concede it just now.

"Well, it turns out that I prefer your bluntness to your cold shoulder. Imagine my surprise."

"I'm not giving you the *cold shoulder*," he said, incredulous. "If anything, I'm lost in my thoughts. Is that illegal in the States now?"

"Spill, Anthony."

He hesitated. Heaved a rough sigh.

"Have it your way. If you must know, I'm wondering if we'll be able to make a go of it after all, because this is all shaping up to be much more difficult than I'd expected."

Melody absorbed this information like a punch to the solar plexus.

He *what*? Was this the end already? Was he about to dump her now that he'd screwed her?

"I've also been wondering if you'll be on another blind date with some other bloke as soon as my plane goes wheels up tonight—"

"I will *not*—" she began, outraged.

"—but I've dismissed that possibility because we've given each other our word and I believe we trust each other reasonably well." His gaze, filled with sudden sensual appreciation, skimmed her up and down, making her skin sizzle. "Besides that, we quite enjoy each other in bed, don't we, darling? We've given each other a lot to think about and a lot to remember each other by until we meet again on Friday, haven't we?"

Melody opened her mouth, feeling a little breathless—

Anthony's lips twisted with unmistakable bitterness.

"I'm wondering why the bloody hell I'll have to spend the week in exile across the ocean, going to meetings most of the time and alone in my drafty cottage the rest of the time while, meantime, you're out having fun with Baptiste and Samira or here in your cozy little apartment with your Christmas decorations, a blazing fire, river views and your amazingly comfortable bed that has the added bonus of having your incredible body in it."

She gaped at him, her head spinning.

"I'm wondering if I could possibly skive off my meetings and just stay here, but my grandmother would have my head. And *then* she'd never let me hear the end of it. My life wouldn't be worth living."

"Anthony..." she said when he paused to catch his breath.

"I'm wondering what you've done to me to turn me into this complete nutter in such a short period of time, because I don't lose my head—about *anything*—nor am I a clingy person." He paused thoughtfully. "*Now,* of course, I'm wondering if it was a mistake to confess my looming nuttery and if you'll use that as an excuse to run in the other direction."

"Anthony—"

"I'm wondering what I've ever done to get lucky enough for a woman like *you* to cross my path, much less give me a chance, and I want to kiss your feet that you haven't written me off now that you know all about both sides of my family. The fact that you've actually met my father and are still even speaking to me qualifies you for sainthood in my book."

She had to laugh.

He watched her, his avid gaze crisscrossing her features. Then he cursed, took her face in his hands and kissed her hard. He eased back to end the kiss, leaving her stunned and hopelessly aroused as he rested his forehead against hers.

"Mainly I'm wondering if it's physically possible for me to survive without seeing your smile or kissing you between now and Friday," he said gruffly. "Aren't you glad you asked?"

Melody paused to smooth his hair and rein in her answering confession, which would include gems like *I want to stow away on your plane* and *I am literally now incapable of thinking about anything but you.*

He wasn't the only one up on a ledge about the future of their relationship outside of the four walls of her apartment this weekend. That was for damn sure.

She let out a shaky laugh.

"You have all that up there?" she asked, tapping his temple. "No wonder you look so pained all the time. There's no room for any fun thoughts."

Crooked smile from Anthony. "You've no idea."

He let her go and sat back, idly twisting her one of her corkscrew curls and setting off frissons of pleasure every time he brushed the side of her neck.

They stared at each other.

"Can I tell you something?" she asked quietly.

His expression softened, as did his voice.

"You can tell me anything, darling."

As always, his use of the endearment made her feel as though her skin glowed.

She stole another quick kiss, lingering over his tender lips because they were so delicious. When they broke apart, she noted, with great satisfaction, that his eyes were glazed.

"I work at the hospital," she said. "*All* the time. I eat. Sometimes I sleep. When I can't sleep, I read my medical journals." She pointed to where they were piled high in a basket. "Sometimes I have a glass of wine. Sometimes I meet up with Samira, but not so much now that she's with Baptiste. And that's it. That's all there is to me."

One corner of his mouth curled.

"Sounds pathetic, to be honest. I never realized you were such a loser."

"Well, I am," she said, managing a quick laugh before her swelling heart filled her throat. Her smile slipped away. It was much too hard to think clearly when he looked at her like that, all steady warmth. "So the next time you feel like I'm having too much fun without you, just remember that I'm either in the OR trying to patch some kid back together or sitting here wishing you were with me."

He hesitated. Ran his hands over the top of his head, ruffling his hair.

"Melody—"

His phone vibrated. They both stiffened.

At that glum moment, Melody would have been happier to hear Jack from *The Shining* chopping through her front door with an ax.

He pulled his phone out and checked the display. "It's Baptiste. He's on his way."

"I know," she said.

To her everlasting dismay, she felt her chin wobble and discovered that she was perilously close to tears. She'd already cried once in front of him (the other day when one of her patients had suddenly died) and had no intention of doing it again. Ever, if she could help it.

The man was going home to London. They'd known this moment would come. No big deal whatsoever.

So she plastered a bright smile on her face and jumped up.

"Did you forget anything? I'd better make sure you grabbed all your stuff."

She hurried into the bedroom, giving herself a swift mental kick in the ass along the way. What the hell had gotten into her? She met a new man and all of the sudden she carried on as though life was a Shakespearean tragedy every time he left her side? Was *that* where this was going?

No freaking way.

Her life did not depend on a man. Her happiness did not depend on a man.

She wouldn't let it.

Tomorrow she would go back to work at the hospital like she always did. Normal life would resume. The birds would still sing in the trees and her curly hair would still refuse to behave. Her entire life had not changed because of this relationship.

Okay.

Focus, girl.

She did a lap around her ultra-neat bedroom with her usual brisk efficiency and noticed it right away: the telltale patch of red plaid under the edge of one of the white decorator pillows on the bed. Anthony's flannel pajama bottoms. He'd be sad if he got back home and they weren't in his overnight bag, wouldn't he? She snatched them up and headed for the bathroom. And there was something else: Anthony's toothbrush in her holder, along with his travel-sized bottle of funky British mouthwash and tube of toothpaste. She grabbed those, too.

Men.

And to think he'd claimed he'd packed. How was it "packing" when you forgot pretty much everything you'd brought with you? Was it a vision problem? Maybe she should hold up a couple fingers and ask him how many he saw—

Anthony appeared in the bathroom doorway, startling her.

She shook her head, disbelieving, and snorted out a laugh as she held the items up for him to see.

"You forgot half your stuff, you silly goose."

But Anthony was evidently in no mood for teasing.

She watched the storm roll in and settle on his face, dimming the vivid cornflower blue of his eyes the way an afternoon rain throws Miami beaches into shadow.

His jaw tightened.

"Why are you getting rid of my things?"

Chapter 2

The sudden rough edge to his voice caught her by surprise. So did the look on his face, as though he planned to call the local authorities if she didn't put his stuff back *now*. A negative electrical charge in the air made nerve endings tingle all up and down her arms and across her scalp.

She froze, baffled.

This whole situation demonstrated, in stark detail, the problem with sexing someone up first, then trying to build a relationship later. The sex, at least for her, kicked the intensity level up to eleven, but the parties involved still didn't know each other well enough to understand whether the inevitable bumps in the road were normal or if they led to hidden sinkholes that could ruin everything.

"Why're you looking at me like that?" she asked. "I'm *not* getting rid of your stuff. I'm making sure you pack it so you don't miss it when you get home."

His eyes flashed. "Why can't my things stay where they were?"

She blinked, bewildered. "I didn't realize you wanted them to."

"Well, I do," he said flatly.

She held her hands up. "My mistake."

He grumbled something indistinct.

"What the hell is going on here?" she asked. "Why am I getting the feeling that your toothbrush is not the real issue?"

"Because you've completely missed the point." He barked. "Some women *want* the man to leave something behind. Some women *want* the man to feel that there's a place for him."

"A thousand pardons."

"Besides. You need the reminder."

"Of what?" she said, still baffled.

"My pending return."

The lingering belligerence in his tone didn't sit well with her. Nor did the *additional* reference to the fact that she hadn't kept the faith the last time he left town.

She crossed her arms, beginning to fume.

"Stop throwing that blind date in my face. And don't bark at me. I'm not one of your soldiers. And you're not General Patton pledging to return to the Philippines."

A flicker of grudging respect crossed over his face. "It was General MacArthur."

"Close enough."

They watched each other, the silence turning wary until a light bulb went off over her head. She snapped her fingers as all the puzzle pieces fell into place.

"Hang on. I know what you're doing. You're picking a fight with me."

His expression became guarded.

"Pardon me? Why on earth would I do that in my last ten seconds with you before I have to leave for the week?"

Look at his face! She was definitely on to something.

"It's part of the separation process. It's easier for people to let each other go and say good-bye if they're angry with each other. I learned about this whole thing during med school."

A dull flush climbed up his neck and resolved over his cheekbones. He cocked his head, squinting at her. "Are you *analyzing* me?"

Meeting his stony expression head-on shaved a year or two off her life. This man gave intimidating a whole new meaning, and she'd been yelled at and humiliated by some of the most fearsome professors Harvard Med had to offer.

Yet she wasn't scared. Not at all. She was exhilarated.

"Am I wrong?"

His jaw began to flex in the back. Maybe that was why it took him so long to speak.

"I hope I haven't reached quite *that* level of insanity and dependency over a woman I didn't know existed two short weeks ago."

The words hovered between them, lingering in the air like a blast from a skunk's tail.

Worse? The veiled implication made her wince. It was all buried in those staccato syllables, something to the effect that she thought a *bit* too highly of herself, or maybe that she read way too much importance and/or permanency into any plans he may have for their relationship.

Whatever it was, it cut far too close to the bone of her sparse dating life and forgettable previous relationships with men. It made her want to duck her head and mumble an apology for letting her narcissistic side run wild.

Then she remembered: she didn't have a narcissistic side.

He *was* picking an argument. No matter how he tried to

dodge and deflect when confronted with the truth. This behavior was a known psychological phenomenon.

Funny thing, though. She still wanted to hit him.

Actually, she wanted a lot of things at the moment.

She wanted him to march his arrogant self out of her apartment and not let the door hit him in the ass on the way out. She also wanted him to stay here forever so she could employ more of her previously undetected intuitive skills and uncover all of his secrets.

Mostly she just wanted a reaction from Mr. Cool and Aloof.

"Tell you what," she said with a sweeping gesture toward the bathroom door. "Why don't you wait for Baptiste in the lobby? Have a great flight."

Seething now, she took a determined step or two away from him.

He made a strangled noise behind her, the only clue that she might have hit a nerve.

Bingo.

She turned back, triumph surging through her as they glared at each other.

One glimpse of those flashing blue eyes revealed everything she could have hoped to know. Honestly, it was like looking into a funhouse mirror of her own emotions. A reflection of everything she felt about him.

She infuriated him.

She fascinated him.

She amused and unraveled him.

He didn't want to leave her.

This thing between them terrified him.

What if it didn't work out?

And, worse, what if it somehow *did?*

This was all too much, way too soon.

Yet he had no intention of backing away from any challenges she might present.

His expression turned determined as he looked her up and down. Hot. Possessive.

There was no mistaking his intent.

She started to shake her head and remind him that Baptiste was probably pulling into the parking lot this very second. The circumstances weren't exactly conducive to her relaxing and enjoying herself. Plus, they'd already had sex roughly eight hundred times in the last twenty-four hours and her intimate lady parts were sore and wonderfully sated. There was a limit to how much her body could take and how many times she could cream and come for him.

Enough was enough.

She started to open her mouth and tell him that now was not the time. But she got exactly nowhere.

Because that was the thing about Anthony Scott.

He had his rough edges and arrogant moments, sure.

But when he looked at her like *that*?

There was only *this*.

She reached for him, palming his scratchy cheeks and pulling his face down for her urgent kisses. He was right there with her, running his hands down to her ass and hefting her as his mouth slanted over hers. She hopped up, wrapping her legs around his waist and reveling in his earthy scent and the size of his erection as he ground against her. His skilled mouth nuzzled, licked and nipped, his tongue growing more insistent and sweeping deeper once he gripped a handful of her hair and tilted her head the way he wanted it.

Just the way *she* wanted it.

She crooned and mewled, choking out little sounds of encouragement that he didn't seem to need as he plunked her on the marble countertop next to the sink.

There was a tiny pause while they stared at each other in mutual astonishment. God only knew what all ran through his mind when he stared at her with such dark intent, his expression vaguely troubled, but she could only manage a single flustered thought:

What is this man doing to me?

Then he unleashed all his passion with a low growl and thinking became impossible.

Never had a quickie been quite so quick or so relentlessly thorough. While she propped her hands on the counter behind her and tried to withstand the onslaught, *his* hands managed to hit all the highlights of her body in sixty seconds or less. They gripped her hair and massaged her nape. Reverently stroked her face and neck, maneuvering her head this way and that for his kisses and nips. Manhandled her breasts and nipples, rubbing and squeezing jolts of sensation out of her body and making her squirm with growing agitation.

Down below, meanwhile, she held his waist in a death grip between her thighs. If this man thought she was letting him hop a plane to London when he belonged right *here* with her, he damn well better think again. But Anthony didn't act like he was going anywhere. He rotated his hips with sharp thrusts, never missing a beat as he unerringly hit the sweet spot between her legs and made her foolish as she panted and moaned incoherently for him.

Then his hands went to the waistband of her yoga pants…

**If you enjoyed this excerpt, read
EVERYTHING I NEED today!**

ABOUT THE AUTHOR

A recovering lawyer, Ann Christopher has been published since 2006 and writes contemporary romance and romantic suspense.

When she's not writing, Ann likes to do the following, in no particular order: read; cook; eat; hang out at Target looking for new stuff she doesn't need; play with her 2 rescue dogs and 2 rescue cats; and travel the world with her family. She lives in Ohio with her family.

If you'd like to recommend a great book, share a recipe for homemade cake of any kind, or have a tip for getting your teens to do what you say the *first* time you say it, Ann would love to hear from you!

Stay in touch with Ann!
AnnChristopher.com
ann@annchristopher.com

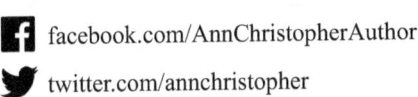 facebook.com/AnnChristopherAuthor

twitter.com/annchristopher